I0731197

MAXIM: SURRENDER

A CLUB XXX NOVEL: BOOK THREE

LANA SKY

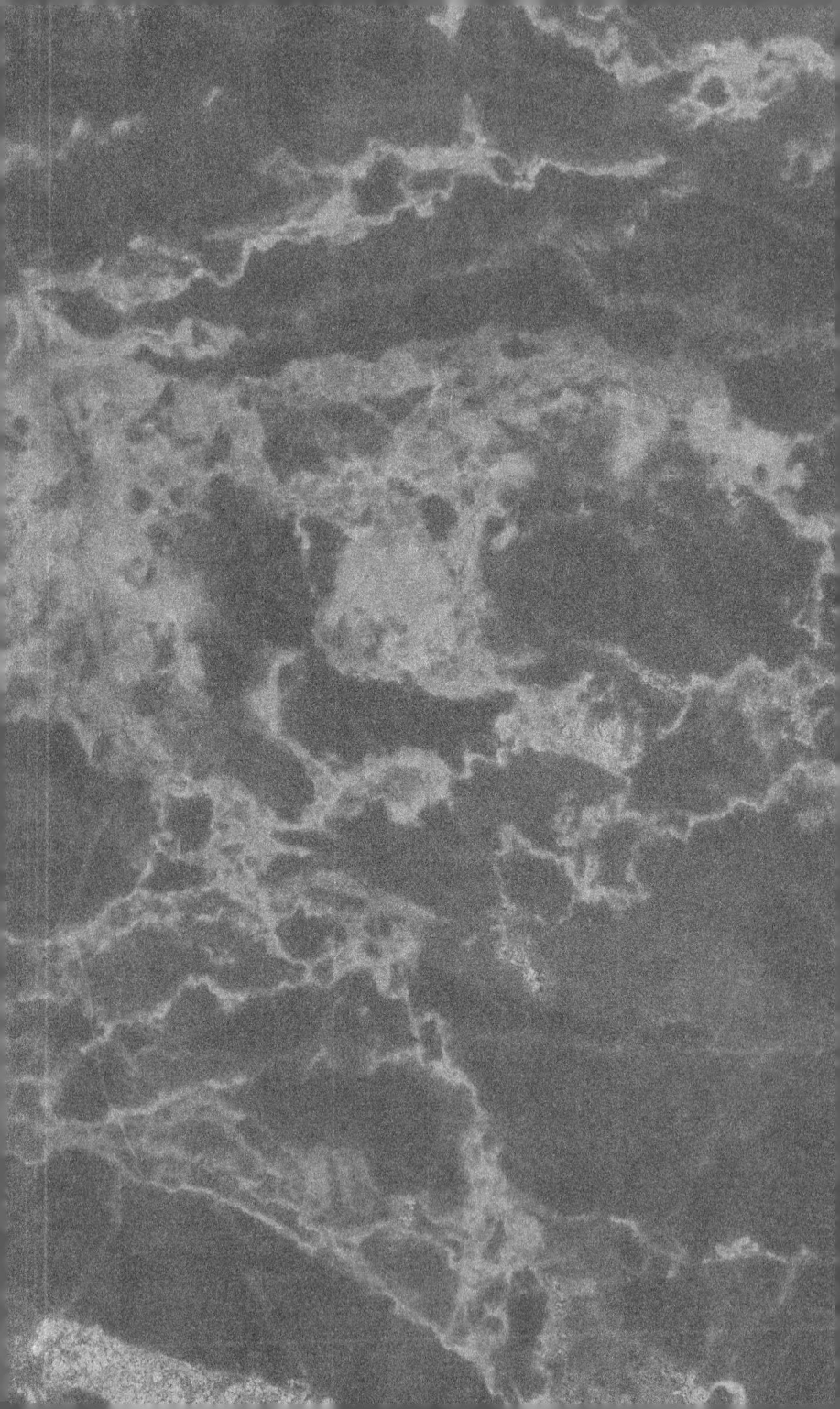

Surrender

Surrender By Lana Sky

Copyright © 2020 by Lana Sky
All rights reserved.

No part of this publication may be reproduced, distributed, or transmitted in any form or by any means, including photocopying, recording, or other electronic or mechanical methods, without the prior written permission of the author.

This is a work of fiction. Names, characters, businesses, places, events and incidents are either the products of the author's imagination or used in a fictitious manner. Any resemblance to actual persons, living or dead, or actual events is purely coincidental.

Cover Design and Interior Formatting by Charity Chimni
Proofreading by Charity Chimni

ACKNOWLEDGMENTS

Thanks so much to everyone who supported this draft along the way, including the many beta readers who provided encouragement along the way! Please keep in mind that this story includes dark, graphic and explicit content matter that is not suitable for readers under the age of 18—or for readers who are uncomfortable with the following subject matter: explicit sex, mentions of sexual abuse, mentions of child abuse, graphic depictions of violence, and mentions of self-harm.

CHAPTER ONE

God has a twisted sense of humor—and for some reason, he seems to enjoy testing my sanity, especially for his amusement. With chaos. With violence. And with scenarios that force me to ask myself questions like—*what do you do after a man proposes marriage while towering over a dead, mutilated body, Francesca?*

The answer turns out to be relatively simple. You stand rigid in a corner while said murderer makes a single phone call, and then you watch him pace circles around his handiwork.

He can't seem to *stop* moving. Raging. Thriving on the stench of blood and the taint of death. He's like an inferno of brutality, burning so bright it hurts to stare at him for too long.

Ironically, I'm frozen in place, incapable of looking away.

The only part of me seemingly alive is my heart, beating in tune to his every footstep. *Thump. Thud. Thump.* Amid the ominous soundtrack, I'm riveted. I'm numb.

Though I should be terrified.

Of him.

Of myself.

In this moment, Maxim Koslov lives up to the worst aspects of his identity I could minimize until now. The criminal who deals in violence and death. The mob boss, dripping blood in his polished suit. The murderer.

As if reading my mind, he inclines his head in my direction, his gaze unreadable. "Leave, if you want. Go."

But he utters no further instructions. Deep in my soul, I know that his driver isn't lurking out front either, and he never offers the keys to his car to drive myself.

The command was a test. Namely, of the fragile promise linking us together amid this chaos. One forged in blood and a vow. My finger aches beneath the figurative weight of it—a marble ring with a single name etched into its surface.

It's so simple in its beauty and so damning in its symbolism.

Marriage.

Corruption.

Surrender.

"I told you to go." Maxim stands by the wall now with his hands braced before him, his back muscles taut. I could trace the line of his spine even through his clothing; he's so rigid. Stone. "You won't want to see what happens next…"

Next. Implying the ultimate fate of the body lying on the floor a few paces away.

I can't look at it. Or give it its proper name in my head. Nope. It's just a thing.

"I won't shield you if you stay, *kotyonok*. I won't. If you run now, I will not judge you, either."

Real urgency laces his words this time. He truly doesn't want me to see this—the twisted aftermath of his violence. The real Maxim Koslov.

But I can't run.

Move.

Breathe.

And with a sigh, he finally acknowledges that fact, though his muscles bulge against his skin as if threatening to explode from it. He's angry. And in some ways, I think he's resigned, too. If I can stomach him at his worst then…

We're *both* fucking insane. It's why I hear footsteps that shouldn't exist, advancing with confidence in our direction.

Then a voice rings out, far too stern to be a figment of my imagination.

"I'm here." We both turn to face the figure who appears at the mouth of the hall. I flinch against the nearest wall, but Maxim looks unsurprised.

"Finally." He nods in welcome. "You came. I was afraid you were away on one of your little trips."

"You were lucky. I just got back." Dressed in a black suit, the tall man cuts a startling figure against the bare walls. Dark hair frames a strikingly familiar face as his eyes latch onto mine before settling over the body on the floor.

"Shit," he says simply. Two bold strides bring him closer, and he nudges Sevastyn with the tip of his boot. I cringe from the sight, slapping my hand over my mouth in grim anticipation. A wave of gagging contorts my throat, but nothing comes up. Yet.

"You could have waited," the man adds. "I would've come sooner if I'd known you were planning this." Disapproval colors his British accent, and I finally recognize him—the figure I saw in Maxim's club during one of our first trips there. The same man who also examined me the last time Maxim lost control. "You know this is something I would've enjoyed watching…" His eyes narrow, disrupting his composure. Then he shakes his head, and all traces of emotion vanish. "We have to move quickly."

"How should we dispose of him?" Maxim asks while turning from the wall. His eyes find me again, even as he continues to speak to the man. "It needs to be clean. I suspect we have less than a few hours before his spies come looking for him."

"*You* shouldn't be anywhere near this to be completely honest." The other man reaches into his pocket and withdraws a cell phone. "Leave. I'll call one of my men—"

"No." Maxim steps forward and grabs his wrist before he can raise the phone to his ear. "No one else. Anatoli has spies watching his own fucking spies. *We* handle this. Alone."

"Fair enough." The other man's eyes narrow, but he slowly returns the device to his pocket. "What do you suggest?"

"I don't fucking know." Maxim turns to the table strewn with tools and grabs one item at random, testing its weight over his palm. As the light glints off a sharpened edge, I realize what it is—a knife. "Whatever we do, it needs to be done quickly."

"And this is a brand-new suit." The other man must know what he intends without him having to say it out loud. Sighing, he snatches his own makeshift weapon from the table and then crosses over to Sevastyn's body. "You can replace it." With clinical detachment, he examines the contorted, battered limbs. Then he looks up. "What about her?"

"Her?" Maxim echoes. He eyes me as well, but his gaze is so distant...

I suck in a breath and press myself against the wall. In the space of a heartbeat, this man becomes as much of a stranger to me as I seem to be to him. His icy glare alone warns me Maxim is gone, replaced by a creature tormented by his past, consumed by the violence of it—all those horrible things his uncle's return dredged up. My lips part, a plea building between them. *Don't.*

But right before I voice it, he blinks...and Maxim reappears, his knuckles stark white over the handle of his blade. Eyes narrowed in concentration, he rips his gaze to the weapon in his hand. "She... She stays."

Without another word, he crouches beside the battered, bloodied mass that used to be his uncle's head. Metal flashes as he lowers his hand...

Desperate to escape the image, I squeeze my eyes shut. I can't watch. *I can't.*

"No," comes a grunted demand, too stern to ignore. "Look. Look at me."

It's not an order—his tone wasn't that whip-like growl. Even more unsettling, I think he meant it as a request, one so dangerous my heart flutters in the face of it.

No, a tiny voice inside me pleads. *Don't.* But as if against my will, my eyelids lift anyway. I fixate on the floor first before inching closer toward that gruesome corner...

Until splatters of glistening red are all I see.

Fucking red everywhere.

"*Kotyonok.*" Blinking, I snap back to awareness as the rest of the room comes into focus. Maxim is still crouched before me. Watching me. Our eyes meet, but something deep inside won't let me flinch away. Perhaps I'm in shock?

The intensity of his gaze is, in some ways, more alarming than the pool of scarlet congealing at his feet or the mass of flesh just a few feet away. One look conveys more than he could ever say. A promise. A threat. *This is what I'd do for you,* that expression declares.

Kill. Maim. Cut. For you. Can you handle that, Francesca?

"Maxim?" As if from miles away, a deeper voice intrudes. "Have you thought this through? You know he won't be missed for very long. I'm sure Anatoli is already calling for his favorite pet," the British man says. "You do realize what this means?"

"It means war," Maxim replies to him. "It means I make my claim now or let that motherfucker win. It means I end this *now*."

Eyeing his blade, he positions the tip against Sevastyn's neck, right below his skull. Nausea makes the room spin around me, but I can't help but register how surely he moves. No hesitation. No queasy unease. Only one explanation makes sense as to why—he's done this before.

"Though how long was it before Anatoli made the first strike anyway?" he muses. "Sevastyn wouldn't dare attack me without his master's permission. He came after me first. He drew first blood. No one can blame me for this."

"Sevastyn…" The other man frowns. "You think he was behind the attacks on the network?"

"He all but admitted it," Maxim hisses, his teeth bared. "As for Anatoli, I'm sure the bastard already knows what I've done. If I know him—and I do—he has half of the family assembling on the next fucking plane. He'll see this as an insult."

"An interesting theory." The other man raises an eyebrow while adjusting his grip over his blade as he scans Sevastyn's pale limbs. "But the man isn't omniscient—"

"He knows." Maxim shifts to nudge the body with his foot, rolling the corpse onto its back. "He knows the same fucking way that piece of shit knew where to strike to provoke me. The way they *all* know."

"Right." The other man's eyes cut in my direction. "I can admit that it is...*unlike* you to keep a companion for so long. But are you sure that they will—"

"Sure?" Maxim laughs, still eyeing the weapon in his fist. "Go on, ask me why Milton. I know you've wondered. Why I would risk everything. My business. My standing—"

"Don't assume. You don't know what I've thought, my friend," the other man says swiftly. "But I'll tell you what's on my mind. We need to get rid of him. Now."

Maxim grunts in agreement. With surgical precision, he lowers the tip of his blade to Sevastyn's throat.

And utilizing the palm of his other hand like a hammer, he rams it straight through the flesh and bone.

CHAPTER TWO

In reference to the dismemberment of a human body, I discover that "now" isn't as speedy as it sounds.

It takes *hours* to render the body to nothing more than bloody chunks haphazardly shoved onto a sheet of plastic for easy disposal. Maxim and Milton work ruthlessly in sync to sever muscle and tendon and bone.

At the very back of my skull, I know the gruesome nature of what I'm watching. I know that the lifeless pieces collecting onto the floor once belonged to a living, breathing human.

I just *pretend* they're nothing more than inanimate chunks of meaningless matter.

Time and space blur into one dizzying realm as I watch the grim display. I'm only aware of the passing hours at all because Milton takes meticulous note of them. "It's been two hours," he says at one point. "Another hour, you think?"

Maxim merely grunted in acknowledgment—though by then, the sound of my pulse surging through my eardrums drowned out any other noise.

I should have vomited at some point. A normal, sane human would. Maybe I did.

By the time the final, grisly piece is shoved out of sight, my knees are buckling. My stomach is a fucking mass of Jell-O balanced between my ribcage. I can't speak. Move. Even scream.

I merely stare as, together, Maxim and Milton bundle the mess between them and haul it to the door.

The sound it makes…

I'll hear it forever. A dragging hiss, followed by a wet, heavy thud.

"Fuck." Maxim hisses, eyeing a trail of ruby speckling the concrete in their wake. He starts to lower the morbid parcel, but I'm already at his side. The world jolts as I sway, off-balance, and clumsy.

I don't know what possesses me. Shock? I'm a mass of trembling, quaking limbs as I wrench my dress over my head and sink to my knees. Wadding the fabric between my fingers, I start scrubbing and scrubbing.

But the stains never disappear. Instead, the red drops multiply into an endless stream.

They're suddenly everywhere, coating everything within sight—blood-red blood.

"Enough!" Maxim rips the fabric from me, and in one quick motion, the red streaks vanish, easily swept away. "Where the fuck do we dump him?" he wonders, directing the question beyond me. "The river? The landfill?"

"We destroy it," Milton calls from the doorway. "I know a guy who runs a furnace. He's good. We won't be traced. I'll make the arrangements while you work on crafting an alibi. Anatoli won't take long to suspect the truth, but you don't have to make it easy for the old cunt."

Coldly and calmly, he wipes most of the blood from his hands with a handkerchief and casually drops the soiled cloth onto the plastic mound at his feet. "And to stop your paranoia from going bat-shit, I'll make some calls to my people. Plant rumors to stall the inevitable. Anatoli isn't a fool. Sevastyn was a loyal bitch, and his master will notice when he no longer comes to heel with his fucking tail wagging. With a little more planning, we could have crafted a more believable disappearance…"

"Go on and say it," Maxim scoffs. "I shouldn't have killed him. Not like this. It's fucking sloppy."

"You shouldn't have killed him," Milton agrees. "But that isn't why I'm concerned."

"Oh?"

A frown distorts Milton's otherwise emotionless visage. "You claimed *Sevastyn* was the one disrupting your supply lines. You sure of that?"

"It makes sense." Maxim returns to his full height and tosses my bloodied dress aside. Concentration consumes him, tightening the line of his jaw. He doesn't even seem to notice or care that I'm entirely naked, without even a pair of underwear. "Why? Have you learned new information?"

"Maybe." Milton looks down at his hands, flexing them one by one. "I didn't want to bring this to you until I was absolutely certain, but my men may have made headway in discovering the true culprit..." He looks up to meet Maxim's gaze directly. "I don't think it was Sevastyn."

"Fuck. Then who?" Maxim's upper lip pulls back from his teeth as he strokes a bloodied finger along his chin. "A rival? No. If it were someone well known, I would have narrowed it down by now."

"Someone we both always seem to underestimate." Milton's gaze drifts toward me and then back to Maxim. "Someone who might enjoy disrupting your supply lines if only to prove that he could."

"No..." Maxim shakes his head. "No. Even he wouldn't dare."

"Wouldn't he?" Amusement tilts the corner of Milton's mouth. "You never could predict Vadim. Though, maybe it's about time you finally set aside your—"

"I said no." The crunch of clenching teeth cuts the silence like a gunshot. "Don't even say his name—"

"Which is why I wanted to be sure," Milton says smoothly. "But even if it is him, he won't take it further."

"Or he could be working for Sevastyn?" Maxim interjects, his voice rasping. "Don't pretend like you haven't kept tabs on them both this entire fucking time."

"No." Milton inclines his head, his lips pulled tight. "He's a clever son of a bitch, I'll give him that, but if anyone wanted to drive a knife into Sevastyn more than you, or myself, it's Dima—*Vadim*."

"I told you not to say his fucking name."

"*Fine.*" Milton extends his arms in a gesture of surrender. His bloodied hands are a chilling reminder of the current situation, almost appearing like a ghoulish pair of gloves to compliment his ebony suit. "Consider the discussion over. For now. We have more important things to do, like focus on getting rid of this wanker. The sooner we finish, the sooner I can call in a team to erase any physical traces."

Wordlessly, he and Maxim refocus their attention on the grisly mass nearby. They both take a corner of the plastic tarp and drag the body into the hall inch by inch, grunting with the effort.

I'm left behind, trembling in the frigid air, naked without my dress. Before I can attempt to move, Maxim's voice reaches back to me. "Stay."

I do, my vision blurring. The only sounds are my ragged breaths scratching at the air as I inhale. Exhale. Faster. God, salt is all I can smell. All I taste.

Maybe I'm overreacting?

Because despite Maxim's comfort with death, this isn't my first time facing it either—a terrifying concept I can't dissect just yet. *No.* So I wait, listening to the scraping of plastic over concrete, desperate for relief.

I find my escape in snippets of murmured conversation.

"You're sure about this?" Milton says, his accent distinct. "We could always attempt to stall. Forge rumors about his whereabouts."

"Like you said, Anatoli is no fool," Maxim replies. "After tonight, it's not like I have a choice regardless."

"So, what now?"

"Now..." Maxim sounds fainter, his words interspersed with muffled grunts and more hissing plastic. "Now, we beat the motherfucker at his own game..."

When approaching footsteps return moments later, I recognize their heavy, ominous cadence before their owner appears alone in the doorway. Bathed in shadow, Maxim inclines his head for me to follow. "Come."

I lurch after him on unsteady, jellied legs. My thoughts are too scattered to make out our surroundings—only he has any definition against a formless, colorless landscape of shadow. Hunched over with my arms around myself, I'm freezing until a layer of warm fabric falls over my shoulders —his jacket, reeking of salt and damp in places...

I gag—but his scent dominates the luxurious fabric despite the wetness. Somehow breathing it in keeps my roiling stomach at bay.

I can resist the terror. He alone is my anchor to sanity, guiding me in deliberate commands and stern touches.

"*Kotyonok*," he prompts as we reach a familiar destination, his car. "Get in."

He opens the door on my end, and I climb woodenly into the passenger's seat. Once we're secured within the confines of black leather and metal, I can finally breathe normally again.

But I'm not brave enough to ask more questions. Like where the body is. Or Milton. Or what happens next.

I close my eyes to shut out the world entirely as Maxim starts to drive. Only now do I realize that I have no fucking clue where he's headed. Despite everything—even the ring on my finger—paranoia sets in, gnawing at my fragile composure. There is one fear I can't ignore when it comes to him…

The unsettling knowledge that he's always on a hair-trigger. Is this the moment when I meet my own end on a wad of sheet plastic? The fear of that fate should bite deeper into my psyche than it does, though. This stupid, internal voice resists it, too naïve to believe but persistent, nonetheless. *He won't hurt me…*

"We're almost there," Maxim declares, breaking the string of morbid thoughts. Like a puppet master adept at his craft, he knows just when to reassert his presence. "Look at me."

When I reopen my eyes, I don't recognize the cluster of buildings around us. They're too tall. Too bright. So we aren't heading toward his usual suite, then. But this isn't the neighborhood where my family is either.

Though, I'm not left to wonder for very long.

As if on cue, he turns a corner, and the car comes to a stop amid unfamiliar scenery. Gripping my seatbelt, I race to piece together our surroundings. Somewhere dark. Enclosed. A garage? Fresh panic sets in, scattering imaginary butterflies in my stomach. Dark spaces have terrible connotations where he's concerned. Especially when he looks like this...

Smoldering in silence. Tense, harboring fire within his gaze as white-knuckled fingers clench in and out of fists.

"Come." He's already exiting the car, oblivious to my reaction. Either that or he's deliberately ignoring the terror I know is etched on my face.

"Come," he commands again, but his back is to me, and he starts across the garage without waiting for me to move.

Before he can leave my line of sight, I stagger after him, a slave to his whims even as my brain stalls.

The garage exits into a darkened hallway closed off by a single elevator. When the doors part several floors later, they reveal another door at the end of a carpeted corridor. Here an eerie sense of déjà vu washes over me. I recall that very first day weeks ago when I arrived as a prostitute before a mysterious, wealthy client who lived in a building much like this one.

Beyond this black door lies a fittingly similar suite—but it's larger than the last. Or so I assume from the echoing, cavernous interior that multiplies our footsteps into a deafening clamor. This layout differs from his old residence in more than just size. The furniture scattered across a spacious entryway is simpler when glimpsed in the dark. Practical.

"We will stay here for now," he explains as he crosses the drawing room. A series of closed doors line a short hallway leading deeper into the interior. His confident steps betray a knowledge of the layout that makes me suspect he didn't just buy it on a whim. "I've already had your things from the old suite brought here."

As he speaks, he opens the door to a room that I assume at first is a copy of my old one. But it's larger. And instead of white or his preferred black, these walls are painted a simple shade of gray. An odd feeling of relief eases some of the stiffness in my limbs.

At least it's not red.

When I breathe in deep, I smell still, scentless air—no salt.

It's a welcome change from that cold, concrete room dominated by a table stocked with weapons. Here, the main piece of furniture is a massive bed positioned near a breathtaking view of the city. It's nearly twice the size of my old one—but it's the open closet that draws my interest.

Of all things to pop into my head, the first thought is fittingly childish after a night filled with death. Daisy would *die* to own a closet like this—one large enough to fit our entire old house in with room to spare. I can't take my eyes off of the clothing displayed in meticulous order for some reason, though. Most of the options on metal hangers consist of his customary dark shirts and slacks.

But they only take up one half. The other side of the space contains an array of delicate, lacy gowns and dresses recognizable at a glance. *Mine.*

And a dangerous thought threatens to disrupt our previous boundaries—this room is *ours.*

Maxim barges into the closet without explanation—as if that little detail means nothing. Sighing, he strips his shirt, and the cadence of his voice snaps me out of my shock. "Take off your clothes. Put them with mine. I'll dispose of them later."

He does the same, but tension contorts his body into a series of rippling muscles. And I'm hypnotized. His scars gleam in the glow of moonlight, betraying a mere hint of the horror he's lived through.

I still haven't moved by the time he throws his wadded shirt to the floor, and wrenches open his slacks. "Did you hear me, *kotyonok*?" He cocks his head in my direction, his gaze indiscernible. "Move."

I jump, too enthralled by his appearance to turn away. Blood speckles his chin. Even more paints his fingers in violent streaks. When he notices me staring, he turns and reenters the bedroom. There must be a bathroom nearby because I hear water running. A few seconds later, he returns, and the blood is gone.

"Look at me," he demands. But I already am.

He hasn't bothered to turn a light on, and only the glow from the floor-to-ceiling windows bathes him in bluish definition. The contours of his body create organized chaos from the hulking mass of bulk and muscle that shape him. He's beautiful, as if hand-carved by an artist intent on crafting a creature somewhere in between a devil and an angel. The only detail out of place is the black binder cinching his waist, obscuring yet another traumatic souvenir from his past.

"*Kotyonok...*" His eyes meet mine, and my heart seizes up at what I find in them. More rage? No. Something far more unsettling. In fact, when his nostrils flare with my scent, it's the most alarming sight I've been faced with all night, and I stagger back a step in the opposite direction.

Lust.

In him, it's an emotion comparable to a match striking a pool of gasoline. Volatile. Like a predator, he advances, herding me into a corner. Within seconds, my back is against the wall, and he's towering above me, rage smoldering off his skin.

But I'm not terrified of what the anger itself does to him. In a way, it's beautiful to witness its impact up close.

His features shift and meld, seamlessly transforming him from man to beast. Gone is the cold, dispassionate mask. Teeth bared, he eyes me with a ruthless flick of his gaze, and I know he's here with me fully—not trapped in the past. But then he laughs, and the sound resonates all the way down to my fucking core.

Sevastyn wasn't the only one to stoke his temper, it seems.

"It's always as though it's the first time. How you look at me," he murmurs, reaching for my chin. His thumb brushes my jawline reverently, even as his eyes glow with that unsteady gleam that heralds disaster. My heart lurches with every careful stroke, and I know better than to say a damn thing. "Whenever you see me at my worst," he explains, lowering his gaze to my throat. "You stare at me, with your eyes so fucking wide. Always as though it's the first time. The first day..."

He laughs again, but it's a bitter sound.

"Those fucking eyes haunt me. I shouldn't even give a damn if you're afraid." He bares his teeth in torment as his finger presses harder, seeking out the bone beneath my flesh. The second I wince, he withdraws. "But I still see what he did to you. What I *let* him do."

My barely healed injuries throb at the reminder, but I don't welcome this biting sort of pain. It burns, summoning tears I have to fight to keep at bay.

"I close my eyes and see it," he adds thickly. "I can't sleep without fucking seeing it. Even now, I can still hear that motherfucker, taunting me with the threat of you."

In a sick way, he resembles someone fighting to stay awake. Like Ainsley when she's resisting a nightmare—but the phantoms in his head consist of horrors no child should ever face. In frustration, his hands unfurl, the nails drawn like claws, and he resorts to the one tool he's relied on until now.

Anger.

"Did you take my ring out of fear?" he wonders, his accent thickening, his baritone deepening. He's hunting for a line of attack, I think—desperate for anything to feed his rage. To distract from the truth—he's losing control. "Is that it?"

"No." He flinches at the sound of my voice, but I finally regain control of my limbs before he can reply. There is only one way to reach him when he's like this—the only language we both understand.

A startled grunt escapes him as I brush my hands over the front of the jacket draped over me. A tailored silk, the fabric easily slides from my shoulders to the floor.

His eyes narrow, tracking the flesh bared with ravenous interest and that wavering darkness slowly fades in favor of a new emotion. He's here again, alone with me in this room —not the past.

I swallow back my relieved sigh and brace. Maybe he's right. In some ways, it really does feel like that very first day all over again. My first exposure to the taste of his brutality. I'm unsure of what to expect from this massive creature who radiates power and control.

And yet for whatever reason, I'm drawn to the flame, even if it burns.

This pain doesn't hurt the way it should.

"Say it," he demands, recapturing my chin in his grasp. With gentle pressure, he pries my jaws apart. "You are mine. Say it."

I rush to obey. "I'm yours—"

"Body and soul," he prompts, each word grated through clenched teeth. His tone alone betrays that they mean more to him than a selfish boast of possession. So much fucking more. They're the reason why I can watch him at his worst, on the brink of madness, and keep what little shreds of sanity I still have left. Why his hands shake as they grasp handfuls of me—whatever he can reach. Nails drawn, he claims every inch of flesh, his eyes fluttering as I flinch.

"Body and soul," I tell him, fighting to form a coherent response.

"And you won't run from this? From me?" He grinds his hips into mine, igniting a tendril of fire in my core.

Clamping my thighs together is the only way to stave off the inevitable inferno.

"I won't."

In a blur of motion, he moves in, claiming my mouth as his hands grip my waist. His tongue barely slips between my lips before he draws back and wrenches me around to face the wall. I suck in a breath, the sound nearly drowning out his appreciative groan. His palm smooths over the flat of my belly, aiming between my legs. In an expert motion, he spreads me open, teasing me with the broadness of his thumb.

I barely adjust to the substitute before the real thing batters against my throbbing skin.

One thrust, and he's so deep I can't even cry out in response. I gasp instead, my lips parted, air trapped in my lungs. Overwhelmed with the feel of him, my brain conjures a million words to describe the sensation—*full, so full. Thick. Heavy. Everywhere.*

Then he moves, bucking into me, forcing my cheek against the ice-cold wall as his body pins me in from behind. He's slow at first, ensuring every thrust stings. Burns, so deep I'll feel him for days. Just as the pain fades into a delicious ache, he moves faster. Harder.

The rhythm lacks the brutal tempo I'm used to. My world narrows to sin and skin, and the wet heat of his mouth latched onto my shoulder, muffling the animalistic grunts he makes with every single thrust.

My nails uselessly scramble over the surface before me, seeking out stability. Security. Anything.

I find neither.

Nothing in the world is stable enough to anchor me against him. I have to endure—every ounce of frustration and fury, slammed into me, straining the confines of my body. The emotions roused by the night's events seep from him, betraying more than words ever could.

Sevastyn rattled him.

Infuriated him.

But what happened after confused him.

And the sight of that marble ring on my finger...it scares him?

There's almost too much to make sense of—too much for him to process alone.

So he spills them all into me one by one, until his release drags both of us under. His grip on my hair tightens painfully as he rams into me one final time, so hard my knees buckle.

He's left holding me, sweeping his hand beneath my knees as he pulls out and lifts me into his arms. Boneless, my head lolls against his shoulder as I find myself focusing on his face first, marveling at what I see. Gone is that twisted, pained expression. I can't resist stroking my fingers along the corner of his mouth, tracing its shape when devoid of a scowl or frown.

For once, he moves free of tension, crossing the room to another door that I hadn't noticed. The bathroom? He shoulders the door open, and I realize that my suspicion was horribly off base.

"I will admit that I prefer to use the club whenever I can," he admits as he steps over the threshold. "But in the interim, *this* will make do for when I need you."

This. A space enclosed by ebony walls and gray marble floors, containing more careful details than the rest of the suite. There are no windows to the outside world. Just closeness and shadow and him. The only real item of furniture is a table in the center made of solid black marble, polished enough for me to make out my reflection as he sets me onto it.

It's cold. A hiss escapes my mouth, and he tugs me closer in response, dominating the space between my legs. Leeching off his heat, I watch him silently explore the surface beneath me. For my benefit, I realize—it's a silent tour of sorts.

Beneath my position, a small ledge extends from the side of the table. I follow the line of his gaze as he runs his hands over the objects strategically placed there, all within reach. One article is a pool of thin, black fabric.

A blindfold? Alarming enough—but the other items are seared onto my psyche even if I don't dwell on their purpose for now.

An unlit candle.

A pair of metal handcuffs, lined with black leather.

And lastly, a knife, sharpened and ready. Maxim grasps the weapon first, testing the weight against his palm.

"Do you know when I first knew it?" he wonders against my scalp. "That you were mine? Do you?" His finger returns to my jaw, urging me closer with a beckoning caress. "It was that first night you climaxed. Do you remember?"

I do, and my throat goes dry at the memory.

"It's not the fact that you got off that made me consider snapping your fucking neck right then and there." His thumb teases the throat in question, tracing the hollow of it as I suck in air, too enthralled by his words to release it. "I could feel it…your greedy cunt gripping me tight. For the first time, fucking wasn't satisfying an urge, no more intimate than pissing or breathing. Your body wanted more than a fuck, wringing every ounce it could from me."

The awe in his tone resonates down to my core. Deep inside, muscles clench in response, my brain buzzing.

"You don't understand it." He looks down at his hands and curls them into fists. "What it feels like to go your entire life satisfying those primal fucking urges out of necessity and nothing more. Before you, I rated the quality of sex based on how efficiently I could get it over with. How much blood I could draw and gasps I could wring from the whore beneath me just to know…I was still there. Still alive. Still connected to my body. Pleasure didn't matter. Lust was a mere byproduct of biology. I was always in control. But that night with you…" His lips purse as he lowers his hand to his glistening cock. "You forced me to feel it, didn't you?"

His eyes cut up to mine accusingly.

"You made me see you. Even now, at the edge, when I can feel myself so fucking close to slipping. When all I should crave is to go numb. To rage, and maim, and kill. *You…*" He laughs in disbelief, shaking his head. The manic gleam in his eye reassures me despite how my heart seizes up. The terror is still there, building in my blood, but that one, searing expression keeps me from succumbing to it.

Because it means he's still here in this moment. Still Maxim.

And he reaches for me like a lifeline, his nails biting into my skin, sealing in his possession.

"I still feel you," he admits. "Like no one else. So hear me now—"A searing pain in my ear is my only warning as he bites down over the sensitive lobe. "Mine," he rasps. "You were made for me. And I will ensure the world knows it. No matter the fucking cost."

CHAPTER THREE

My memory goes hazy after that, devolving into snippets. More sex. Restless sleeping. Waking. More sleeping. When I fully regain my senses, I'm lying on a substance so soft that I swear I'm floating. Falling. My fingers fan out, scrambling for purchase against something solid. And I find it.

Warm, flexing, heavy…

Confused, I open my eyes, enthralled by the vision before me. Maxim Koslov, in stark naked glory, save the black binder around his waist. Golden hair fans over his forehead, obscuring his eyes. But they're closed and his chest rises and falls in a steady rhythm. He's asleep. And that fact alone transforms him into another fucking person.

My breath catches as I find myself inching closer, riveted by his face when devoid of a glare or scowl. Someone like him can never be at peace—not fully. But this may be the closest I've seen him come to it.

And the sight leaves me stunned. My fingers fan out without my brain telling them to, smoothing over his cheek. I barely touch him before the moment shatters. He springs into awareness, grabbing my wrist, but when his eyes finally open, his fingers relax, releasing me.

We're on the bed, I realize.

Our bed. Sweat and musk flood the air—me and him combined into one indiscernible aroma. Gone is the distinct, invisible barrier that always divided his old suite, separating him from me.

This place is different.

And he's still here, lingering beside me in a way he rarely has. Nostrils flared, he inhales my scent as his other hand grazes my waist, dragging me closer to him. Like a dog on a leash. I arch into the touch, savoring the satisfied grunt resonating in his chest.

"So much like a kitten," he murmurs thickly. "My *kotyonok*. Snuggling close to me when she should turn tail and run. Now more than ever."

For once, he doesn't sound angry, and he doesn't roll me beneath him in a sexual frenzy either. *This* is somehow more unsettling. Him lying here with me. Breathing me in. Feeling me. Torturing me.

"I scared you tonight," he says, his cold eyes blinking once. "I saw how you looked at me. Like I lost my goddamn mind. But, you were not the catalyst for this... I used to dream of killing him." I marvel at the raspy cadence of his voice, devoid of hostility. I think he's half-asleep still, but for whatever reason, he feels compelled to share. Something. Anything.

So I hoard every scrap he's willing to give.

"I planned it down to the last fucking detail," he continues, absently stroking the side of my hip. "How I would make him suffer. Make him scream. For over twenty years, I've dreamt about it. But there are rules when it comes to revenge. I alone was never worth the risk…"

He settles the palm of his free hand against my cheek. Though he may have cleaned them of blood, violence resonates in his fingertips, impossible to erase. I can feel the power weighing down every inch of flesh and nail and bone. It's intoxicating in its potency.

But intimacy shouldn't feel like this—like a drug—I know that. Going off depictions in movies, I should crave heartfelt embraces and passionate cuddling.

I should crave normal, wholesome affection.

Not the caress a murderer can impart just as easily as ruthless brutality. He frowns, seemingly just as confused as I am by my reaction. My chin tilts, seeking out the contact, extending it.

"So greedy," he admonishes. "You take only what you can in the moment. Maybe it's for the best," he adds. "Dwelling on the past is for the weak. Don't make the mistake of assuming that's why I did it. I didn't kill him because of what he's done—but because of what he was. A wolf too much of a fucking coward to hunt in the light, so he thrived in the shadow, picking off weak prey. *You* appealed to him. He hurt you, and yet you look at *me* with pity."

His voice catches on a dangerous, unstable note I know too well.

"I don't crave your pity." I flinch as his fingers brush over my cheekbones, but I don't pull away. Nails drawn, he probes me mercilessly. Whatever he seeks must lurk in the corner of my mouth. He slides his thumb along the seam, blinks...and he's back again.

"And yet you offer it, anyway." His nostrils flare, his voice hollow. "It's the one thing you give me freely, other than submission. Your pity." I can't tell if that angers him or not.

In the end, he merely sighs and eases the hair from my face with the tip of his finger.

"That motherfucker didn't make me. I made *him*. I ended him. He didn't fucking win. They won't win. And whether I seek out Dima or not, nothing changes."

"Dima?" I risk asking. He's mentioned that name before to Milton. "Who is—"

"No one," he snaps, but the viciousness in his voice warns of the opposite. "The past cannot be undone. So there is no point in regret. I never owed him a damn thing. I still don't."

My lips twitch. I need to say something else. Comfort him, I think.

Before I can get a word out, he rolls onto his side with his back to me. I barely mourn the loss of his touch when he hooks his arm around my waist, dragging me to him.

Tethering me to him.

"I chose you over him. Over them." I can feel the vibrations rumbling through his back with every grated word. It's more than a boast. More than a promise. It's a warning. "Don't forget that. Don't ever forget that. I chose *you*. I will fight for you."

Saying it out loud must comfort him in ways that even bashing Sevastyn's skull in didn't—because within minutes...I know he's asleep.

I WAKE up again to golden daylight flooding in through the window, but I don't have the strength to even move, let alone get up. I'm so fucking tired. My muscles ache, my mind exhausted. For a second, I think I'm still dreaming, imagining the snippets of conversation drifting on the edges of my consciousness.

"...A message came this morning," a man confesses, his tone cordial. *Lucius?* "You won't like it. Should I convey it regardless?"

Someone grunts in response. That guttural baritone needs no introduction.

"Anatoli has demanded your presence," Lucius continues. "Far be it for me to make a suggestion, sir. But if you were planning to declare your independence from him, now might be your chance. My contacts have already picked up on chatter within the network, speculating on Sevastyn's sudden absence over the past twenty-four hours…"

If Maxim replies at all, I don't hear him, imagined or otherwise. It could be because my brain shuts down, cringing from any mention of that name. *Anatoli.* If I'm still dreaming, the image creeping into my mind would surely reinforce this moment being a nightmare—a man with cold, lifeless eyes so similar to Maxim's it's chilling. Like he's doomed to one day reach the same level of callous, inhumanity.

I squeeze my eyes shut, blocking out the memories. Rolling over, I press my face against a mound of silken sheets. Just as I start to drift off again, a familiar command cuts through the exhaustion like a knife. "Come."

Still half-asleep, I scramble from the sheets and find a black robe draped over the end of the bed. It's silk, tailored to my size. Made for me.

Cautiously, I enter the hall wearing it and find Maxim in an enormous dining room adjacent to an open floor plan kitchen. A row of windows displays the city of Fair Haven from its very heart. From the bay to the glittering center, all the way to a glimpse of the slums on the very outskirts.

Attacking his uncle may have been the opening salvo of a so-called war, but Maxim certainly isn't in hiding. This bold, new residence makes one fact painfully clear—he's ready for a fight.

And this view serves as the perfect backdrop for the breakfast of a man hell-bent on domination. What might fuel such an enigmatic figure? Two plates before him contain the answer—poached eggs over a rare steak sliced to perfection.

"Sit." He nods to the chair beside him. When I comply, he picks up a fork from the table, twisting it between his fingers. He's been up for a while, already fully dressed in a black suit, his hair damp and freshly washed. The sight of him makes me keenly aware of the grime still clinging to me. Namely, the rust-colored gunk caked beneath my fingernails.

I try scratching it away, but the stain remains no matter how fiercely I dig. It hurts, but I can't stop scraping. Probing. Bleeding.

"I have business to attend to," Maxim informs me, and I look up, forcing my hands flat against the table. "Meetings. I'll be gone until tonight."

I nod absently, still processing the past twenty-four hours. My brain struggles to digest the tonal whiplash. Murder one moment. Breakfast the next.

And brutal sex replaced by casual conversation.

"Lucius will accompany you today," he continues. "But you will be on your own for most of it."

That sounds like more than an afternoon spent here waiting for him. I brush my tongue along my lower lip before replying. "For what?"

Rather than answer me immediately, he drags my plate toward him and cuts the meat into even smaller pieces. Then he nudges it in my direction with a grunted command, "Eat."

As I shovel a piece of steak into my mouth, I catch him watching every fucking move I make, missing nothing.

"Swallow," he prompts, once I've taken a few mechanical chews. Satisfied, he adds while my mouth is full, "I'm sending you for a dress."

A dress. Maybe his penthouse and our relationship isn't the only thing that has changed after last night? He thinks I need a new wardrobe as well. I'm partially through chewing another slice of meat when I finally process the deliberate way he pronounced that word, however. Dress.

A dress.

The dress.

I swallow too quickly and wind up choking. Eyes streaming, I gulp at a glass of water shoved in my direction. Once I stop sputtering, the only thing I can think to say is, "But I haven't even told my family."

About the true nature of my relationship with him.

About why our lives have changed so drastically.

About…

"Did you change your mind?" he wonders, his tone eerily level. "About marrying me."

I flinch and set my fork aside. Even thinking in those foreign terms heats my skin. It sounds unnatural. Me *married* to Maxim. Him, waiting for me at the end of an aisle. Signing up for forever at his whim.

It sounds fucking insane.

"If your siblings are your main concern, we can arrange for you to tell them before then," he suggests while stabbing at his own piece of meat.

I feel my brows furrow. "Before what?"

"The ceremony." He pauses to chew a bite of steak. As he swallows, he dabs at the corner of his mouth with a white cloth. Then he continues, "I've arranged for it to take place by the end of the month."

"So soon?" I sound more panicked than surprised. So soon. A wedding.

"The sooner, the better," he insists while slicing off another piece of his steak. He makes it sound so simple. Like a walk in the park. A necessary chore. Business—but the more he broaches the topic, the harder it is for my brain to comprehend. "It is not enough for me to merely claim that you are mine," he says. "I must prove it. Publicly, in terms that men like my grandfather will understand. In my family, your worth only extends to the power of the name attached to it. If you are to be protected from now on, you must take mine. Eat."

I force down another bite while observing him. It's going to storm today—literally and figuratively. Already, dark clouds shroud the sun, choking out the daylight. A cold, overcast gray replaces it, reflecting off the angular features that make his face so expressive and so beautiful.

Even while he's brooding.

Aware of me watching, he shifts, angling himself toward me. "A month might seem 'soon' from your position, but trust me, it's a gift. Even a week's delay is wasted time." He takes a sip from his own glass of water as his eyes flicker over mine suddenly guarded. "The sooner you become a Koslov in name, the better."

Though, in a sense, I already have his name. Absently, I trail my fingers along my bare inner thigh, tracing a series of healing welts. Lines. When viewed at once, they proclaim ownership. His. "Why so fast?"

I'm not brave enough to mention the conversation I may or may not have imagined. Could his accelerated timeline have something to do with his grandfather's demand?

"Why?" He cocks his head and observes me from the newer angle. "Consider it like another transaction. I give you security. In return, I know you are protected."

"But why rush?" I say, probing him as much as I dare. "We barely even know each other."

Which is a goddamn lie. In some ways, he knows me better than I know myself. And as for him…

I know that he's someone who would never offer a "transaction" like this to any other woman.

"Your feelings or mine have nothing to do with it," he says, scoffing at the prospect. "This would be a transaction. Nothing less, nothing more."

"Okay, but…" I shake my head. "What about my family?"

"It's simple. They become *my* family."

"And the house? Will we stay there—"

"Nothing else will change," he snaps, shoving his plate aside. "Think of it as merely an extension of our previous arrangement."

"Through marriage…" My head is spinning. I lean over the table and cradle my temple against my palm. "A wedding," I repeat, tasting how the word sounds out loud. Terrifying, that's how. "Are you just going to take me to the courthouse or something?"

"I don't think you understand the situation." His tone softens a fraction, sounding damn near gentle. "Killing Sevastyn didn't end this. It started it. If I don't make my intentions known now, they won't just kill you. They'll take pleasure in using you against me any way they can. They'll sell you. Beat you. Destroy you." He glowers into the distance, seeing his hypothetical threats unfold. "So, trust me when I say that a month isn't soon enough. Regardless, you still have time to tell your family."

"And then what?" There are ways to sugarcoat it—but I doubt Daisy and Mikie will buy that I would meet a man and marry him in less than a year. They *shouldn't*—even if said fiancé purchased a new house and enrolled them in schools, we could have only dreamed of them attending a few months ago.

Melanie did shit like that. Not me.

"Then..." Pulling his plate back, he glowers at the meat before slicing through it. "Then you'll be protected. Nothing else will change. And Sevastyn can rot in the ground like the rat he is while Anatoli twiddles his thumbs in the front fucking row before the altar."

I flinch at the imagery. I don't think he even realizes the irony of it—in one breath, he makes being a Koslov sound synonymous with envious security. But in the next, he refers to his own family members in terms most people would reserve for mortal enemies. Melanie had a habit of hitching up with men she barely knew—but here's the funny part. I know even less about Maxim or his past.

But some topics are better left broached when he doesn't have a knife within reach.

"I'm guessing I can't just wear a dress from Kmart?" I say, clumsily changing tact.

He raises an eyebrow. I caught him off guard. No, it's stranger than that—I've amused him. "Not exactly." His hand shoots out, and he snags one of my curls. As I watch, holding my breath, he tucks the strand behind my ear. "My wife deserves something a bit grander than that."

Goosebumps rise over my skin at how dangerous that word sounds coming from him. *Wife.* His tone caresses it like a noose, strangling any warmth from every single syllable. It's not a title. It's a life sentence.

"You're serious about this," I rasp.

"More than serious." He grasps my hand, extending the fingers for his inspection. The one wearing his ring trembles beneath his scrutiny. "I told you once, in so many words—I do not offer what I am not willing to give." He strokes his thumb along the gleaming marble for emphasis. "I am offering you this."

This. Him. Our lives. The possibility of those two things no longer being mutually exclusive.

The possibility of tethering myself to him in ways more binding than a stupid piece of paper.

The possibility of complete and total surrender beyond the boundaries of sex.

"It's a lot to consider overnight," I croak—but it's another lie. I've had days to reconcile my relationship with him well before now. Hours of dwelling on him. Endless minutes of contemplation of what my connection to him means.

And I've avoided thinking of anything beyond the here and now.

"Did you think I was lying?" he wonders as if reading my mind. "Or making a boast in the heat of the moment?"

"No," I say quickly. "But…"

"Or perhaps you don't understand just what it is I'm offering. Do you think I was my father's only child?" He stands and storms over to the windows. With every step he takes, tension ripples down his spine, enhancing his bulk until he appears ten times larger. Massive. "Of course, I wasn't. He had more bastards than a stray mutt drawn to any bitch in heat. But *I* am the one with his name. I was the one legitimate enough to supplant him. I am a *Koslov*." He makes it sound so much more than a title. It's his identity. In a way, I think he's proud of it as much as he hates what that very name makes him.

He is Maxim Koslov. In his world, that gives him meaning. Purpose. Enough for him to adhere to its archaic rules.

And prize its twisted perks.

"Even Anatoli cannot deny that fucking birthright. Once you are my wife, no one will be able to touch you outright. No matter who I kill or what I do. You won't have to fear a fucker like Sevastyn ever again…" He frowns as if unconvinced of his own words, but the subtle tensing of his jaw reveals that he's already made up his mind. "I would like your permission," he adds, clenching his hands so tightly the knuckles crack in unison. "But don't presume I need it. If need be, I can drag you to the altar."

"Really?" I feel hot. My body reacts to the warning, tensing up. Unease thickens my throat. All I can choke out is a stupid, pathetic question. "Is that what you really want?"

"No," he confesses—and for what it's worth, I believe that he means it.

Regardless, I can't take my eyes off his ring. Like magic, it morphs, becoming a ball and chain, making my hand impossible to lift.

"Don't forget that you've already accepted this," he points out. "You've accepted me. And yet there it is. Those eyes—" He glowers at me from over his shoulder. "Always so fucking surprised. I kill a man, and you strip yourself naked to assist me with the mess. Only to pretend that you have no idea what staying by my side at all *means*. Have we really come back to this?" He sounds so empty. Maybe because those are the exact words I asked myself last night.

Which brings this whole conversation to a morbid full circle.

Unsure of the answer, I meet his gaze and shiver at the secrets I find lurking inside it. Going off of my experience when he's angry, he should frown, or flash that disapproving glare I've grown accustomed to. Anything but tilt his head away from me, disguising any potential reaction I could decipher.

"Tonight." Turning on his heel, he starts for the foyer, flexing his arms to adjust his suit jacket. One of his hands brushes his collar, smoothing the lapel flat while he shoots me one last searching glance. "We will discuss this tonight. Everything. *After* you return from the fitting."

Even if I felt brave enough to, he doesn't give me the chance to argue. With his back stick-straight, he marches to the front of the suite. A second later, I hear the door slam.

And I'm alone.

CHAPTER FOUR

Our impending discussion doesn't include the potential of whether or not I'll need a dress—the matter has already been decided. Like always, some aspects of Maxim Koslov are nonnegotiable—what he wants, he gets. Within seconds of him leaving, his trusted henchman is already knocking on the door.

"Ms. Marconi," Lucius greets me with a small smile. "I will allow you to get dressed, and then we can be on our way."

After a quick shower in a luxurious bathroom off the master suite, I change into a simple black dress and join Lucius in the car.

Minutes later, we reach our destination.

"I'll be waiting whenever you're ready, Ms. Marconi," Lucius announces from the driver's seat. He eyes the building straight across from where we're parked. It's simple, made of brick, positioned between some of the more upscale buildings in the affluent part of the city. Places I used to only glimpse in magazines.

My heart pounds as I exit the car and cross the busy street, bustling with the height of afternoon traffic. Trust Maxim to pick such a place—exclusive and excluded, yet unabashedly public.

Through a pair of gleaming black doors, I find an interior of dark walls and plush carpet. A woman comes to greet me from around a wooden podium, her outfit a crisply tailored black. "You must be Francesca," she says, clasping one of my hands. "This way."

She leads me into a wide, open area displaying a rack of fabric along one wall and a row of mirrors along the other. My reflection taunts me from them—an army of pale, wide-eyed figures gaping as the world shifts around them.

"Mr. Koslov had a list of requirements sent over," she explains while fishing a slim black notebook from an apron slung around her waist.

"Requirements?" I sound surprised, but deep down, I'm not. Maxim leave something as personal as a wedding dress up to me? Never. Like everything else in his life, he seems to have it planned to the last meticulous detail.

"Oh yes," the woman gushes, oblivious to my confusion. "The designer can't wait to get started. We drooled over the sketches last night. Not many people opt for traditional gowns nowadays. And attempting a Russian style gown will be a unique challenge, especially."

She pauses expectantly, but all I can do is blink and force a smile.

"Yes…well…" Clearing her throat, the girl steers me before the wall of mirrors and withdraws a tape measure from another apron pocket. "Today, I will just get your preliminary measurements. You don't have to lift a single finger. Shall we begin?"

Eyeing my reflection, I nod. The girl in the glass glares at me, her gaze revealing everything I'm too chicken to say out loud. *Don't be stupid. You're not really surprised, are you? Emotion has nothing to do with it.*

In Maxim Koslov's world, relationships are tethered to contracts. Sex is a primal release, no more intimate than breathing.

And marriage is a business transaction.

Nothing more.

HOURS LATER, and I'm still staring at my reflection—a stranger draped in yards of ivory lace. If I ever were to imagine myself wearing a wedding dress, I wouldn't pick white as the color.

It makes my skin look sallow, and my hair duller than usual. My curls are a frizzy cloud barely able to support the thin, sheer fabric thrown over them as a makeshift veil. Not to mention the dress itself.

Grander, Maxim claimed. Maybe his real meaning got lost in translation—extravagant. Swaths of silk and taffeta extend from my waist. It's the skeleton of a ballgown ripped from one of those princess movies Ainsley loves to watch.

The designer is crouched beside me, sticking pins into a massive skirt. She works efficiently, but one thing is clear— my input isn't needed. While I may be the one meant to wear it, this dress is a token in the same vein as my ring. Maxim has his own plan set into motion. I'm just a pawn being moved across the board.

"We're all done for today," the woman announces, rising to her feet. She swipes imaginary dust from her knees and then helps me remove the pieces of the dress. "Your next appointment is in a week. Mr. Koslov has already made the arrangements."

A week. The timeframe feels like an ominous deadline. One I'm keenly aware of as I exit the boutique and find a black car waiting for me. Before I can take a step toward the curb, a voice calls out.

"Mrs. Koslov? Mrs. Koslov!"

I turn to find the seamstress racing from the boutique, a white piece of paper clenched in her fist, and a shopping bag dangling from her opposite hand. Even as she rushes toward me, I can't bite back the instinctive need to correct her. "I'm not—"

"Here," she insists, shoving the items into my hands. "Mr. Koslov wanted me to pass this message along, along with this dress. Have a nice day."

I stare after her, my heart racing, my throat dry. Inside the shopping bag is a white box tied with a black ribbon. A building sense of dread churns in my stomach as I shove my hand between the edges of the box, just enough to catch a swath of dark fabric inside, nestled within tissue paper. Whatever it's meant for, I doubt it's intended for the wedding. Something less formal, then? Like another meeting with Anatoli…

My grip tightens, and it takes everything I have not to drop the bag onto the sidewalk. The note, however, turns out to be relatively simple once I unfurl it with trembling fingers. *You're shaking now,* he wrote, and the back of my neck prickles with awareness. A glance over my shoulder reveals that no one is there—but I sense the extent of his control, nonetheless. Especially as I read the next written line. *But get accustomed to how it sounds, Mrs. Koslov.*

"Ms. Marconi?" I look up to find Lucius watching me from beside the car. "Are you alright?"

"Y-Yes." I stagger the rest of the way toward him. "I'm fine."

"Good. We have a few moments to spare before Mr. Koslov suggested you return. In the meantime, I can take you by your family's home," he suggests while ushering me into the backseat. "I know that Ainsley, for one, can't wait to see you." A rare grin tugs at his mouth, and I force a smile in response.

"It feels like ages since I've been home," I admit.

Ages since I've had to clean up decapitated Barbie dolls or break up fistfights. Since I've had to confront my family and lie to their faces.

And it feels like it's been even longer since I've had a say in my own wardrobe. The item within the box turns out to be a dress after all—black velvet with a high, modest collar. The kind of outfit someone might dress his supposed fiancée in while parading her before a man who raised a family of monsters and murderers.

"Ms. Marconi?" Lucius asks. "Was that a yes?"

"Y-Yes! Thank you. That would be great." I look down, and my gaze drifts from the black dress to my ring. My ears are still ringing with two ominous words. *Mrs. Koslov.* "I need to talk to them."

"That you do. But if I may make a suggestion…" Lucius eyes me in the rearview mirror, and a frown strains his normally professional expression. "Mr. Koslov can be insistent when it comes to his point of view, but if you are uneasy with the pace of current events, you must tell him."

"Uneasy?" I echo. Though it's no use feigning innocence when I can barely look at the item of clothing on my lap.

Lucius nods while effortlessly melding into the thick of traffic. "I saw your face just now, if I may be blunt. After the fitting. You seemed uncomfortable."

Shock paints my cheeks scarlet. "I... I..." I don't know what to say. "You aren't just talking about the dress," I finally croak. "Are you?"

"I'm afraid not." He clears his throat, and I sit forward in anticipation. Rarely does he reveal snippets of his secretive employer. I think the only other time was during one of our first meetings when he issued a warning—*my client has unusual tastes, Francesca.*

"I've been working for Mr. Koslov for over ten years," he continues. "I would like to think I know him better than most—so when I say that the effect you have on him has been...dramatic, to say the least, I hope you take my words at face value. And I hope I may take this time to impart a bit of advice."

I swallow hard, wringing my fingers together. The note caught between them is crumpled in the aftermath, made smaller and smaller the more I twist and pinch. "What do you mean?"

"While I may have known him for more than half of your life, I suspect that you know more of his past than I will ever learn. More than I care to know, if I'm being frank. He's not an easy man to work for, but he is a loyal and just employer. If he happens to have a few...quirks that may make him seem unapproachable to most, well, that is beyond my place to say. But everyone, no matter who they are, needs an outlet. A release. Someone." His tone deepens with unsaid meaning, and seconds pass without him saying another word. Then he sighs, and that single sound betrays just how old he really is. How exhausted he is. "A life devoid of that simple luxury, can make a man act out in ways he might regret. I am well aware of what happened last night," he adds, shocking me with how unperturbed he sounds at the prospect of murder. "It wasn't the first time he has called me to clean up such…lapses in judgment. Those calls have not stopped since you've been with him, either. But the nature of them has changed. He has changed. You may not notice it. And with everything you've been through, maybe you don't care to. That is your prerogative, to be fair. But…" He sighs again before confessing, "I feel like I sound a bit like a gossiping old woman, but I think you need to hear this. Heed this one piece of advice—be honest with yourself. Be honest with him. It may seem impossible now, but a man like him has built his entire life around rejection. You can trust he knows how to survive it. But deception?" He tilts his head, his brows furrowing. "*That* would inflict a wound I doubt even Mr. Koslov could come back from. And deception can be an innocent thing at first. One might not even realize that their intent is insidious at all. Lying to someone," he adds with a shrug. "Pretending to feel things that you do not—or even worse. Lying to yourself. Misrepresenting your emotions because you cannot face them. Take charge of them. You are too wracked by fear to take ownership of what you desire while understanding what it *truly* is at its core. Do you understand what I mean?"

Our gazes meet in the rearview mirror, and I nod once. A creeping, aching sensation spreads throughout my stomach. *Deception.* Is that what I've been doing?

"I don't want to hurt him," I admit, my voice hoarse.

"Of course, you don't." He sounds like he truly believes that. "But tell me something. A hunter comes across a wolf and learns to care for it. He feeds it. Nourishes it. And then he locks it in a small cage because it is a difficult thing to care for a wild creature. To understand the freedom it needs. To trust that it will always return to you. That hunter may admire its beauty, and its power, and its brutal strength. But how can he trust that such a creature won't turn on him? And the wolf, it cares for the hunter as well, you see. But even such a creature can sense the fear in the other. So it tries to deny its nature and pretend it enjoys its life within captivity. But instinct can only be ignored for so long... Until one day, the wolf lashes out from behind its bars, mortally wounding the hunter. And they both die, each never truly knowing the other."

"What are you saying?" The picture he painted is in my head, replaying in a morbid loop. *Death. Death. Death.*

"I'm saying that love is in trust," he warns. "*Not* fear. Though that was merely a silly story, of course. And you must recall that you're relationship with Mr. Koslov was built on a contract first and foremost. An understanding. From the outside, it might have appeared odd. Imbalanced, even. But was it?"

He waits long enough that the resulting silence demands an answer.

"No," I admit. "I could always walk away."

"And you still can," he warns. "I apologize for the aimless chatter. Nonetheless, I appreciate your time. We should be arriving shortly."

He refocuses his attention on the road, and his professional demeanor returns. In some ways, it feels like he's drawn an invisible curtain between us, cutting off my chance to reply.

Beg for more.

More snippets of a man who hoards his past so fucking jealously.

But I'm desperate enough to risk it, testing the bars of my own invisible cage. "What if, in your story..." I lick my lips, they're so fucking dry. My hands shake, and the crumpled note falls to the floor, bouncing beneath the driver's seat. "What makes you think the hunter loved the wolf?"

Seconds tick by, but he doesn't answer. Only the hum of the engine fills the silence between us—and my heartbeat. It beats faster. Harder. It's all I can hear. *Thump. Thump. Thump!*

Reaching out, I place my hand on the back of Lucius' seat. "Please—"

"A hunter's nature is to kill," he says softly. "*Something* in the wolf made him forsake that purpose, even for a second. Even if his following actions were misguided. Something in the wolf made him, for a moment, question his sole intent. It might not fit the average definition, but why, in his viewpoint, would the mere desire to spare that one wolf, not be worthy of being called love?"

I inhale raggedly, my mind buzzing. "Do you know what—"

A classical ringtone cuts me off, and Lucius fishes a cell phone from his pocket, answering it one-handed. "Sir? You mean… Understood." His jaw clenches, concern clouding his weathered features. "We're already on the way. Yes, sir."

He hangs up, and the car lurches forward as his speed noticeably increases.

"Is something wrong?" I ask, scrambling for my seatbelt.

He doesn't respond.

Within minutes, we reach the building housing the new suite. Lucius takes the dress and ushers me from the car, up to the penthouse. I follow him inside, but my footsteps falter before I truly process the scene before me.

Maxim's thunderous bellow reaches me first. "Find him *now*, Milton," he growls. "I want his fucking head on a platter… No! Don't lie to me. You've always pitied him, coming to his rescue. Little Dima. I *know* you're aware of where he is. Do you think Anatoli is cunning enough to plan this on his own? No. Someone is pulling his strings— don't talk to me about strategy!"

He stands in the large sitting room off the foyer hunched over a black end table, a cell phone held to his ear. His posture alone sets every nerve in my body on high alert.

He's trembling, his fingers grasping the edge of the table so tightly it rocks on its axis.

"Find him! I want a location by tonight—you owe me this. But it might be too late, even then. They all know it by now. They'll be coming for her. *Fuck!*" Hissing in rage, he rips the cell phone from his ear and throws it across the room.

I take an instinctive step behind Lucius before I even think to focus on what might be the source of his rage. On the table before him lies a square-shaped object I can't make out at first. It's gray, made of metal. A briefcase?

As Lucius continues to advance, Maxim looks up and his eyes... I don't even think he sees us at first. Just phantoms from a nightmare he can't seem to wake up from.

"Sir," Lucius calls to him, his tone level. I can tell from his careful stance that the words he spoke in the car weren't bravado. He's used to dealing with Maxim in this state—a caged, feral wolf. For one, he wisely keeps his distance. "Can I be of any assistance?"

"Lucius." Maxim blinks and refocuses his attention on the older man. "*This* was delivered to one of my offices," he hisses, gesturing to the case. "It came from Anatoli himself. It seems the bastard couldn't wait for me to come to him. I'm sure you know what it means."

"I believe so, sir." Lucius' jaw clenches in recognition. "I'll review any breach in security immediately. As for this. I can remove it—"

"Like it would do any fucking good. Leave," Maxim demands. "But you—" He turns to me. "You stay."

"As you wish, Sir. I'll make adjustments to your security immediately."

"The house first," Maxim snarls. "They may start there."

"Of course. I'll double the detail." With a wary glance in my direction, Lucius retreats from the suite. In his absence descends a silence so heavy it's suffocating.

"What's going on?" I manage to rasp. *House.* That word won't leave my fucking brain. The only one I know of him owning just so happens to house my entire family.

As I watch, Maxim braces his hands on the table, his expression like thunder. Slowly, he nudges the case, tracing the corner of the lid with his thumb. Then he lifts it, revealing a sliver of plain, gray material and a flash of red. That's all I see before he slams the lid shut. His eyes cut to mine, and I swear my heart stops beating.

It's like my entire body can't function again until he turns away, his shoulders hunched, hands curling into fists. "I changed my mind," he snaps. "Go! I need to be alone."

I flinch toward the door without actually taking a step. The tormented figure who devised the phrase "hot and cold" had to have Maxim Koslov in mind. In some moments, his apparent need for me burns so fucking hot, I can pretend it means more than lust. More than a sadistic whim. But then his gaze can go so cold. Like now.

And it's like I don't even exist.

Lucius referred to a wolf and a cage—but the analogy he should have used was that of a doll and a child who can't decide if he wants to play with it or smash it to pieces.

"Is something wrong?" I ask, taking a cautious step toward him. "What happened—"

"You got your wish," he says, his mouth twisted in a cruel sneer. "There won't be a fucking wedding. So smile. You can remain as nothing more than my whore. What?" He cocks his head as I stiffen. "That's what you wanted, isn't it? Well, now you have an excuse to turn tail and run. Though, I suggest you don't go too fucking far."

He's right. Hurt pride could drive me away from him now. Make me run. It's what he expects.

And it dawns on me that it's exactly what he *wants*.

"What's wrong?" I ask instead. The strength in my voice surprises me almost as much as it seems to surprise him. "You let me go to the fitting," I point out. "So whatever changed, it had to happen—"

"I said leave." He shifts onto the balls of his feet, ready to storm away himself.

"Talk to me," I beg, switching tact. "If something is wrong… If my family is in danger, I need to know. Just talk to me."

"*Now*, you want to talk." He strokes his chin with one hand while the other tears through his hair. "Are you sure you don't want to tremble and stare and cower? Like you don't know *who* I am…"

This is about more than a mysterious case or a phone call.

Images from last night flood my brain in ominous snippets. How easy it is to lose him to anger, contrasted with the only method capable of bringing him back. In some ways, Lucius' words feel more like a warning now than a comfort —*you've changed him.*

But not for the better.

"Tell me what's wrong." Before he can reply, I approach the table containing the case. My rebellious fingers brush the metal surface, and his reaction makes me suspect that I'm not the source of his unease after all. "What does it mean?"

"You want to know?" Finally, he faces me, devoid of any expression whatsoever. No hate. No anger. No mercy either. "Open it."

An ominous thrill shoots down the fingers I use to pry the ends of the case apart. As the lid rises, I hold my breath…

Only to release it in a puzzled exhale. The inside of the box is lined with gray velvet, betraying a formal purpose, but all it contains is a single strip of blood-red fabric. Confusion displaces some of my fear. Enough that I can eye the item objectively. It's silk, cool to the touch, and deceptively luxurious.

I flip it over and notice a design embroidered on the other side in a slightly darker shade of scarlet—an intricate series of conjoined circles resembling a cross.

"What is it?" I ask. A scrap slightly too small to be a handkerchief or anything useful from what I can tell. Almost like a sample swatch, one might use to order a couch or carpet. Or a dress. I look up at Maxim only to find him watching me. But the look on his face now…

His eyes are black holes constricting even darker pupils.

"*That* is a death sentence," he says. "*Krasnyy konets*, the 'red ending.' An old archaic tradition, but one still alive and well in certain circles. Within families. My family." He extends his palm—a silent command for me to relinquish the cloth. When I do, he eyes it with an expression that makes every hair on the back of my neck stand up. I've only witnessed him deploy that glare at his uncle.

Or his grandfather.

"This is a mere symbolic token. At its core, the purpose is to signify a bounty. An insurmountable one, no amount of money, can outweigh." He forms a fist, crushing the fabric within it. "And it should have come for *me*. I was expecting it. He should have… No one would confront *me* out in the open, blood price or not."

I swallow hard, eyeing the case again. From what little I know of his family, I sense grand displays of murderous threats are nothing new. But this… This is different. It's evident in Maxim's hostile posture. The rage spilling from his eyes, barely contained by his obsessive restraint.

He's more than angry. I think…

I think he's terrified.

"What does that mean?"

"It came for *you*. And the bastard doesn't truly want you dead. Oh no…" He exhales a growled chuckle and turns, lumbering toward the far corner of the room. A virgin section of the white wall draws his notice, and he braces his hand against it. Then he forms a fist and strikes the surface, so hard cracks appear in a spidery web. Lashing out a second time, he shouts in a way I've never heard. A howl. A hiss. A broken, maniacal laugh all in one.

His following sigh resonates like the first raindrops falling in a breaking storm. One I'm naked in the face of. My only course of action is to brace at the mercy of the tempest.

And pray, I survive it.

"If it came for me, I could resist him. Fight him," he explains. "He would be declaring war, and no one would get in my fucking way if I went for his throat. I could rip him apart at my own fucking discretion, and not even God could say a damn thing." He laughs again, his body locked in the violent pose, his knuckles trembling against the wall's surface. "But now? He doesn't have to kill you. He doesn't even have to lift a finger. You're already as good as dead. So much for my protection. I couldn't even fucking outsmart him."

He turns, crossing the room in an instant. I don't even have the sense of mind to run.

"No one will acknowledge you," he snarls, snatching my wrist, his focus honing on my ring. "No one will accept you. With this, you will never be a Koslov, and I couldn't even avenge you."

He rips the ring from my finger and throws it so hard it ricochets across the room, its progress tracked by faint musical pings.

"So much for a fucking wedding," he growls amid another unstable bit of laughter. "In my world, you no longer exist."

Fear weighs me down, almost too powerful to overcome. Inhaling shallowly is the only way to combat it. One deep, slow breath right after the other.

Until eventually, words form, escaping my throat before I even register them. "What are you saying?"

"I'm saying that there is no point in a wedding," he hisses. "No point in a ring. No point in a fucking engagement. Everything my name could give you means nothing now. Anatoli has won. The only thing I can do now is keep you from being killed."

He stalks toward the door, creating a noise comparable to thunder. The force of his rage strains the entire room at its seams, too wild to be contained. A part of me fears the windows might explode beneath the pressure.

Or I might.

"Is that the only reason why?" My voice echoes back to me before I realize I've spoken at all. My words play amid an eerie backdrop of silence as Maxim freezes.

"What did you say?" he demands.

"I…" Instinct warns me to run. Back down. I lick my lips tentatively, but something won't keep me silent. I break. "Is that why you wanted to marry me? Power?"

"No. For *security*. Why else?" he counters, driving that point home. "With my name, no one could touch you. Is there any value in a ring more than that certainty? Tell me you're not so sentimental."

His steps reverberate through the floor, advancing toward me. I couldn't escape him, even if I tried. My body jolts as he touches me. One brush of his finger feels comparable to a hot poker jabbing against the chilled flesh of my throat.

But it's not the sort of pain I've come to associate him with. Whippings, biting, and beatings feel nothing like this— emotions utilized more ruthlessly than any knife. *Is there any value in a ring?*

"You would always be protected as my wife," he says, tightening his grip so that I'm forced to face him. "But now, a few vows will change nothing. As much as I loathe the motherfucker, I can't go against Anatoli on my own—and married to me or not, nothing would change as far as my family is concerned. If anything, they will make a game out of trying to use you against me. And Sevastyn… He was the tamest among them."

I cringe at what that implies. A family of people more evil than a child abuser. People so ruthless even Maxim seems shaken at the prospect of them coming for me. And yet a family he seems desperate to make me a part of. A name he cherishes above all else.

"So, the ring means nothing?" I reiterate.

He inhales as his fingers twitch against my throat. "You're upset." He sounds more confused than alarmed by that realization. "I don't understand why..."

"I'm not upset," I clarify. I've been touching my ring finger as I spoke, something I only realize as I look down and observe the pale naked flesh. "It's just a lot to take in." My ragged laugh proves that I'm not lying. I sound fucking insane. Manic. "First, you want to marry me. Then you don't—"

"And you ask why?" He starts for the door again. "What use is a fucking worthless token without the power it conveys?"

I don't know why I follow him, no match for his ruthless pace.

"So, what happens now?" I ask, watching the muscles in his body coil as his hands curl in and out of fists.

"Now? I need to get you somewhere safe." The callous phrasing conveys a million different meanings. Somewhere safe. Away. Out of his hair. Like a nuisance fly, he has to trap in a jar just to keep it from getting smashed.

"Where?" My brain spins with the possibilities. Somewhere out of the city? The country? "What about my family—"

"They'll be fine. I'm already moving them to a new location. But I… I need to think this through. Alone."

I flinch at the barely concealed warning. Everything about him broadcasts a blazing, ominous warning. *Run. Retreat. Let him brood and rage in peace.*

"I want you to tell me something," I croak instead, still frozen in place. "If this never happened. If what you think your ring means was still the same, what would change?"

"What?" He scoffs. "You would be protected."

"But nothing else?" I don't know why I'm probing him at all. Where I'm going with this line of questioning. What drives me to ask next, "So you would continue to make decisions for me without including me?"

Despite all the appearance of power and security, as his wife, I would be powerless. An animal in a cage like the one depicted in Lucius' story.

"I don't know what you expected from me." He sounds so damn tired. If the threads of his control were visible chains, I can imagine them straining. Cracking. Breaking.

"Our first contract was always prefaced on the understanding that I could always walk away," I say. It sounds so strange to recall that fact after weeks of being at his virtual beck and call, under his mercy always. But

Lucius was right. "You laid out the risks and the benefits. You gave me a choice. I could leave if I wanted to—"

"Is that what you want now?" The hollowness of his tone sucks any warmth from the room. I'm shivering. "To leave me?"

"No." I start toward him only to falter paces away. He's still within my reach though, a raging shadow in the waning daylight, but my fingers twitch uselessly at my sides. His anger radiates, forming an invisible barrier too dangerous to breach.

"Then what are you saying?" he demands.

"I'm saying that what we had before is the kind of security I need now." Even if I don't know why. "I want to know the risks if my life is in danger. I want you to explain. I want a…choice."

"Choice?" He whirls on me. "Your only choice is to stay with me or die. The bounty is on your head regardless. I cannot fix this."

And that lack of control is consuming him like nothing else. I've never seen him so resigned. Except maybe once before in the face of his uncle.

Before he beat him to death with his bare hands.

"I want to stay with you," I admit, marveling at the contrast between my voice and his. I should be the one straining, my words faltering. I should be the one trembling beneath the sheer insanity of my fate.

Slowly, I reach out and settle my hand against his forearm. He stiffens as if his first instinct is to shrug me off. I can physically feel the jolt of muscle tensing and then relaxing.

"Talk to me," I beg. "Tell me the risks. I want that choice."

A sound resonates low in his chest. Another laugh? I can't tell as he inclines his head without looking in my direction. "You want that choice? Well, here it is. Anatoli ensured that I can never give you the safety I want for you. Even if I kill him, the fucking mark stands. You will never be seen as a Koslov by the people who matter. To them? You will always be a fucking whore."

And that bothers him. More than he will admit out loud. So much is simmering beneath his surface fury, boiling over in ways he can no longer control. I suck in a breath as he faces me directly and brings his hand to my cheek, tilting my face for his inspection.

"I want more for you than that," he swears, brushing his thumb against the corner of my mouth. "But first, I will get you and your family somewhere safe. Then I will reach out to some contacts in my network. If Anatoli wants to play this game, then we will play. Though nothing I do will really matter in the end. The family won't move against him. Fuck!" The tension drains from him as I watch, and his lips part into a terrifying grin. "He's won this round, I will give him that. To challenge him, I would need another Koslov. I would need…"

His fingers snatch at his chin, stroking the stubble there as he thinks. "I would need an ally who is blood. But would he... No—" He shakes his head, breaking off whatever thought he may have had. "I will make the arrangements for you to leave within the week. It's safer, the less you know."

"Safe?" Again, I barely recognize the woman speaking. Her voice doesn't tremble or falter. Each clear tone resonates as strongly as his does. "I trust you," I race to clarify before he can reply. "I do. I don't even know why I do. But I can't live my life being treated like... Even when I first came to you, you forced me to become a player in your game. You didn't leave me in the dark like this."

"Didn't I?" A wicked, soulless smile shapes his mouth as he balances my chin on the palm of his hand. "Don't fool yourself, little kitten. You were always a pawn."

"Or a bullet," I croak, shocked that I'm challenging him at all. "We were always playing Russian Roulette."

He frowns at the comparison. Against me, his fingers twitch, part caress. Part lashing, his nails nipping deep. "And yet you still want to play?" he wonders.

"I could... If you tell me what you want from me." I try my best to meet his stormy gaze without flinching. Maybe I succeed because he doesn't hiss in disgust. For a second, I can glimpse a hint of the turmoil lurking beneath those dark irises. The pain. The frustration.

"What I want?" He shakes his head as a growl rips from his throat. Within a heartbeat, his entire posture changes. It's like watching a chain on a raging, barking dog snap. He's loose, barreling off in a random direction.

A thunderous sound echoes as he strikes the wall again. Again. Red streaks paint the surface when he withdraws, and the same liquid coats his knuckles, dripping onto the floor. Blood.

"I want to rip that bastard limb from limb. Can you give me that?" he demands. "Can you? I want to set his entire fucking empire on fire and force him to watch it burn. I want the power to destroy him! Can you give me that?"

"No," I admit hoarsely. I sound like myself again, but when I approach him, I don't hesitate to reach out, brushing his forearm. "I can't. But I can give you something else."

"Like what?" he snaps.

Lucius, in his own quiet way, gave me the answer.

"Control," I say softly. "A release. You don't have to keep this in—"

"Release." His gaze cuts to me as calculating as a predator observing fresh, bleeding prey. "You want me to hurt you, little *kotyonok*?" His bloodied knuckles boldly brush my cheek, daring me to flinch. "I'm more than capable of doing so. You want to get off on my anger and then run like you didn't enjoy every fucking second of it? Maybe that is why you stay—"

"No." I reach up and settle my fingers over his scarred, bloodied ones. They twitch at the indignation of being trapped against my skin—but he doesn't pull away. "I want to give you what you need."

"Sex?" His accent thickens over that single word, stressing its pronunciation. Like that, he gives it another connotation that triggers an answering shiver through my entire body. *Pain.* "You think that's what I need? That I won't hurt you? Do you think that in this moment, if you beg me to stop that I will?"

I take in his unfocused, wild stare and manic grin. A part of me whispers in horror, *No. He won't stop. He'll go too far again. He's insane. He'll more than hurt me. He'll kill me.*

For an instant, I'm in that cold, terrifying room with the plastic tarp all over again, watching him brandish a knife, knowing that he's too far gone to reach. He's nearly as unhinged now as he was then.

Do I trust him anyway?

"Yes." I swallow hard and meet his gaze unflinchingly. "I know you will."

His eyes narrow, displacing some of the anger with…shock? I can't be certain because he snatches my jaw the next second, dragging me to him. He slams his mouth to mine, claiming my lips with devastating blows from his tongue. Sharp, his teeth sink into my bottom lip, making me jump. In retaliation, I grip his forearms, sensing the power coiled in every single muscle.

But the balance of power is his to claim this time. To do so, he shoves me back, tearing at my dress in the same ruthless movement.

"There have been things I've wanted to do to you," he chokes out, grasping at any part of me he can reach. My breasts. Hips. Hair. His fingers claw at each additional piece of me, using them as a leash to yank me toward him. Harshly. Harder. Viciously.

"I've thought about it," he adds, finding my ear. His teeth skewer the lobe, sowing another sharp burst of pain, scattering my senses further. "I'll do it now."

He backs away and grips my shoulders. A taste of his strength forces me down to my knees before him. I'm stunned by the shift in position, still struggling to keep up.

But knocking me off balance is his favorite part of the game.

"Stay," he growls, turning on his heel. My heart stutters as I watch him follow the hall to the master suite. I ignore the devious suspicions running across my brain, taunting me with what he could be getting. Seconds later, he returns with something dangling from his right hand. Not a whip or a knife. This is something different. Long and heavy, it drags along the marble floor in his wake.

A rope? No. Craning my neck, I can make out gleaming links of metal forming a slender, but still substantial chain. Alarm prickles through my belly. Only God knows where he had it hidden up until now.

"Up," he commands, bending his fingers in a curt motion. "Look at me."

I look up, desperately hunting his expression for any sign of…something. Malice? Rage? His mouth flattens into a firm, cold line, withholding any hint of his intentions from me.

Slowly, I shift on my knees, wincing as my weight bears down against the hard, unyielding marble. The icy cool contrasts with the heat sweltering beneath my skin, growing hotter, the more my brain scrambles to reconcile his aim with the length of chain.

With one hand, he sweeps the hair from my face and cradles my throat. His thumb caresses my quivering windpipe. It would be so easy for him to crush it. Break me. He strokes me instead, tracing a path from my collar down to my left breast.

A gasp escapes me as he teases the aching peak with the tip of his nail, coaxing the flesh to stiffen. He's gentler than he's ever been—even as his eyes bore into me ruthlessly. My back arches, my body heating to his touch. I can't deny the reaction he inspires within me—burning, vicious need. Aware of his effect on me, he nods, a satisfied hum reverberating through his chest.

Without warning, he crouches and grips one end of the chain. I only make out something small and silver attached to the end of it before he brings it to my breast. To tease me, like he did once with ice?

No. Fire sears through my nipple so intense I cry out, jerking back. I don't even go an inch before his opposite hand snatches a fistful of my hair, locking me in place.

"Don't." The low, dangerous rasp in his voice, spurs my heartbeat into a frantic rhythm. "Don't move. Don't look down—" He captures my chin, smoothing his fingers against the flesh. "You look at me."

Him. A man so alarmingly on-edge that his body sways with every breath. Alight, his eyes lazily dip lower, relishing in the freedom he's denied me. Whatever he sees makes him groan, biting his lip between clenched teeth.

"You are so beautiful," he praises thickly. "Like this. Red. Swollen. Bitten..." He drags his thumb over the stinging wound in my lip, left by his teeth. "Mine."

My body radiates with tension as he reaches down, lifting the chain in his fist. *Fuck.* My eyelids flutter. I feel every twitch in every goddamn link. Through my nipple, down my spine, into my core. Slick with moisture, my inner thighs rub together as my cheeks catch fire. I've never felt... *Ever.* My thoughts dissipate as my breaths feather. Already I'm drugged on this pain.

"You enjoy even this," he remarks, sounding smug. "Fuck, I knew you would. But stay with me, *kotyonok*—" He tugs again...harder. "We aren't done yet."

A whine tears from my throat, high-pitched, and broken. I can't think. His face is my only anchor to sanity. In a beautiful display of flesh and bone, he eyes me reverently, his lips parted, eyes wide and unfocused.

"You can take this for me," he suspects. "You will. So good..."

He doesn't sound angry anymore, but a part of me clenches in anticipation of the emotion that replaces it. Hunger. Excitement. Lust.

His nostrils flare as he fingers the chain again, keeping it raised within my line of sight. Each deliberate caress roils through me, raising goosebumps over my sweat-misted skin. The reaction must cement some dark suspicion of his because he nods. "You can handle more."

Handle... Can I? He doesn't give me a chance to decide. The chain rustles, tugging...pulling. I grit my teeth, hissing out a breath. I don't register what he's done until it's too late.

He lifts the chain higher, displaying it curved around his finger, held taut at *both* ends. And an inferno rips through my body. My head swims, my heart pounding madly. I can taste my pulse in my fucking throat, hammering through each nipple. He did something to them. *Clamped them,* I realize as my eyes rebel against his command, glancing down. Metal beads surround both peaks, crushing them into tiny points.

And the resulting sensation intoxicates me.

"I warned you." Maxim tugs a fraction harder. I whimper, digging my nails into my hips—it's the only way to stop myself from reaching for the chain. Tugging it back. Tugging it more. God, I can't think.

"Do you want me to stop?" he wonders. How his voice cuts through my broken, splintered brain? I'll never know.

"Yes…" I croak, but just as quickly, I stammer, "N-No…"

He winds the chain between two fingers, and I go rigid, shaking my head frantically.

"No! No!"

"You want it." He tugs so hard my body lurches across the marble. As if from far away, I hear a scream echo off the walls, nearly drowned out by my own hammering heartbeat. The next thing I know, I'm quivering in a ball, my head resting against a thick, hard thigh propped beneath it. Soothing and tender, warm fingers run through my hair as a deep voice offers endless praise.

"So good for me. Always so good… More than I wanted— always more I want to do to you. But fuck you make me…"

Crazy. In the same way, he makes me mindless. His words dissolve into meaningless grunts as he slides his hand between my legs, hissing at what he finds.

Soaking, aching flesh—his to claim. His to take.

He has me in his arms within seconds, moving too quickly for me to process his next actions in order. We're racing down the hall. Then crashing inside the bedroom. I've barely regained my senses when I land on the bed face down as his weight slams against my back.

Panic sets in before I can smother it. He's crushing me. But then his fingers sink into my hair, grasping a fistful that he uses to wrench my head back, allowing me to suck in air as he nudges my legs apart. I quake from head to fucking toe, assaulted by too many sensations at once to pinpoint them individually. His weight. His skin rasping over mine. The pull of the chain swaying against my chest, enhancing every single fucking movement to an agonizing degree.

And finally, his cock rips into me, demolishing every other feeling like a wrecking ball.

My eyelids flutter as I focus solely on breathing, allowing my body to adjust to his size. *Massive.* He thrusts in hard without restraint, hissing out his pleasure. Jolted by every bucking motion of his hips, I wind up lying on parts of the chain, straining others, and I lose track of the sounds I make. My throat aches, throbbing and raw as he grips my hips, fucking me in earnest.

If I were a normal lover, he would hurt me, there is no question. But his voice drips into my ear, an awed growl, revealing the difference that makes me just as deranged as he is. "So wet for me." He inhales sharply and then groans with another brutal thrust. "Always so wet for me."

His mouth finds my ear, nipping at the lobe as his mangled, grunted words punctuate the movement of our bodies. "You know what I need, don't you? You give it to me. You take me... Fuck! You aim to tame me..."

I close my eyes, savoring the violent contrast of gnashing teeth, and broken groans, and sweat as his body ruthlessly claims mine. The sex isn't about pleasure—I know that. I'm climaxing anyway, biting a mouthful of sheets to silence my cries as every muscle goes taut. I see stars, speckling my vision as he grunts, slamming inside me one final time.

His release is that in every sense of the word. The tension leaves him as he collapses beside me. His fingers remain in my hair, preventing me from facing him. The heat and sweat of his body assault me in an overwhelming barrage as his mouth finds my shoulder, his teeth teasing the flesh.

"You can fuck me like this," he says, almost amused despite the growl reverberating in my skin. "Let me use you any way I fucking want—" His finger slips beneath me, teasing a length of the chain just enough to make me shudder. "But if I offer you more, you hesitate. And yet when I refuse to give you an empty fucking vow…you challenge me."

I'm too exhausted to move, awed by his tone—part sated lust, part smoldering fury.

"Do you want me to marry you?" he wonders musingly. "Or collar you? State your preference now, so I know whether to offer you a ring or a leash. Say it. No?" He chuckles while I pant, too breathless to reply. "I'll tell you what it is you crave. Ignorance. For years you wore yourself down caring for your siblings. They've drained you—so you chase any vice you can find to take the pain of it all away. To let the world crush you rather than spend your energy carrying the weight of it on your shoulders. I make it easy for you." His lips brush my shoulder, a mocking kiss. "Don't I? You question my intentions for marrying you, but I have no doubts as to what I want. But what is it *you* want from me? Tell me what happened at the club was a lie."

Was it? The other day feels like another lifetime now—coming to him of my own volition. Promising complete and total surrender. Have I been lying all along like Lucius insinuated?

"No," I admit, uttering the truth as much to myself as to him. "I meant it."

"So perhaps it isn't fear then," he suspects with a puzzled grunt. "Tell me what you want from this, if protection isn't good enough to tempt you."

"I want…" Not for the first time, I don't even recognize the sound of my own voice. This new, braver stranger must have been born in the aftermath of Sevastyn's death—like watching the whole gory affair killed something inside of me as well. Or awoke something. Something so deviant it thrills at the agony only he can arouse within my body. "I want clarity," I tell him. "About everything."

Everything I can discover about Maxim Koslov and what makes him tick—and not out of mere curiosity either. Maybe because his anger matches mine—the horrific magnification of the twisted shit I never faced within myself before him. The flaws only he has ever called me out on.

The selfishness.

The self-hatred.

The blind, consuming rage.

I could be the world's most pathetic masochist, thriving off the manifestations of my own internal bullshit. But I'd be lying to myself if I accept that explanation—the easy solution to what exactly draws me to him.

Because even now, I'm not really afraid. My heart may be racing, palms sweating, and my entire body tense on red alert. But deep down, the real name to call this emotion by could be…excitement. Guilt. Jealousy.

As long as he feels the twisted, dark shit festering beneath the surface of his soul…

I don't have to face my own.

"Clarity, how? Answer me." He grips my chin, forcing me to meet his gaze, but there's no real strength in the contact. He merely eyes me as if I'm a mirror, utilized the same way I might be using him.

Is there any true connection mingled within it all?

I want to say no. But my heart pounds against my ribs, hammering out a silent answer—*liar, liar, liar.*

"Marriage is status to you. But…" I lick my lower lip, tasting my answer before I have the strength to utter it out loud. "I don't even know what it is to me. My mother didn't exactly model healthy relationships."

Though what does that say about not only me? Daisy, Mikie, and the others have never known stability either. A loving mother is a foreign concept in our world, let alone a father.

"You value your name, but I value my family. I don't want to make the same mistakes Melanie did."

And what little I know of marriage comes right from her playbook. Melanie had been married at least four or five times. Hell, to be honest, I've lost count. In her view, being a wife was nothing more than a fashionable accessory. A game. A way to chase off boredom.

But I've never even had a serious boyfriend. I've had partners. Clients. Johns.

I've had Maxim.

Only one of those options has lasted longer than a handful of hours at a time.

"Deep, down, I always told myself that I never wanted more," I confess. "That life was enough. Scraping by and depending only on myself was enough. I don't know anything else."

"But I can teach you, little *kotyonok*," he finally says, satisfied by my answer. "There is so much I have yet to teach you."

He nudges me onto my side, tracing my sore nipple with the tip of his thumb. In one swift motion, he releases the clamp, and my head swims.

"Holy shit!" I nearly crawl off the fucking bed to escape the unbearable sting—he has to press on my hip just to keep me in place.

"It will hurt," he warns, soothing the abused flesh as blood rushes back to the area. "I think you might enjoy this more than a whipping." He spares a glance at my trembling knees, fighting to stay together. "Next time, I will..."

He trails off, letting my twisted imagination fill in the gap.

A whine breaks from me as he releases the second clamp, but then his hands settle over my hips, drawing me into him.

"I can show you the lengths a man will go to in order to prove his claim to the entire fucking world," he swears. "But I won't call you my wife without the power that title deserves. I won't." He drags his fingers along the side of my face, down to my throat. "So if you want it...then fight *with* me for it."

"How?"

"There is someone I could use as an ally," he admits, and I marvel at the change in his tone. Gone is the bitter anger. He's the composed, calculating game master again. One with a new strategy in mind. "Finding him will be difficult," he adds. "But if you want a partnership? Then come with me when I eventually do track him down."

"Really?"

"Yes." I shiver as his fingers soothe my burning scalp, replacing the violent tugging with a rare, addicting softness. "He would never agree to meet me alone. And you... You will fascinate him." A growl mangles the words, making them anything but a compliment.

His touch turns possessive as his nails nip at my flesh in a silent warning. *You're mine.*

"Who is he?"

All at once, he withdraws from me and leaves the bed altogether. His footsteps retreat toward the doorway, but I know better than to chase him this time. I merely roll over and watch him go, his body dominating the door as growing darkness shrouds the room in shadow. Near the threshold of the hallway, he hesitates.

"He... He is someone I mistrust even more than Anatoli. And he is the only other bastard crazy enough to stand against him."

He enters the hall, and his echoing steps track his progress throughout the suite—but he never leaves.

And I don't sleep. I just coexist in a silent dwelling that I know he still occupies, fuming in some distant corner. I can smell him. Sense him. It's like my body stays attuned to his presence even if he isn't in the same fucking room.

I'm draped in invisible chains this time, tugged and twisted at his discretion.

And right now, he is twisting hard.

CHAPTER FIVE

For what feels like hours, all I can do is lie still, listening to the cadence of his footsteps echo. He's pacing. It isn't long before his voice reaches back to me, though directed at someone else.

"You found him?" he demands. "I knew it! Where? Don't bullshit me, Milton, your men are more accurate than that. No, I won't kill him. Yet. And why even ask? Don't tell me that after all this time you still harbor some ounce of pity for the son of a bitch? I didn't think you were so sentimental. You were children then, after all…"

He must hang up. After a few minutes of silence, heavy footsteps fill the absence in the wake of his baritone, advancing slowly in my direction. He takes his time, lingering in the hallway, just beyond the door. He's testing me, I think. Knowing I'm awake but wanting to draw out the tension and extend every last second of brutal anticipation.

Unchecked, my pulse flutters beneath my skin, each frantic beat counting the seconds down. *Thump. Thump. Thump…*

"Your family is safe," he finally says. "They're in a property outside of the city. I'll take you to them in the morning. Together, you will be moved to a more secure location."

I sit upright, still draped beneath the bedsheets. The darkness shrouds him well. I have to strain my eyes before I spot him leaning against the wall, his arms crossed. "Thank you."

"But tonight…" He shifts, and I sense him mulling over his next words, debating uttering them at all. "I have a lead," is all he says. "Come with me if you want—"

"Where?" I'm already scrambling to my feet.

"Get dressed. Meet me downstairs within ten minutes. Or not. You have a *choice*."

I flinch, recognizing my own plea being thrown back in my face. Still, I can overlook the jab in favor of the larger prize.

Answers.

For once, tangible, real answers.

What kind of man might someone like Maxim Koslov seek out for help against his grandfather? How does this figure tie into his past? My brain spins with a million potential possibilities as I race into the closet and tug on a dress at random. It's too tight. My nipples throb, forcing me to switch to one with a looser neckline. When I finally join Maxim in the garage, I'm panting.

He, however, sits calmly in the back seat of his car while a dutiful driver claims the wheel. The door on my end is already open, and I climb in without a word, settling beside him.

"If there is one thing you are, it's eager," he murmurs. He reaches for my left hand, and his thumb strokes my bare ring finger. "Perhaps, I may have broached the subject from the wrong angle?"

My heart clenches. Is this an apology?

"I forget… In some ways, you are so young—ignorant," he continues as the driver guides the car into the street. "More often than not, it seems I misjudge you."

He's thoughtful tonight, his expression pensive as passing streetlights illuminate his face in various shades of neon red and green. A lack of tension makes him seem more open than usual as well. I can't stop staring. It's such a contrast to even a few hours ago.

"There are some things I don't have to explain to you. But others…" He runs his fingers along my shoulder and parts my tangled hair. "You have no idea as to the lengths I would go to keep my word. Do you? Just know that when all is said and done, God himself won't be able to dispute my claim over you. Do you understand? I need you to say it out loud—" His hand cups my chin, gently lifting it higher. "Can you give me this? Time?"

I have to inhale deeply and form each word in the base of my throat. "Y-Yes. But—" His hand stills against me. "I need to know everything. I don't want to be *ignorant* anymore."

"Fine." He turns away, letting me go, and my entire body slumps in the wake of his touch. "But first, you promise me one last thing."

"What?"

He leans forward and grunts something to the driver. Simultaneously, the car lurches forward with a sudden burst of speed, and I scramble for my seat belt.

"I'll let you ask what you want. I'll answer your questions. But you keep those wide eyes in check," Maxim warns. "If you think you can stomach my world, then you accept it. All of it. No more flinching. No more running."

"Okay."

"So now, ask your questions."

"Where are we going?" I ask—a neutral enough starting point.

"Outside of the city. I have a general area of where to look," he admits, eyeing the world racing past beyond the window. "But no key destination. Admittedly, one could say that I'm shooting in the dark."

"Who are you looking for? One of your uncle's men?"

"Not quite." He leans back against the seat, tilting his head away from me. "Sevastyn was never interested in surrounding himself with *men*."

Mayday. Unease floods my belly, and I flick my tongue along my lip to delay posing another question. Dealing with him sometimes is like pulling the lever on a slot machine—I never know what prize I'll get.

Such is the risk when it comes to roulette.

There is no time to think.

Or regret.

"Tell me about him," I ask, pulling the trigger.

"Sevastyn?" He makes a sound in his throat somewhere in between a grunt and a scoff. "He served as a liaison between my grandfather and the more senior members of the family. That position made it ideal for him to use blackmail as his weapon of choice. So like any snake, he traded in sin, tempting powerful men and women with the kind of debauchery most only acknowledge on their deathbed to a priest…"

He told me more than he meant to. Confusion disrupts his icy gaze before he refocuses it on the road. Around us, the buildings gradually decrease in height. We're nearing the city limits.

"How do you know Milton?" I ask, aiming my focus at a less volatile target. Or so I think.

"Milton?" He grits his teeth—a habit I'm starting to connect to when he's suppressing an instinctive need to lash out. Evade. "You could say our upbringings were similar," he admits to my shock. "I've known him since I was a child.

As it turns out, our goals in life converged as well. I trust him."

It's a surprisingly chilling concept—a child Maxim forging a friendship that would include future bonding experiences such as the dismemberment and disposal of a body. I try to picture him as an angry boy with flashing dark eyes and white-blond hair.

But I can't.

I recall how he interacted with Milton instead. In some ways, he seemed more at ease than he is even around Lucius.

"He's your friend?" I ask.

"He is my partner." His tone gives that word far more reverence than the one I used. "Apart from my family's holdings, everything in my business was built between the two of us. Everything."

"Like the club?"

He nods. "It's as much his as it is mine."

Given how comfortable he feels there—especially in his private room—that simple acknowledgment conveys so much more. The place has more value to him than some piece of random property.

"What does the name stand for? XX—"

"An X for every partner with skin in the game." He flexes his fingers, observing them one by one. "We combine our resources. Think of it as an alliance."

"Three men for three Xs," I deduce. "You, Milton, and…"

"Another investor." He shrugs, crossing his arms. "I don't know his identity. Everything goes through Milton. As long as the money flows and our business interests remain unchallenged, I don't need to know the details. The third member has remained anonymous since the start."

"Milton knew Sevastyn." Or so I'm assuming from his apparent disgust when he saw the body.

"He did," Maxim says. A dare lurks in the ensuing silence. *Do you really want to know how?*

Given what little I know of Sevastyn already, I don't. Two men with similar upbringings—one of whom I know was caught up in the web of a child molester.

Ignorance may be preferable in this instance.

"I believe it's my turn to ask some questions of my own," Maxim says, reclaiming the reins of the conversation. His inflection doesn't change, but I recognize the shift in subject as a warning. A plea. "I never asked you about the dress. What did you think of it?"

"It's…white." I gauge his reaction in glimpses snuck from the corner of my eye. "I don't know much about religion, but I don't think someone like me is allowed to wear that color in a church."

"Allowed?" He raises an eyebrow. Have I surprised him? Or annoyed him? A searching look later and I'm still not sure.

"I don't think you understand the irony. As my wife, no one will dictate what you are *allowed* to do. Not a priest. No one."

"No one but you?"

"You think I tell you what to do?" He laughs, but there's no warmth in the sound. "You... Who stayed when I first told her to run? Who questions my intentions to give her the highest thing of value I possess in my name?" I jump as he grabs my hand, dragging it onto his lap. His heat floods my blood like poison, enhancing my awareness of him. He sits rigidly, but not out of annoyance. His thigh muscles tense in a way that makes me suck in a breath. "The woman who, with one look, can make me fuck her like an animal when I desire control," he adds softly. "But yes, I control *you*. Starting with keeping you alive. You will leave the city tomorrow night. I've already contacted Gemma so that you may resume your lessons while away."

I grit my teeth, unsure of how to respond. "I—"

"Stop here," Maxim snaps, directing the order to the driver. Just like that, the brief display of intimacy is over. As if a switch is flipped, his jaw tightens, eyes narrowing. He's in business mode, fixated solely on whatever motive drew him here in the first place.

Here, being a seedy-looking bar on the edge of the highway. We're just beyond the city limits. In the distance, skyscrapers pierce the horizon, pointed like daggers. The imagery makes me shiver. A poetic observation, or an omen?

"Come." Maxim exits the car and extends his hand for me to follow. I step out onto a narrow curb in his wake, taking in whatever I can.

At a glance, this place is no match for his elegant club XXX, that's for damn sure. Made of brick, the building itself is square-shaped with a broken neon sign reading *Money's*, instead of the intended *Montey's*.

Inside, plumes of cigarette smoke choke the narrow barroom, so thick I can barely see the figure beside me. Dressed in a crisp, black suit, Maxim stands out among the shadows—an angel in hell. Coifed blond hair and a blood-red tie give him a harsh definition against the monochromatic backdrop.

Which only confuses me more when my own appearance is factored in. Given his usual obsessive attention to my clothing, he must want it this way. My dress is a plain, shapeless gray. Still mussed from our stint in bed, my hair is a mess. If I wanted to be self-deprecating about it, I look like I belong slobbering over one of the truckers camped out near a pool table at the back of the room—not on his arm.

His palm cups my waist possessively regardless, forcing me to match his pace as he draws up to a chipped, wooden counter. A man stands behind it, rubbing a filthy glass with a filthier dishrag.

"Can I help you?" he wonders without looking up. It's funny how, after all this time in Maxim's world, seeing someone dressed casually in a pair of jeans and a T-shirt stands out as odd. At least in comparison to the polished suits everyone down to his drivers seems to prefer.

"I believe you can." Maxim reaches into his pocket and tosses something onto the bar. My eyes widen as I identify it —a wad of cash, neatly constrained by a silver rubber band.

"I'm looking for someone," he continues. "Calls himself Vadim. *Dima*."

The bartender's movements slow as he assaults the same crusty stain over and over. Finally, he looks up and shrugs. "Don't know anyone by that name. Sorry."

"Is that so?" Maxim laughs and returns his hand to his breast pocket. This time, he withdraws a second wad of cash, noticeably larger than the first. "Does this refresh your memory?"

The bartender glances over his shoulder. Then he swipes his hand across the bar, dragging the money toward him. "Heard of a Dima," he admits while stuffing the cash into his pocket. "Showed up a few weeks ago, I think. Didn't cause a lot of trouble. He owe you money or something?"

"How do I know your memory isn't faulty?" Maxim wonders. His upper lip curls back from his teeth, and the other man flinches, nearly dropping a wad of bills before he can fit it all into his pants. I don't blame him. Maybe I flinch too. It's chilling how easily the figure beside me can switch from suave to menacing. "Describe him to me."

"Tall, um... Lanky. A bit of an oddball—" The bartender twirls his finger beside his head and raises an eyebrow.

"Kept to himself, like I said—"

"How do you know it was him?"

"His name," the bartender says, shrugging. "He didn't exactly make a secret of it. And he was damn good. That's why I asked about the money. He would come in some nights and fleece the shit out of my regulars playing pool." He nods to the table in the corner. "Damn smart, that guy... He might have looked scrawny and all, but I ain't never seen anybody play like that. It was like he was reading fucking minds and shit. And tough, too. One of the guys tried to have a go at him after he won. But that Dima guy, he just gave him a look, ya know? Billy went to prison for attempted murder, so he ain't no chicken shit. I never seen him back down from a fight like that." He shakes his head and snatches up his rag. "But he hasn't been here in a few days."

Scowling in concentration, Maxim braces his hand against the bar. "And you're sure of that?"

The man nods. "Positive. But ah, if you want, I can keep an eye out." He eyes Maxim's bruised, bloodied knuckles and swallows. "Let you know if I see him."

"Good." Maxim fingers his lapel and turns his attention to a nearby booth. He moves boldly, drawing attention from every patron in the entire damn room. "I'll have a drink."

He sits, pulling me down beside him and withdraws a cell phone from his pocket—a different model than the one from the other day.

"Lucius," he snaps, bringing the receiver to his ear. "Switch out with Victor. We need to talk."

He hangs up and eyes the silver watch on his wrist and then refocuses his gaze over the center of the room in a way that makes my stomach twist into knots.

One by one, he eyes the few other patrons huddled in the bar, scanning their faces with ruthless focus. The longer he stares, the harder his expression becomes. After about an hour, he stands, tugging me after him.

"Come."

Once we return to the car, the other driver is gone. Instead, Lucius patiently inclines his head for instruction. "Where to, sir?"

"I don't fucking know." Maxim swipes his hand through the air as he reclaims the back seat. He looks ready to pounce through the windshield, hungry for a fight. "Drive around. And as you do, you can explain why Dima has been here for weeks, and I haven't heard a fucking word."

"That is news to me as well, sir." Lucius calmly pulls into traffic, heading toward the main road. "I know for a fact he hasn't been spotted in the city." A rare note of sternness colors his tone. He's confident of that. "But if he has been on the outskirts, I will have my men extend more resources immediately. Any lapse in vigilance is unacceptable."

"I should have known it seemed too damn easy," Maxim hisses. "The bastard knew I was coming. He's probably in fucking Moscow by now. I should have known Milton would protect that piece of shit… But you are no lazy hack, either," he adds, speaking to Lucius. "The only way for this to go under your radar was if someone *helped* sweep it under. I paid one of the men off, but I could tell the fucker's been bought before. Only one man I know is cunning enough." He strokes his chin, his eyes gleaming murderously.

"Sir?" Lucius inclines his head. "You don't mean—"

"Milton has always had a soft spot for Vadim. They were in the same batch, you remember? In Europe. Kept like prized rats in a cage to be bought and sold amongst the same fucking 'clientele'…"

He glowers, staring beyond me, and this car and anyone else. The past surrounds him, and he bares his teeth against it.

"I thought time may have broken that pathetic sense of pity in him. But I was wrong." A single twitch of his frown betrays just how deeply that fact unnerves him. "When it comes to Vadim, I can no longer trust him."

"Sir?" Lucius inclines his head. "What would you like for me to do?"

"You have full reign," Maxim replies. "Do what you must to hunt him down—but don't kill him. I want you to give him a message." He laughs in a way that will haunt my fucking nightmares. "Tell him to stop hiding like a boy and face me like a man."

His voice resonates with more vitriol than usual—even for him.

"Let's see how the rat reacts when presented with a pile of cheese."

"As you wish, sir. But Ms. Marconi?" Lucius clears his throat, and Maxim flinches at the subtle reminder.

"Bring her to her family," he commands, returning his attention to me. "Then take me back to the city."

"Yes, sir." Lucius nods. "Right away."

DAWN PAINTS the horizon as the city skyline looms in the distance. Fair Haven, as a whole, looks surprisingly cold when viewed from here. A lifeless jungle of concrete I've been stuck in for my entire life. Before Maxim, I think I would have sold my soul to escape from it.

Maybe I did, shedding my old life and neighborhood for something new.

Glimpsed from the perspective of a brutal billionaire, Fair Haven contains a darkness far more terrifying than the prospect of wasting my life as my mother did. It reminds me of Maxim in a way. Beautiful from afar. Terrifying and cold while up close. Impossible to leave for reasons I can't really explain.

The fact that our destination is beyond the city limits unsettles me in more ways than one. It's symbolic, in a sense. I've craved my freedom from the place for so damn long…

But as it turns out, the world beyond my home is flat, boring, and devoid of the chaos I've grown accustomed to. When we arrive at the property, I assume my family is sequestered in, I'm even more unsettled. No one would ever guess the true owner of the quaint dwelling enclosed by a wrought-iron gate. Hell, add in a white picket fence, and the place would look tailor-made for some rich soccer mom and her brood to inhabit.

Not a crime lord with a preference for penthouses.

The only glitch in the façade is a security booth guarding the entrance, staffed by two men dressed in black. They nod solemnly as the car advances past them, down a paved driveway and up to the front of the house.

"The extra security measures are temporary. As for the house, I admit it's not my usual taste, but it's secure," Maxim explains as I take in the white mansion with black trimming. He must sense the skepticism my expression can't disguise. "Get some rest. Your family is already settled in. I've asked the guards to remain out of sight. Lucius will come by later."

He doesn't bother to explain what will happen after that. He doesn't have to, considering that my experience with his controlling nature is enough for me to fill in the blanks—tonight, we'll be on a plane to only God knows where. Though, to be fair, in Maxim's world, God himself sits beside me, so convinced of his own power. Any slight violation of his wishes equates to a mortal sin.

Like daring to question him. "What about their school?"

"The arrangements have been made," he says, prepared for me. My punishment is his thumb tracing my lower lip as if savoring my rebellion. "As for your siblings, they've been told you're going on a surprise family vacation."

Surprise. Our first trip from the city ever is anything but a "vacation."

It's petty to focus on that point. To be irritated by it. After all, what is a trip somewhere new in relation to a pre-designed wedding dress, or a disposable ring? Petty, fucking concerns. It's even pettier to needle him for no damn good reason. "What if I don't want to leave?"

A low sound resonates in his throat. "Don't." He meets my gaze directly, his stare fathomless. "You feel comfortable enough to question me. I can respect that. But don't ever doubt me or my intentions toward you. When you are safe, I can turn my attention to Anatoli without any distractions."

"So, you're staying in the city?"

"Keep the car running," he tells Lucius before exiting the car. To me, his tone is far more curt. Another warning. "Come."

I trail him up the walkway, allowing him to take the lead. Beyond the front door is a layout similar to that of his previous house. Faint noises from various directions betray the presence of other occupants, awake despite the early hour. Running water. A muffled television. High-pitched bickering over toothpaste.

A sense of relief nearly barrels me over, and I forget my annoyance. I've spent these past few days so wrapped up in myself. I didn't have the time to truly fear for my kids—or feel the gratitude for the man who has kept them safe all this time.

I glance at him only to catch him observing me in return. Dark, his eyes brim with an unknown emotion. One too dangerous to decipher on a whim. Rather than try, I reach out, brushing my fingers along his forearm. "Thank you—"

"Frankie!" I turn to spot a tiny blur of pink and blond racing down the stairs in my direction. "I missed you!" Ainsley declares while throwing her arms around my waist. "Where are we going? I've never been on vacation before!"

"Um, it's as much as a surprise to you as it is to me," I confess. But I force a smile and try to bite back any doubts. "Are you excited?"

"Why do you look so funny?" She wrinkles her nose and tugs me along. "Never mind. Hurry up. I want to show you my new doll. Are you going to stay over?"

"I think so…" I look back for confirmation, but Maxim is already gone, vanished without a goodbye.

And I barely catch the door closing behind him.

CHAPTER SIX

It's scary how easy it is to fall into an old routine. To take on another persona as though it's a well-worn role in a tired play. I've been away from the kids for days, but in little over an hour, I've broken up two fights and played referee during three shouting matches.

Some things never change. And in Maxim's world, maybe that's a *good* thing.

"Damn, Frankie," Mikie grumbles from across the living room. He lies across a couch so expensive it probably belongs in a fancy boutique rather than here. His bare feet are propped on one of the armrests, and I nearly rip his legs from their sockets as I knock them off.

"Have some fucking manners," I snap at him. "We don't live here." And I can't shake that fact no matter how comfortable they seem. The beautiful, priceless furniture serves as a mocking reminder that it's not truly ours. It's borrowed.

"Chill," he says, laughing. "I almost forgot what it sounds like to hear the master utilize ten different curse words in one sentence. Bravo."

"Fuck off, smartass." My jaw aches, but when I rub the sore muscle, I realize why. I'm smiling.

Maybe because this feels good in a way I don't expect. No talk of weddings or gowns. Normalcy.

But there is always an undercurrent that reinforces one thing—this newfound security is possible at the behest of one person. The man who pays the bills. The puppet master who ensures that I don't have to craft a lunch of burned macaroni and Pop-Tarts like I used to.

In my new reality, a chef appears from nowhere to announce that brunch has been served in a dining room set exactly for seven. In lieu of paper plates, fine cutlery and expensive china adorn each place setting. No roaches are scurrying in the corners to set the mood. Instead, a bay window overlooks a meticulously crafted garden of fancy, colorful flowers.

Trust fund babies, eat your heart out.

"Hey!" Mikie snaps, slapping at one of the twins' hands as they reach across the table. "Use your goddamn manners and say please. Right, Frankie?"

Something inside me aches as he eyes me as if for permission. While I've been gone, I have no doubt as to who had to step up to fill my shoes.

"Right," I croak.

"Taste this," Ainsley squeals, shoving a forkful of her food in my face. The menu ironically consists of a fancier version of macaroni and cheese with vegetables on the side instead of sugar.

I choke down a bite. "It's good."

"Yeah! I didn't know anything, but pizza could taste so good," Ainsley chirps in agreement.

"Pass me the bread, *please*," Mikie says while reaching for a porcelain saucer. "So where are we going, Frankie? I never thought we'd be the kind of people who 'go away' for summer break."

I can't tell if he's horrified or excited by the prospect.

"It's a surprise, right, Frankie?" Ainsley pitches in.

"Do I have to eat this? I read in a magazine that dairy isn't good for your skin," Daisy muses, eyeing her plate. "Though the sun isn't either, so if we're going to a beach—"

"What's a little more acne, pizza face?" One of the twins snipes.

I sigh and reach for a fork. "Cut it out. Let's just have a nice, normal fucking…"

Something in the window catches my eye. A shadow, displacing the pretty flowers and manicured lawn. No. A person…running?

"Frankie?" Someone taps my shoulder. "You okay?"

"I…"

Suddenly, two men race into the dining room and lunge toward the window. One of them bites out a shouted command, "Get down!"

And everything goes to shit.

Glass shatters. Screams echo. Something slams into me from the side, knocking me to the floor. I scramble for balance, dazed as a million different things happen at once.

Racing footsteps. Another monstrous, echoing sound. Noise. More screams, high-pitched and deafening. I can't see. Think.

Then a hand comes from nowhere, yanking me to my feet. "This way," someone commands into my ear, their tone familiar. Lucius. He throws his arm around my shoulder, pinning me to his side. "Keep your head down. I've got you."

He nudges me toward the exit, but I turn back, barely recognizing the room behind me at all. Glass decorates the table like confetti. One of the chairs is broken, and flailing bodies clamor for the doorway. It looks like a fucking bomb went off.

"Ainsley?" Panic breaks my voice into a hollow rasp. "Daisy?"

"Come!" Lucius grabs my arm. "Everyone is safe, but we need to move. Now!"

I follow him blindly. Wherever we go, we move too quickly for me to track our progress. All I know is that when Lucius finally stops, we're in an enclosed space illuminated only with fluorescent lighting. A basement?

One by one, the kids stream inside, flanked by several men I don't recognize. They're dressed in black, each openly sporting a weapon. Guards.

"What's happening?" Ainsley demands. I look down to find her clinging to my waist. Her eyes are wide, staring blankly. "Frankie, what's happening?"

"A minor gas leak," Lucius explains calmly. "It most likely caused a small pipe explosion. Nothing to worry about. Ms. Marconi, if you don't mind, may I have a word?"

He heads into the hallway, past the guards. The second we're out of earshot, I reach for his hand, forcing him to face me. "What's really going on?"

"Someone just tried to kill you," he explains, his tone eerily blunt. "It was a lazy attempt to be sure. A warning more than anything, but Mr. Koslov will want you brought to him immediately."

"No." The world spins. I have to hunch over and cradle my head in my hands just to keep standing. The floor sways beneath me as a tattered giggle escapes my throat. Maybe I'm in shock. From here, I can hear Mikie demanding answers amid a thin, terrified cry. *Ainsley.* God, she's never sounded so frantic before. Standing upright, I start in their direction. "I'm not leaving them—"

"Trust me, it will be for the best," Lucius insists, grabbing my hand before I even make it a step. Frowning, he withdraws a handkerchief from his suit pocket. "You're bleeding. If I may—" He dabs at a patch of flesh above my left eye, but I don't feel anything. The cloth, however, comes away red. "Don't be alarmed," Lucius says, stowing the stained fabric within his jacket. "It's merely a superficial laceration. Nothing too serious. Still, I'll have a physician meet you at the club."

"The club?" My thoughts congeal within my skull like jelly. He's speaking too quickly. I can't keep up.

"Yes." Lucius nods. "I need to get you to Mr. Koslov immediately. And I know you're concerned for your siblings. I will stay with them. And, if I may be blunt, they'll be safer apart from you for now. Tomas?" He directs his attention to one of the men dressed in black who steps forward. "This is the head of security," Lucius explains to me. "He will bring you to Mr. Koslov. Now go."

But I never have a choice. Tomas takes my arm and steers me into another room before I even realize what's happening. I start to protest, but one last look from Lucius makes me go limp, resigned.

It's the same way he looked at me in the car after dispensing his "advice."

Without judgment or irritation. No anger, either…

Just pity.

TOMAS DRIVES me to the club in a vehicle I don't recognize. Rather than a sleek sports car, I find myself in the back seat of a bulky van with tinted windows that paint the world beyond in dark obscurity. Rather than to portray luxury, its purpose is far more utilitarian—safety.

And urgency.

Forgoing about a million traffic laws, Tomas whips the van over the courtyard of the club and parks mere feet from the entrance. A heartbeat later, he's already at my door, moving to shield my body with his. "This way, Ms. Marconi."

We barely enter the building before Maxim appears as if conjured from thin air. Wild with rage, his eyes trace my face, narrowing over the blood drying on my forehead.

The next second, I'm in his arms, my head on his shoulder. His pulse hammers madly beneath his skin as he carries me down a darkened hallway and into the secluded bedroom, I know to be his.

"You're bleeding… Damnit." He makes me sit on the edge of the mattress, his focus on my forehead. "Are you alright?"

"No," I croak, but the blood dripping down my chin barely fazes me. In fact, the only thing I can seem to care about is a simple statement Mikie said. "It's almost summer break."

Maxim frowns, scanning my face. "How do you feel? Is your head—"

"I mean, my kids should be in a fucking amusement park or something." My hands are shaking. Balling them into fists isn't enough to stop the tremors wracking me from head to toe. My teeth chatter, breaking my words into a series of jagged syllables. "They deserve a normal vacation. School. A *real* home. Not getting s-shot at—"

"Breathe," Maxim warns, stroking the uninjured side of my face. "You're in shock—"

"You think I want protection?" I'm babbling. I can barely make sense of my own damn words—but I can't shut up, either. "I want normalcy! I want my sisters to grow up in a normal fucking environment, and my brothers shouldn't see me covered in bruises... I want them to have bedtimes, and allowances, and take walks in the park. Shit normal people do. I want them to have what I didn't. Not this." My eyes burn, and moisture spills from them the second I blink. "Not borrowed mansions, and fucking fear."

Maxim watches me cry, his expression unreadable. Then he crouches before me, and his heavy sigh ruffles my wayward curls. "You were right to question me," he admits, bringing his mouth against my ear. "Separating you from me was foolish. It won't happen again."

"Who was it?" I ask as the chaos replays in my mind over and over. "Was it your grandfather?"

His upper lip pulls back from his teeth. "I don't know," he snarls. "But I will find them. They will pay—"

"Sir?" The door opens, and Tomas enters.

"What the hell is it?" Maxim whirls around, but before he can utter another word, Tomas approaches him and whispers something into his ear. Whatever he says makes Maxim's entire body stiffen. The next second he's barreling into the hallway, and I have to run to keep up.

At first, I don't know what makes him stop at the edge of the club floor. His erect posture is alarming, but nothing compared to how I'd assume he'd act in the face of an armed intruder. For one, he doesn't draw a weapon. Instead, his body ripples with barely concealed tension—but that's the odd part. He's trying to *hide* it.

I discover the answer to the mystery once I spot the lanky figure leaning against the bar, admiring a bottle of liquor. He's tall and alarmingly thin. His body barely shapes the gray sweatshirt he wears paired with light wash jeans. Wild dark hair obscures his face from this angle, but his pale fingers betray an unusual grace as he twirls the bottle between them.

"I hear you've been looking for me," he says without turning around. "Well, you've found me, little Maxi. What do you want?"

Maxim observes the other figure in a way that can only be described as hostile. His fingers flex at his sides as if he has to consciously keep them from forming fists. "It's about damn time you've crawled out of hiding, Vadim."

"Oh?" Vadim cocks his head, still facing away from us. "Unlike you, I don't dwell in the lap of luxury. I am, in the open, as they say. Easy to find." He has an accent as well, though it's less pronounced than Maxim's and harder to place. British? Russian? French? He speaks with a blend of several different inflections. "And it's funny that you sought me out. Considering you threatened to kill me if I ever set foot in your precious city again. I took your sudden change of heart as an invitation to visit. Nice place—"

"You know what the fuck I want." Maxim advances a dangerous step, but Vadim doesn't seem to notice. Or care. He lazily tosses his bottle into the air, catching it one-handed.

"Enough games," Maxim warns. "Let's cut to the heart of it. Stand with me against Anatoli. You know I will make it worth your while."

"Is that so?" I jump as Vadim barks out an unexpectedly harsh note of laughter. Compared to the musical quality of his voice, the sound rings like an off note in an otherwise pretty piece of piano music. "You think I give a damn about your money?"

"No." Maxim flexes his arms, adjusting the fit of his suit. "But did I say anything about money?"

"What else could you be willing to offer? Hmm?" Vadim finally inclines his head to observe us with the same scrutiny Maxim inspects him with. I feel my mouth fall open as I take him in. He's beautiful—but in a different way than Maxim could ever be.

Instead of harsh, violent appeal, this man could only be described as *delicate*. His swanlike throat and graceful jaw are comparable to meticulously crafted glass in contrast to Maxim's powerful bulk. But his eyes…

They're a shade so dark they seem to glow, even from this distance.

"Do tell," he prompts, waving his hand expectantly through the air. "You have my full attention."

"I'll give you a piece of my so-called empire," Maxim replies, crossing his arms. "That's what you crave, isn't it? That which was always *mine*."

"Oh no…" Vadim leans back against the counter, still fiddling with the bottle. The motion displays him from a different angle, making it apparent how young he is. Maybe in his early thirties, like Maxim. Or even younger—but whatever his age, he's nowhere near naïve. A guarded calculation shapes everything from his perusing gaze down to the quirk of his chin. He's ready for an attack at any moment. "Crave? I think the correct phrasing is 'what I'm owed.'"

"Discuss my terms, and you can have it," Maxim suggests. "What little scraps I'm willing to give."

"Scraps…" Vadim runs a hand through his hair, parting the thick black strands. He observes a particularly long section, his nose wrinkling in disapproval. "You must think I'm stupid, Maxi," he says, returning his attention to the other man. "A stupid fucking prick, huh? Even from my little hidey-hole, I've heard the rumors. That lately you've started collecting your dolls, rather than just fucking them." He eyes me pointedly and sighs. "An amusing little anecdote. Following in the footsteps of our dear old man, I see? What is she? Some obscure countess you aim to impregnate before chopping her to pieces—"

"Is that what the rumors say?" Maxim interjects—but my brain remains stuck on three words. *Our old man...* I barely comprehend what he says next, "I knew you were wallowing in your shame, Vadim. But obsession? It's beneath you."

"So is lying, Maxi," the other man scolds, wagging his finger. Was his insinuation a joke or something more? I can't tell. The only similarity I can find between the two is icy, ruthless confidence. "But you've always been good at that," Vadim adds. "Lying. Scheming. Backstabbing. How does the saying go? You can take the boy out of the whore, but not the whore out of the boy—"

"Enough." Teeth bared, Maxim advances another impulsive step. "Watch yourself."

"I've *also* heard that someone's pissed off the old man," Vadim says, seemingly unconcerned. "He doesn't seem to care who you fuck, but the day little Maxi decides to take a wife? The old man issues a bounty. Have you stopped to wonder why? It isn't like him to panic so easily. Not to mention, his favorite doggie's gone missing. Though you wouldn't happen to know anything about that, would you? While he may let you run your little empire on the side—" He gestures around us with a wave of his hand, indicating the club itself. "Anatoli wouldn't react kindly to a direct challenge. And you've been such a dutiful servant all this time. Why risk it now?"

Maxim says nothing, but Vadim nods as if he has.

"Ah… I see. You were *sloppy*." He grins, displaying perfectly white teeth. "Sloppy and reckless. If I can suspect as much, you can believe the old man has. It's why he's gone out of his way to bring you to heel. Oh yes, you've been a bad boy, little Maxi—"

"And you need to decide what role you want to play, *Dima*," Maxim snarls in a tone so harsh I suck in a breath. "As a player? Or as the stray mutt, you've always been? Milton can't protect you forever."

"Maybe." Vadim flicks his tongue over his lips. "Milton wants me to play nice and assist in your little war. What he really wants is for you to break from your chains and claim the city for yourself so he can stop worrying where your loyalties lie. But me? Maybe I should watch Anatoli rip you apart and find another whipping boy to serve as his figurehead? One could say I've dreamt about it…"

"Funny. I would dream about amassing my own power. But some things never fucking change, do they?" Maxim reaches into his pocket and withdraws a small, rectangular item that I recognize as a business card. From this angle, I can only make out a silver letter X gleaming on the front of it. "When you get tired of hiding behind another man's pant leg, you know where to find me—" He tosses the card onto the floor. "Come when you've made your choice as to what role you'll play."

"What about as a spectator?" Vadim laughs again, but there's no mistaking the sound for what it truly is. A growl. "The decision as to 'where I stand' was made for me a long time ago—I am no Koslov. And you've always made sure to remind me of that. Haven't you?" He extends his throat, drawing my attention to a reddish scar stretching from his jawline down beneath the neckline of his shirt. It's nasty, betraying the severity of the wound that made it.

I swallow hard and run my fingers along my own neck. Images sneak into my skull before I can fight them back— the feel of a knife, biting into my flesh.

"Pretty, isn't it?" Vadim's eyes flicker toward me, meeting my gaze directly. Maxim snatches my arm, pulling me to his side, but something won't let me turn away. It's his expression. He doesn't blink, his stare open and raw. With one look, I get the sense he understands all too well. "And I can tell your little friend has already gotten a taste of your... let's call it, *affection*—"

"You speak to me," Maxim demands in a hiss. "No one else."

"If only you listened. But you are right. Let's cut to the heart of it..." Vadim turns his attention to one of the intricate silver chandeliers hanging overhead, his frown wistful. "As much as I'd like to see the old man burn in hell, I don't have a problem with Anatoli. In fact, you could say I've made peace with the idea of letting his time run its course—" His lips twitch in a fleeting smirk. "As for my help, tell me how someone as lowly and worthless as I can be of service to someone so great?"

"Cut the bullshit." Maxim releases me and takes another step in Vadim's direction. Mere feet separate them now, and for the first time, the other man displays a hint of wariness. He sets his bottle on the counter, freeing his hands. "I know Milton has been protecting you—"

"Milton is Milton." Vadim lifts his arms in a casual shrug. "And as far as I know, he's made his choice of alliance *very* clear."

"Then you know as well as I do whose side that is. You've been attacking my network. Don't insult my intelligence by insisting that he just found out recently. He knows your handiwork better than anyone. I'm sure he's been aware of your scheming since day one," Maxim continues. "You must have some resources to hide your tracks so well. Though scheming from the shadows isn't too much of a stretch for a rat."

"What can I say?" Vadim smiles, and the slight tilt to his mouth transforms his face. He's a different man in a heartbeat, charming and bright. "I was taught by the best. You should know—he trained you too. Good old Anatoli. Tell me something." He strokes his chin, suddenly thoughtful. "When you brought your new 'friend' to him— and I use that term loosely, all things considered—did he fuck her first? Or did you toss her to Sevastyn to have her broken in?"

A roar of anger reverberates like thunder. Maxim. In a blur of motion, he lunges at Vadim, his arm raised, fist poised for a blow.

But Vadim stands calmly in the line of fire. Right before Maxim can touch him, he says, "You *did*, didn't you?" A shadow falls over his face, enhancing the nuances of his expression concealed until now. He's not afraid. He's angry —but in a different way from the furious figure standing between us.

Where Maxim radiates fire, this man is cool, controlled ice.

"You threw her to Sevastyn." Awe paints his tone, mingled with horror. "Either that or you failed to protect her from him. For some reason, Maxim, I never pegged you as a womanizer to quite *that* extent. Even with your quirks…"

Maxim says nothing, his fist still raised, body trembling with tension.

"I thought it was a lie, the last, juiciest bit of gossip fluttering around about you," Vadim adds. "I guess not. Anatoli *has* put out a bounty, after all, merely to spite his golden boy. A hefty one."

"Oh?" Maxim lowers his fist but doesn't back away. If anything, he towers over the slender figure, but the pairing doesn't seem quite as unbalanced as it should.

Maybe because his opponent meets his glare unflinchingly.

"A blood price to be exact. *Krasnyy konets*," Vadim says. "So archaic and dramatic of him, but somewhat fitting in this sense. How else can he better define the rules of that precious family? *Koslov*. Otherwise, it's figurehead may get the urge to induct some unworthy whore into such a stoic bloodline, and the world will fucking end."

"Watch your mouth," Maxim snarls.

"You know it's true," Vadim taunts. "Even in his old age, the man can still read you like a book, Maxi. You *finally* move to declare your independence from him, and he issues you a spanking you can't ignore. A blood price is no small offer considering the old man—bless his soul—could keel over at any moment. I could claim the bounty now, for instance, and earn my place in the family, right over your head. In the event of Anatoli's unfortunate demise, I might even be able to take the reins of the entire precious Koslov empire. Such a prize."

"Am I supposed to feel threatened every time the old man decides to test me?"

"Oh, but I didn't say the bounty was on *your* head." Vadim's gaze finds me again, glinting with renewed curiosity. "Did I? I see now, why you picked this one. A wide-eyed innocent little girl who won't ever question her master. Who stays by your side, even when you toss her to the wolves. How much was she worth? A few grand? You wouldn't pay any more than that—"

"Enough."

"Yes. I've had enough." Sighing, Vadim easily slips beyond Maxim's reach and starts for the exit. "Goodbye for now," he calls with an enthusiastic wave. "But we really should do this again. It's been far too long...*brother*."

Shock nearly robs me of the balance I have left. I almost miss Maxim's reply. "You are nothing to me," he hisses. "You want to play games? Get the fuck out."

"Ah, yes, well, we can't choose family, can we?" Vadim confidently strolls for the archway connecting this part of the club to the rest. "Oh, and I won't be needing the calling card. I'll just name my price outright. Since you like to whore out your woman, then that's what I'll take. An hour with her, alone—"

An object hurls through the air and smashes to pieces above Vadim's head. A torrent of clear liquid and broken glass miss him by mere inches, but his steps don't even falter.

"That's the price," he says, oblivious to the murderous glare Maxim directs his way. "And don't think about having me followed. Your men are good, but they aren't the sharpest tools in the shed, so to speak. Invest in more skilled minions if you hope to find me. I'll await your real answer once you've thought on it. *Dasvidaniya*."

"Follow him," Maxim growls the second he's beyond view.

"Yes, sir." Tomas leaves, followed by two men.

"Fuck!" Maxim rakes a hand through his hair, his shoulders hunched away from me. When he finally looks back, I can't read his expression. I don't want to.

It's funny in a sick way. These past forty-eight hours have desolated my sanity. My security. My sense of self. But out of all of the twisted revelations I've been forced to reconcile, only one lands the heaviest blow.

"He is your brother." Like a broken record stuck on repeat, I can't stop blurting it out loud. "You have a *brother*—"

"No," Maxim growls with barely concealed restraint. We're alone now, and his voice echoes to the furthest reaches of the club floor, easily dominating my hollow whisper. "My father had a *bastard*. Vadim is nothing more than a mutt. Look at me. Fuck, you're still bleeding—"

"You never mentioned him," I point out. God, I sound so dazed. Like I'm sleepwalking in a nightmare, half convinced that none of this is real. "I've told you everything about me. Everything about my family, but I didn't even know you had a brother—"

"Vadim is not a factor in my life." He snatches a handkerchief from the breast pocket of his suit and grabs my chin, keeping me still. "*Your* family is my only concern. Stay." He dabs at the wound above my eye, his eyes narrowed. "Your pupils are dilated. You could have a concussion."

"I'm fine." I try to turn away, but his fingers skim my hair regardless.

"The doctor will examine you—"

"Just stop!" I cringe from him this time. Alarm renders him frozen, and he doesn't reach for me again. "Please…"

"Alright." He tosses the bloodied cloth aside. The fact that he backed down at all shocks me. Almost as much as how he stands there awkwardly, his fingers clenched into fists. "Lucius sent for a doctor," he says after a second of silence. "When he gets here, let him examine you—"

"I need to go home. I need to… Ainsley was crying. She needs me." More tears spill down my cheeks, startlingly hot. All this time, they've never stopped falling. "I need to make sure my family is okay. I need to comfort my baby sister, who had a bullet whiz past her head. I need to…" A sudden urgency spurs me to stumble for the doorway. "Take me back."

Maxim doesn't move. "I can't."

"Why not?"

"Because…" I look back, and his gaze reluctantly meets mine. "They're already on a plane."

A tattered laugh escapes my throat as I stagger, my knees trembling. Before they give out, my back strikes the nearest wall, and I cling to the cool surface.

"So, you've just kidnapped them." At the back of my mind, I know I'm overexaggerating. Logic can't pierce this fog of sheer, fucking panic. I can't stop shaking. My chest feels like a brick is balanced on my ribcage, crushing it. No matter how quickly I breathe, I can't find enough air.

"You're hyperventilating." Maxim places his hand on my shoulder, but I wrench away from him, and I have to brace myself against the wall again just to keep from falling.

"Don't touch me! You've kidnapped them because that's what it's called when a stranger takes your family members away, isn't it?"

"*Kotyonok*—"

"I don't know you!" I bury my face in my hands, blocking out the sight of him. Something Vadim said serves as a morbid fucking key, unlocking the twisted, horrible memories I've done my best to lock away. "Is that why you wanted me to go with you?" I have to grit my teeth to keep from gagging. Vomiting. "You knew what he'd ask for. You said it—I would fascinate him. Was that it? You wanted... You wanted to w-whore me out—"

"Look at me."

"Don't!" I throw my hand out, keeping him at bay. "I don't know you. I don't know your past. I don't know who your friends are. I didn't even know until five seconds ago that you had a brother. Maybe it's best if you don't marry me." I stare at my bare finger. This pinching, aching sensation in my chest, could be relief—not agony. "I think I'd rather be your whore than your property—"

"Enough!" Eyes flashing, he moves in on my position. Despite how I cringe from his touch, his hand sinks into my hair, forcing me to face him. "Vadim is no one. You care for your siblings, and I respect that. But him? *He* was a tool. One of my father's many bastards. If anything, he was a whip that Anatoli used to punish me, serving as a reminder that I could always be replaced. Our relationship extends to nothing more than the shared blood of the monster who sired us. Do you understand?"

His nostrils flare when I don't respond. Readjusting his grip, he wrenches my head to the side, and his opposite thumb traces the space above my left eye.

"You want to know why I brought you? Because if I didn't, I would have lost my fucking mind, and I would have killed him. I would have lost control..." His voice breaks, followed by a laugh and then a sigh. "You say you don't know me—but you do. You know when to ask me fucking questions I wouldn't tolerate from anyone else. You know how to use those fucking eyes so that I can see myself reflected in them. You keep me here." His tone deepens with unsaid meaning. *Here.* In the present, away from the horror of his past.

"And I know that *you* don't panic easily. I know when I've pushed you too far... And I know that I won't lose you like this. Not because of him." He releases me, only to grab my chin and coax me into meeting his gaze. "I want more than protection for you," he admits, lowering his lips to the uninjured side of my forehead. "I want..."

His nostrils flare, inhaling me, and he says nothing else as if the act speaks for him. He wants my scent—skin and sweat and a hint of blood.

"You want your normalcy?" He finds my earlobe with his mouth, nipping it with gentle pressure. "Then you will have it. No matter what it takes."

But, as if to counter that promise, slow, heavy footsteps advance on our position from the direction of the entrance hall. Maxim tenses just as the newcomer appears in the doorway. Dressed in an ebony suit crowned by a blood-red tie, the man cuts a striking figure against the gray backdrop.

"Milton…" Maxim withdraws from me, lowering his hands to his sides. The posture is a stark contrast from his hostility toward Dima—but not completely relaxed either.

"I came as quickly as I could," Milton explains, fingering his collar. His eyes dart cautiously around the room before settling over the broken glass on the floor. "Vadim was here?"

"Don't pretend like you don't fucking know," Maxim says with a scoff. "I'm sure he didn't learn this location through luck."

"It's your right to mistrust him," Milton says with a nod. "But can I make a suggestion?"

"Like what?" Maxim cocks his head. "Say it."

"Give him what he wants. End this feud."

He makes it sound so simple. So easy. Maxim doesn't seem to know whether he's joking or not. A rugged sound escapes his mouth in response—part laugh, part growl.

"I'll assume that you don't know what he requested," he concedes in a lethal tone. "So, I will let that insult pass."

"And you can't give up anything, not one fucking thing, in exchange for a truce?" Milton's eyes narrow, revealing the briefest hint of anger. A heartbeat later, it's gone. "Dima has vital insight on how to defeat Anatoli—"

"Dima," Maxim echoes, an eyebrow raised. "You still call him that."

Sighing, he crosses to the bar. Putting his palms flat on the surface, he observes the liquor selection with his back to us. "I don't ignore my past. Not that it lets me. Some days it bothers me, I won't lie, but I've made peace with it. I don't let it define me now, and I don't dwell on it. If I choose to refer to Dima as *Dima,* so be it."

"And I do? Dwell?" Maxim strolls toward the pile of glass on the floor and nudges a chunk with the toe of his boot. "Tell that to the mess he's always left in his wake. The past does not define me, either. I have just never made the mistake of forgetting it."

"Anatoli threatens my livelihood as well, or did you forget that?" When he turns from the bar and meets Maxim's gaze head-on, Milton's noticeably colder. "Despite his faults, Dima knows better than anyone how to... let's call it, circumvent overwhelming odds. With his help, you can make Anatoli bow with little bloodshed."

"So, you want to play peacemaker?" Maxim laughs, shaking his head. "Don't talk like a pacifist, Milton. It's beneath you."

Milton flashes a disarming smile. "Alright, then, let's cut the bullshit. You don't have what it takes to defeat Anatoli on your own—" his voice deepens, losing any ounce of congeniality. "You and I both know it. Running from him will only delay the unavoidable. In his arrogance, Anatoli will see it as an opportunity to force you to surrender. The old bastard will get spiteful, placing us *all* at risk. You do realize that?"

"Go." Maxim turns away from him and observes my forehead, frowning in concentration. "Get out. We will discuss this later."

"Will we?" Milton starts toward the entrance, his steps deliberately slow, skepticism darkening the shadows on his face. "I'll leave out of respect for the circumstances—" he points his head in my direction. "But I won't let you ignore me this time. I mean it. You have my loyalty, but I'm not above making my wishes known in ways you can't ignore. Understood?"

He passes through the archway, and the second he is out of view, I remember how to move.

"Are you alright?" Maxim reaches for my forehead, but I recoil, nearly tripping in my rush to back away.

He follows, his eyes narrowed, jaw clenched. "Don't move—"

"I'm tired." My fingers tremble as I brace them against his chest. I'm too weak to push him off, but he withdraws regardless. "I… I just want to see my family."

He eyes me for so long. I'm numb when he finally nods and turns away, his expression blank. "Clean up—" He gestures to the rag on the floor. "I'll bring the car around. We'll leave soon. Together."

I watch him go, storming off to take charge once again.

But I have no desire to follow him this time.

CHAPTER SEVEN

I could never hold onto anger the way Maxim does. At least, in the sense that I don't acknowledge it at all. Feel it. Let it consume me. If anything, I've always been a doormat, swallowing down my emotions. Choking on them. My pain. My hate. If I didn't, I doubt I would have survived up until this point.

Melanie may have been a cunt, but she wasn't stupid—and she wasn't inclined to get arrested for child neglect either. She knew which kid to shoulder her responsibility on. She knew whose personality she could meld and shape and beat into submission.

She knew that as much as I hated her, I loved the kids more. Enough to willingly suffer anything for them. Anything... and devotion was one surefire thing she could always bank on—even when the shitty marriages and stolen money ran out.

And now, she's laughing at me from her spot in hell. *I never got them shot at, Francesca,* I imagine her taunting in that smug fucking way only she could. *I never put their lives in danger. I was a selfish bitch, but I never entangled them in a mafia war. What does that make you?*

It makes me crazy.

It makes me guilty. So fucking guilty…

And it makes me more selfish than she ever was.

I'm blind to everything but the gut-wrenching panic building within me, as Maxim's doctor finally arrives and examines my injury. His determination is a mild concussion, nothing serious. Once I'm deemed able to fly, Maxim ushers me into the car, and we leave for the airport.

The following hours pass by in a blur too dizzying to interpret. I'm left with just snippets of memory. Entering a private jet. Staring blankly from a window, aware of Maxim watching me. I don't even have the sense of mind to acknowledge another of the many firsts I've experienced with him—my virgin plane trip.

I'm numb when we land, and I nearly lunge out of my seat the second Maxim stands. Exiting the climate-controlled cabin for a sweltering, oppressive heat feels like entering a parallel universe. The sun is so bright I have to shield my eyes with my hand and take in our surroundings in bits and pieces.

No city, for one. No skyscrapers and lifeless concrete. Instead, I see endless blue—sky, water—everywhere, reflecting sunlight like glitter. The taste of salt teases my tongue and triggers my curiosity. We're somewhere tropical. Near the ocean?

Maxim pushes ahead without revealing the answer, and I don't ask. As we descend the steps to the tarmac, I spot a black car waiting nearby, along with a familiar face.

"Sir. Ms. Marconi." Lucius nods to us in greeting, but even his warm smile can't disguise the exhaustion hammered beneath his eyes in purplish bruises. I doubt he's slept at all since I saw him last. As dutiful as ever, he opens the door to the back seat. "Once you're settled, we can go."

Maxim extends his hand for me, but I stare ahead and enter the car on my own. He follows me in without a word, and Lucius commands the steering wheel.

"Your siblings are safe and sound," Lucius declares before I can get a single word out. "Everyone is settled in. They know to expect you shortly."

"Thank you." God, I sound worse than he does. My eyes burn as I rest my head against the window on my end. I can't even tell how long I've been awake. An eternity, it feels like.

"Sir," Lucius begins, shifting the conversation. "Mr. Hood has been persistent in his attempts to reach you."

"Milton?" Maxim's voice is a passionless hiss. "Tell him I'm otherwise engaged."

"I have," Lucius admits. "But I will say that he seems... unwilling to be pacified in this instance. I know for a fact he's tracked the jet out of the country, an action he doesn't normally take—"

"Did you make the arrangements I requested?" Maxim interjects, forcibly changing the subject. *Arrangements.* I make a half-hearted attempt at guessing what he means. More security? More shuffling my family around like pieces on a gameboard? More lies?

Wary, I eye him through a crack in my eyelids. Though he sits beside me, we could be an entire fucking world apart. We don't touch, our bodies poised on opposite ends.

"Yes, sir," Lucius replies. "I will admit it was a challenge, but everything is in place."

"Good."

They continue speaking, presumably about business, but I stop listening. I must drift off because when I snap to awareness, Maxim's hand is on my shoulder, and the door on his end is open, letting in a wave of stifling heat.

"We're home." Something in his tone catches me off guard. The softness, maybe?

I inhale in the wake of it, my fingers fluttering toward him. But then I remember Vadim's "price," and I shrug him off and exit the car on my own, clinging to the side of it for balance. His eyes track my every movement, dark and unreadable.

In a bid to ignore him, I focus on our surroundings.

It looks to be late in the evening now. Despite its intensity, the sun has gone down compared to when we first landed. A brilliant, reddish-orange paints the horizon, threatening to swallow it for good. I can't tell how long we were in the car.

Or where we are now, exactly.

Somewhere luxurious, seemingly private, and far from civilization. Around us lies a courtyard enclosed by palm trees and white stone architecture. A path leads off into what seems to be a garden, bathed in shadow. I can just make out a gurgling marble fountain and countless, sprawling plants in the fading daylight.

Behind me looms the real attraction, however. Towering at least three stories, the structure is composed of the same white stone as the courtyard—a mansion expensive enough to star on the cover of some fancy billionaire magazine—the exotic beach home edition. Massive windows promise a view of the ocean I can see looming beyond the trees.

It's breathtaking.

"You and your family have the run of the place," Lucius announces, drawing up beside me. He eyes the house objectively, stroking his chin. "There is a pool. A courtyard. Plenty of rooms. Several acres of property for recreation—"

"I just want to see them," I blurt out, starting forward. "I need to see them."

A passing figure manages to beat me to the front door. Maxim. He opens it without a word to me, revealing a wide entryway.

I barely register the layout at all. I can't fucking *breathe* until several figures rush toward me all at once, shouting my name. Before I know it, I'm assaulted by all six kids, and I gladly allow myself to be crushed within the rush of hugs and the barrage of questioning.

I can't stop touching them. Feeling them—and they hold me even tighter in return. A part of me shatters at that fact. I did this to them. I put them in the middle of this mess.

And I refuse to fail them ever again.

Fresh tears slide down my cheeks, obscuring my vision as I bury my face in Ainsley's hair, inhaling her scent. Even so, I'm painfully aware of a certain figure who keeps his distance from the fray, eventually leaving the vicinity altogether. His absence reinforces the truth I think we both know at heart, and the ache in my chest could be resignation more than anything else.

This is where I belong.

With my family—not him, a man who sees those around him as tools...

And nothing more.

CHAPTER EIGHT

Children are so easy to fuck up. Traumatize. Hell, I should know that better than anyone. Melanie left scars on my psyche that probably deserve intense therapy or some shit.

But history has a way of repeating itself. Of rubbing your nose in your own mistakes and taunting you with the aftermath.

Right before she started talking, Ainsley went through a clingy phase—but without her real mother around, she attached herself to me. *Separation anxiety*, I think one of her social workers called it. Whatever the fancy term was, she'd panic if I wasn't within reach.

At the height of it all, I had to carry her into the bathroom with me. Eat with her in my lap. Bathe with her. Hell, it got to the point where she would only sleep in my bed.

It went on for four months, being her entire world. At least until I stole a night light from the drugstore, and she stopped having nightmares.

Until now. Roughly a day after being shot at, we're back at square one.

She's the first kid to swarm me when I arrive. With hugs at first—then death grips on my arms and eventually my waist until I can't pull away. It's nearly an hour before she lets me go just long enough for me to escape into the bathroom.

Finally alone, I splash water on my face and inspect the wound above my eye in its full glory. It's a thin scratch, superficial like Lucius said, but I can't stop touching it out of morbid curiosity. It's going to scar, joining the many already scattered on my skin. I've grown accustomed to ignoring my old cuts. The ones made "accidentally" intentionally with a knife or my nails—anything sharp I could get my hands on. They're mostly silver now, faded with time.

My newer wounds are more severe in both number and brutality. Injuries left by Maxim. Bruises inflicted by Sevastyn. And now this…

"Frankie!" The door shudders, assaulted by someone's pounding fist, and I nearly jump out of my skin. "Frankie!"

"Coming!" I leave the counter, passing a sunken tub and polished white marble tile to reach the door. My hand shakes as I wrench it open, dreading what I might find on the other end. Broken glass? Another shooter? Maxim?

My knees knock together as I face the inevitable. "W-What's happening?"

Ainsley is the only one standing on the other end. I barely take a step before she throws her arms around my waist so tightly it hurts to walk, but I don't go far. The bathroom is just off the open living room on the first floor. Whether intentional or deliberate, the color scheme is night and day to Maxim's grim monochrome.

If an insanely rich mafia boss were to read a manual on what décor might less alarm six children, this room would be on page one. Beige walls blend in seamlessly with pale hardwood floors, creating a brighter, cozier interior than that of his penthouse. Instead of a king's perspective from the heart of the city, the view from here is of the night sky, glimpsed from beyond a landscape of palm trees. It dawns on me as I settle Ainsley onto a white leather chaise near the windows, that I haven't even explored the rest of the property yet.

Even if I wanted to, Ainsley claws at my wrist until I finally relent and sit beside her.

"Don't go." Wider than ever, her eyes fixate on the window. "What if bad people come back?"

"No one's going to hurt you." I pull her into my arms and run my fingers down her back. She's shaking. "Ever."

"Is the man going to protect us?" she asks. "Is that why he's here now? He can fight away the bad people?"

"The man?"

She buries her face against my chest rather than answer. I have an idea of who she's referring to, however. Should I be relieved that she associates Maxim with protection? Maybe. Maybe I'm more alarmed that she noticed him at all despite his intermittent presence these past few weeks. I'd been an idiot to hope that they all wouldn't. Not yet.

Not when I have no fucking clue where he even fits into our lives. Or where I fit into his…

"Close your eyes, baby," I murmur, running my fingers through her hair. "I'm not going anywhere. I promise—"

"You should get some rest," a deeper voice suggests. I stiffen, though the speaker's identity is no mystery—his shadow looms over the polished floor beneath my feet, inescapable. "You need sleep. Both of you. Lucius has coverage on the house from every possible angle. A fly won't get inside unnoticed."

"We're fine." I tighten my grip on Ainsley and close my eyes, nestling my nose against her scalp. If I inhale her deeply enough, I can ignore everything else—including the masculine musk threatening to invade my nostrils by the second.

My sister smells sweeter. Like sugar and toothpaste. And…

I recoil, my nostrils flaring. *Shit.* She smells like pee. Like she wet the bed overnight, but no one else had noticed or forced her to wash up well enough. Guilt hits me like a punch to the stomach. I can't even be angry. It was a habit she had grown out of after a year of constant vigilance and

enough pull-ups to last a lifetime. We worked damn hard—
the two of us—until she stopped.

My eyes burn, but I blink any new tears back without
saying anything. I don't have the heart to. Not even to drag
her into the bathtub. Not yet.

I owe her one fucking night of peace, at least. For now, she's
breathing normally, her hands in my hair, already asleep.

"There is a room for her upstairs," Maxim continues. "She
has a bed. Her clothing has been brought from the—"

"She needs *me*." I pull her closer, cradling her in my arms.
"I'm not leaving her."

"There is a room for you as well." His tone falls flat, far
more level than I'm used to. "You can share it with her."

"Right now, all I need to do is keep her safe. Make her *feel*
safe. No one else can do that. A fancy bed or a fancy
fucking house, doesn't change anything." My voice rings
out, harsher than I've ever heard it.

In the end, I don't know how long it is before Maxim finally
retreats. Minutes? Hours?

I force myself not to care, pouring my sole focus into my
sister.

What I said to him was the truth. She needs me more than
anyone else. *They* do.

And I've already failed them more than once.

I STARTLE AWAKE to the sensation of my skull on fire. More specifically, like someone is trying to rip a chunk of my hair out. Panicked, my eyes fly open, my body hunched defensively—but my only assailant turns out to be the tiny blond curled on my lap. Still asleep, she moans, grasping for any part of me she can reach.

"You're having a nightmare," I murmur, shaking her awake. "Open your eyes, baby. It's morning."

Soft yellow light seeps in through the windows. As Ainsley rubs her eyes, I stand up.

"Don't go!" She all but climbs onto me before I can go a single step.

"You're okay. Hold on—" I bite back a sigh and lift her into my arms. Her smell hits me like a punch. The house is air-conditioned, but a ruthless humidity magnifies every ounce of sweat and grime.

"Where are your clothes?" I ask.

She shrugs, but I carry her up a modern-style staircase to the upper level of the house, recalling Maxim's mention of a room. It doesn't take me long to find the one meant for her and Daisy to share. Daisy's still asleep in one of the beds, huddled beneath yellow sheets.

The whole room is decorated in shades of pink and yellow, somehow suiting them both. A large window overlooks a clearer view of turquoise water and a distant, white beach.

Wherever we are, it's breathtakingly gorgeous—like a goddamn living postcard.

Once I shake off my shock, I find Ainsley a fresh pair of clothes from a jumble of suitcases stacked in the corner of the room. Then I take her into an attached bathroom every bit as luxurious as the one downstairs. Oddly, this feels like falling back into yet another routine from our old life. Cleaning her up. Scolding her for not attending to her hygiene properly while gingerly showing her the correct way to.

"No one shows me like you," she says as I drag a washcloth over her back. "Daisy's always too tired. I was *trying*. Honest."

"I know." I brush my fingers along her delicate cheek. "But you should have told me. I would have helped you. You know that."

She shrugs, sending water sloshing over the rim of the tub. "You weren't there."

I freeze, still holding the cloth against her back. "I'm sorry."

Maybe I'd assumed that Daisy would have been watching her more closely all this time. Or that one of the maids Maxim supplied would know how to coax a six-year-old who didn't understand the concept of soap and body odor fully.

Assuming as much might have eased some of the guilt for staying away.

But not anymore.

"I'm not going anywhere," I whisper near her ear. "I'm not going anywhere ever again."

"Really?" A small smile shapes her lips. "Promise?"

"Yes, baby…" I run my fingers through her damp, tangled hair and sigh. "I promise."

After I dry her off, I help her dress in clean clothes and carry her downstairs. Someone else is already in the living room, peering from a section of windows that overlooks a different view of the outside.

"Hey, Frankie," Mikie calls to me despite his face being practically pressed against the glass. "Have you fucking seen this? Holy shit! I know that guy is loaded as fuck, but damn!"

"What?" Alarm spurs me over to him, only for my mouth to drop open once I reach the window.

I don't even have the sense of mind to scold him for cursing. "Holy shit."

The house has a massive pool that pales in comparison to the view of a sandy beach and the ocean beyond it—but I barely notice those features. Because on the lush green lawn below the terrace, someone dropped a random carnival.

I rub my eyes. I'm delirious, that explains it. But when I look again, nothing's changed.

"This is insane," Mikie exclaims. "The twins are gonna lose their shit. They've been begging to go to shitty Fun Mountain for weeks—" He eyes me from over his shoulder, suddenly serious. "If this is your rich boyfriend's attempt at buying our affection, then consider me fucking bought. This is *insane!*"

Insane is one way to put it. Colorful tents stand erect in the morning light, bathed in the shade of massive palm trees. An actual fucking carousel and some kind of spinning ride add to the impossible illusion. Staff in fitting costumes mill about, setting up machinery and equipment.

And standing stoically amongst it all, I spot a lone figure directing the chaos.

"He gets mad points for this," Mikie adds, his voice dripping awe. "Even if he is in the fucking mafia—"

"Watch your mouth!" I flinch, pressing Ainsley to my chest, though she's seemingly too busy eyeing the scene beyond the glass to listen. "What are you even saying?"

"Frankie. I'm not fucking stupid." He shoots me another brutally honest glance, and my cheeks catch fire. "Normal people don't dress like him. He has a private jet. Armed security. And..." His eyes skim the length of me, surprisingly sharp, missing nothing. "You're always on edge around him—"

"Here." I do my best to hand Ainsley to him. "I'll be right back."

"No! Don't go!" She squirms, but Mikie's strong enough to hold her. Regardless, I have to rip myself away, and her nails sink into me one final time, drawing blood.

"Go ahead. I've got her," Mikie insists, wincing as she claws at his arm next. "It's okay. Right? *All of this* is okay?"

I turn away, unable to answer him. My heart pounds as I race deeper into the house and eventually find a set of French doors that exit onto the terrace. A wall of heat hits me like a slap, and sweat instantly slicks my skin. My brain buzzes with the scent of sea salt, and I sway, blinking to adjust. It's like I'm in a different world entirely from the cold, gray realm of Fair Haven.

One presence serves as my anchor to this reality, however. He stands near the edge of the pool, his back to me. Presumably, due to the heat, he wears a crisp white linen button-down and slacks instead of a suit.

"You're awake." I stiffen at the formality of his tone. He barely inclines his head in acknowledgment as I approach. "How did you sleep?"

"Fine." I cross my arms over my chest, self-conscious of my rumpled clothing and messy hair. At his subtle reminder, my back throbs in full force, sore after sleeping upright. "But what is this?" I gesture to the scene unfolding before us. "Where did you even—"

"This?" He sounds as though waking up to find a popcorn machine in your backyard is a totally normal occurrence. A boring one, even. "This is...*amusement*," he says. "Though I hope you realize why a visit to a real park is out of the question."

"What?" I stare, stunned. Then it dawns on me, what I said to him in the club. *My kids should be in a fucking amusement park or something...*

"No." I shake my head, tearing at my hair. "You didn't..." The insanity of it all is harder to process when viewed up close. The scent of cotton candy and popcorn taint the ocean air. It's as if he really has transported an amusement park here, to only God knows where. Just for the kids?

No. A telltale pinch in my chest warns me that isn't the only reason.

"I was just... I was being hysterical," I croak. "You didn't have to—"

"Get dressed. I need to ensure everything is in order." He turns his attention to one of the passing workers, leaving me behind.

I watch him go, my throat tight. A man of his resources is capable of making the unbelievable possible daily. Like committing murder undetected. Or making problems disappear. Moving families across the world on a whim seems to be his favorite pastime lately. But of all of those actions...

I can't fathom this one.

Confused, I return to the house and enter one of the bathrooms. I wash up at the sink, but without any fresh clothes, I keep on the same dress and comb my hair with my fingers. By the time I return outside, all of the kids are already fully dressed, descending on the lawn. Racing past me, they fan out, rushing from attraction to attraction, all while laughing. Fucking around. Taunting each other in a way they did back in our shitty living room while fighting over video games.

I didn't realize until now how long it's been since I've heard them like this...

They actually sound happy.

And the lone figure responsible stands apart from them, silently watchful. The heat is affecting him as well, gluing the hair to his shoulders and making him glisten beneath a sheen of sweat. He doesn't look anywhere near as rough as I do, though. It's like he thrives within the change of environment, dominating the world even beyond the city. Untouchable. Unfazed.

Unreadable.

Lucius stands beside him, speaking intently. From this distance, I catch snippets of what he's saying. "...Mr. Hood called again this morning, sir."

Maxim grunts in acknowledgment, but he doesn't turn his attention from two workers currently setting up some kind of machinery.

"He was insistent, sir," Lucius adds. "He said if you didn't return his call by this evening—and he specifically accounted for the time difference—then he would, and I quote, 'take matters into my own hands.'"

"I'll handle him," Maxim says, still surveying the surrounding activity. When his eyes find me, he stiffens. "That will be all, Lucius."

"Yes, sir." Lucius nods and crosses the terrace, entering the house.

Alone, Maxim says nothing, but he doesn't turn away. An odd feeling thickens my throat as I take a tentative step in his direction. Gratitude? Guilt? I only make it halfway to him when another voice rings out.

"Frankie?" I bite back a groan as Ainsley spots me from near the carousel and races over. The closer she comes, however, the more relieved I feel. Her eyes are bright, a crooked smile shaping her mouth. "Do you see? There's ice cream!" She excitedly points to a booth across the lawn, staffed by a smiling server. "Can I have some now, even if it's breakfast?"

"Yeah… Just this once." I let her take my hand and follow her over. Not only is the ice cream booth fully stocked, but with an impressively vast selection. So much money must have gone into this. And effort.

I remember something Lucius said in the car after collecting us from the airport. *Everything is in place.*

Were they in on this together?

"I don't know which one," Ainsley whines, drawing my attention back to her. "There's so many. I can't pick!"

I crouch beside her, reading the advertised flavors. "Just pick whichever one you like the best, baby."

"Or…" It's only when a deeper voice replies that I realize she wasn't talking to me. "You can try more than one." Maxim stands nearby, just beyond physical reach—and I can finally put a name to his tone. *Cautious.* "As many as you like."

"Really? Okay!" Beaming, Ainsley turns to the server and proceeds to order a cone topped with five different flavors. The resulting creation is a massive stack she struggles to hold upright. After a few careful licks, she turns to Maxim and flashes a crooked grin. "Yummy! Which one is your favorite?"

"I don't know." His dark eyes scan the ice cream menu, devoting far more attention to the deliberation of dessert flavors than I suspect he usually would. "I admit that I've never tried it."

"What? No ice cream? Never?" Ainsley's eyes go bug-wide as melted chocolate dribbles down her chin. "You should try vanilla, right, Frankie? It's my favorite, and it's the safest bet—"

"Ainsley!" Mikie shouts from across the yard. He, Daisy, Eric, and the twins stand before a toy shooting range, complete with a selection of stuffed animal prizes. "Come see this! I'll win ya whatever you want."

"I want that bear!" All thoughts of ice cream forgotten, she races off, a different girl from this morning.

Four months of progress in four minutes. I know this won't last, but still... A wave of gratitude nearly knocks me over. I have to grip the edge of the ice cream counter for balance. In an instant, I sense a presence nearby, and someone's hand brushes my shoulder.

"Are you alright?"

"I'm fine." *Damn.* My voice echoes back to me, so fucking bitchy. "I'm sorry." But should I be? In frustration, I rip my hands through my hair. "I mean, I'm sorry for what I said last night. But I have to think about what's best for—"

"I could leave now," Maxim suggests. There's no anger in his voice. It's not a threat, but an offer. "Say it, and I will be on the next plane within the hour. You can stay here."

Here in paradise, freed from his presence. But would the distance prevent another attack in the name of his grandfather?

"I..." My mouth is suddenly too dry to speak. I have to moisten my lips with the tip of my tongue, weighing my potential answer. And as I do, Lucius' words come back to haunt me once again. *He can handle rejection...*

"Ainsley thinks you can protect her," I rasp, jerking my head in her direction. I could blame her newfound attitude on the random carnival—but that's not it. My sister isn't that fucking fickle. In the presence of Maxim, she feels safe for whatever reason. Safe enough to let her guard down. "Can you?" I demand. "Can you let her get attached to you without revealing what you do in your spare time? Can you give her stability—and you know I'm not talking about an army of strangers with guns camped outside our house, or a million fancy mansions. I come with *them*. All of them. Do you really understand what that means? You won't open up to me—" Gritting my teeth, I choke down my own hurt in favor of what really matters. "But can you include them into your world? If you can't, then maybe it's best if…"

"If?" His eyes narrow a fraction, fathomless in the sunlight. The more seconds of silence that tick by, the dizzier I become. My chest feels tight, like my heart might explode after the events of the past forty-eight hours.

Should he leave? Stay? I'm on the verge of deciding either way when a guttural voice cuts the tension.

"I will try vanilla," Maxim declares. He's speaking to the server, apparently to order a single scoop of ice cream on a cone.

My breath sticks in my throat at the sight. For a man who can wield a chisel as a weapon, it's nearly impossible to fathom how awkward he looks now. He eyes the cone warily as if skeptical of the purpose of dessert as a whole. Regardless, he brings it to his mouth anyway.

"I confess that I never found the appeal of the concept," he says, this time to me. "*Vanilla.*" His tone betrays a different context for that word, far beyond ice cream.

Without elaborating, he extends his tongue. At the same time, his eyes flick up to mine, and something inside me tightens. I choke down a lump in my throat, incapable of reading his expression. Not even as he tilts his hand, silently offering the cone to me.

"I… I'm good," I stammer, shaking my head.

"You don't appreciate the taste of *vanilla*, after all?" He definitely isn't talking about a shitty frozen treat anymore.

"I-I do." My fingers shake as I curl them over the base of the cone, overlapping his. If I aimed to prove him wrong, I fucking regret it instantly. The heat of his hand is a furnace, melding with the scorching sun.

"Then taste," he commands.

Sweat beads over my forehead as I copy him with my own brief lick. *Vanilla?* This is a version of it I've never experienced, that's for damn sure. The taste flooding my mouth feels anything but *safe*.

"It's good," I agree, drawing back.

He samples another taste for himself. "It's sweet," he declares after swallowing. "I could see how some men prefer this overall."

"For some people, that's all they need," I point out. My gaze drifts beyond him to where Mikie and Ray swing Ainsley between them, while Daisy carries Eric on her back. "Boring. Easy. Safe."

"Safe? Appealing to some, yes. Though I think I will always prefer another taste…" A low sound resonates in his throat as he laps up an entire section of ice cream in one ravenous swipe. Another. His gaze doesn't leave mine once, feeding a dangerous curiosity.

What taste could appeal to him more?

The dessert is already starting to melt, dripping in rivulets down his knuckles, conjuring sinful imagery. *Glistening fingers, assaulted by his tongue, coated in a liquid far different from this...*

I exhale sharply as he takes a step back. I can breathe again. But the reprieve comes at a cost. His entire posture shifts. In an instant, he towers above me, no longer the aloof carnival director. In his gaze lurks a dare he doesn't pose out loud.

Come. His chin tilts, beckoning me closer. Closer. Closer.

I comply before I truly register advancing toward him. Eventually, we wind up yards away from the commotion centered around the kids, and I'm faced with the sheer size of the property. A row of swaying palm trees and a wooden shed obscure us from view now. Happy squeals and joyous shouts make me suspect we won't be missed for a while.

"Maybe your sister had the right idea?" Maxim proposes. His voice sounds closer to its usual baritone, though still cautious. "More than one flavor. A mix. A harmony—" He offers the melting cone to me again. "*Taste.*"

I lick.

He inhales, his eyes gleaming in the sun.

"Would you really be okay with that?" I swipe my hand over my mouth. "Adding *vanilla* into your life?"

"I am not unwilling…" He steals another bite of ice cream, his expression contemplative. "But there will always be parts of me that I cannot change. Certain tastes I cannot compromise for anyone. Can you understand that?"

The cone returns to my mouth. I barely feel the chill wafting off it amid this heat. The suffering mass of ivory symbolizes so much more—no match for satisfying Maxim's true appetite. A wolf can't subsist on vanilla ice cream forever.

But the fact of him even trying it at all might be enough…

"Yes," I whisper. "I understand."

He nods to his hand. "So taste."

I lean in, but at the last second, he moves the cone out of reach, and our lips meet instead. I stiffen at first, only to relax into him. Groaning, he shoves his tongue inside me, snatching me against his chest. The cone falls, but he turns his attention to savoring a different taste. Sugar and sin.

Me. He licks at the sweat dripping down my throat. Down my chest. Between my breasts. My dress is a cumbersome obstacle, no match for him. Fabric rips, and his hands eagerly replace the material, groping. Grasping. Taking.

But even from here, Ainsley's laughter tickles the air. Too close.

"Wait—" I barely voice the plea as he tugs me into an enclosed space. Somewhere hot. Stuffy. The shed?

I only make out a row of hooks on the wall, sporting an array of clothing before his fingers are inside me, his mouth near my ear. "Relax," he growls. "We're alone. Fuck... Always so wet for me."

He's right—and the intensity of his touch takes my breath away. There is no restraint to each violent, brutal thrust of his thumb. No care to disguise the lust edging every hoarse sound to leave his throat.

He devours me.

And some sick part of me is desperate to be consumed. My inner muscles clench around him. I'm wetter by the second, melting in his fucking hands.

"My little kitten," he grates as if in agony. "Always so fucking greedy."

Our eyes meet. Lips again. Panting, I tug at his shirt. His pants. The second his cock is free, I rock my hips, and he enters me. It's fire. Gasoline meeting a lit stick of dynamite.

He feels so good. Too good—despite there being no pain to feed off of. No nipping nails. No bitten flesh. Just him, slamming inside me in a ruthless rhythm. Like he's too drunk off the feeling to crave the violence.

His fingers, slick with ice cream, paint a trail up and down my hips, grazing my nipples, heightening every sensation. Marking me.

Maybe it's the heat or the sweat, but I've never been so wet. He's never felt harder. Deeper. We move in sync, my body gripping him in desperate, grasping convulsions. And yet at the same time, there's a rightness to it. A knowledge deep within that every quivering, yearning inch of flesh belongs to him.

I'm offering it to him.

And his answer lurks within the way his release floods me in waves of scorching fire.

He'll take it all.

CHAPTER NINE

"I may become a fan of vanilla yet," Maxim murmurs against my throat, his fingers entangled in my hair. "Admittedly plain, but…" His lips ignite a fiery path up to my ear, down my jaw, and finally, claim my mouth. "Satisfying," he says, pulling back as my lips burn in the aftermath of his kiss.

"Where are we?" I eye a mass of pink sequins dangling from a hook above my head. An unusual design choice in his world.

"On a private island in the Caribbean."

"Oh." I ferret away that bit of information for later. "But, I mean, now?" I gesture to the view before us—a deconstructed clown costume piled against the opposite wall.

"A staff lounge," Maxim explains absently. "Something about occupational code. Lucius insisted I needed one for the workers, even for a day."

Which reminds me of the insanity that is this morning. "I can't believe you did this—"

"Can't believe?" He lifts me and spins me around, placing me on a flat surface that creaks against our combined weight. A table? I'm too distracted to be sure. His eyes track a white bead of liquid dripping down my chest, and he lunges for it, laving a path with his tongue.

"Still so doubtful of my limits. Though, I do *believe* I am a new fan of ice cream. A rare admission," he confesses against my navel. Before I can recover, he crouches down between my legs, wrenching them apart. My cheeks catch fire at the way he eyes me. Like someone starving. Depraved.

I arch my back, craving the act he promises with a pointed flick of his tongue against his lower lip.

But then I hear it. Voices, calling out desperately. For me.

"Frankie? Where did you go?"

"Shit." I lurch upright, and Maxim returns to his full height, blocking me in.

"Relax." He grabs my arm before I can race for the door. "Listen. They aren't in danger."

He's right. The kids call playfully, but they seem close. Too close. Right when I'm sure they'll barge into the shed, their voices fade, sounding further away.

"An hour's absence," Maxim says. It's only when I notice the thoughtful tilt to his head that I recognize the statement as a proposal. "They will not miss you for that long. They have diversions…"

And even Ainsley can survive for an hour without me in a private, personal carnival.

Could the possessive master be asking for permission?

My heart skips at the possibility. Finally, I trace my lower lip with the tip of my tongue as my gaze meets his. "An hour," I concede.

His eyes flash as he stoops and fishes something from the floor. His shirt. Unfurling it, he coaxes my trembling, languid limbs into the sleeves. Then he redons his pants, and we creep to the door of the shed.

Maxim peeks out first. After a few seconds, he inclines his head for me to follow, and we cut across the terrace for the house at breakneck speed. I don't think it dawns on me until we finally pry open the French doors and slip into the air-conditioned sanctuary what we're doing—sneaking around like horny teenagers desperate for a minute alone. That is, if I had ever been a normal horny teenager who did normal teenage shit.

I doubt he was either.

Still, I can see the appeal of it as Maxim takes my hand and pulls me across the living room and up the stairs. In the absence of his shirt, his muscles ripple with his every movement, devoid of tension for once as he heads in a direction different from that of Ainsley's room—and the other kids' for that matter.

Conveniently out of earshot of the rest of the house, this hallway leads into a semi-private wing. A single door opens onto a space that I presume, given its size, to be the master suite.

It's large enough to fit at least ten more beds, apart from the massive one dominating the center of it. Floor-to-ceiling windows display an intimate view of the surrounding landscape, and a clean, simplistic color scheme fits in perfectly with Maxim's taste.

Black, black, and more black.

Sliding glass doors open onto a secluded balcony containing only a lounge area shaped like a bed, covered in a delicate canopy.

That refuge isn't his intended hiding place, however. On the edge of the suite—coincidentally facing a view of the beach the other rooms only hint at—is a bathroom fit for a mafia prince. Ebony marble reinforces his unique tastes, combined with golden fixtures and a huge sunken bath designed to have an uninterrupted view of the ocean.

I'm so entranced by the sight, I barely notice as thick fingers gently remove his shirt from me, tossing it aside. Naked, I'm at the mercy of his scrutiny. Maxim's breath scorches my overheated flesh, growing harsher the more of me he inhales. Starting at my neck, he skims the width of my shoulders and then back again. Despite our self-imposed deadline, he takes his time, and my thoughts dissipate with every passing second.

Eventually, he manages to get the water running and eases me into the basin of the tub. He sits at the edge, and I settle between his legs, aware of the parts of his body he doesn't bother to disguise for once. His binder which chafes against my back. His bare legs positioned on either side of me, riddled with scars. His cock, hardening already, straining against my hip. I'm a glutton for this moment, hoarding as much of him as I can steal beneath the tips of my fingers. They skim him greedily, unrestrained for once.

God, he's a creature formed of beauty...

And brutality.

My heart lurches the more of him I explore—awed and terrified at the same time. I tentatively trace a stretch of his inner thigh, emboldened when he growls in appreciation. But then my fingers catch a gnarled, near-invisible scar, and I recoil. It's so jagged, betraying a long, agonizing healing. God, I can't even begin to guess what could have made it. Something *painful*. So painful...

"A whip," he explains as if reading my mind. His fingers find mine and force me to touch the scar again. It's as if my curiosity enthralls him almost as much as it consumes me. "Anatoli," he adds. "He liked to embed metal in the tip. That time, I served him a meal without showing the proper respect—I didn't kneel deeply enough."

He sounds so cold. Like someone telling a normal, boring anecdote from his childhood. Not a snippet of horrific, traumatic abuse.

"This upsets you," he deduces, fingering my fluttering pulse. "I will spare you any further—"

"No!" I grasp him in return and tilt his hand, revealing the calloused palm. It's as brutalized as the rest of him—a map of a million unknown injuries. "I want to know."

A deep sound rumbles from his throat as if questioning. *Oh?* I sneak a glance at his face, surprised to find him watching me, an eyebrow raised in confusion. Could that be why he's so fucking secretive? Not because he's trying to hide his past, but because he can't fathom the idea of someone wanting to know about it. About him.

"I want to know everything about you." I hate how it sounds when uttered out loud. So desperate and pathetic. But he doesn't scoff or hiss in annoyance. Taking a risk, I finger a scar slicing across his palm and propose my first request, "Tell me what caused this one."

"A blade, I think." The rising water around us sloshes as he shrugs. He's skeptical of this game of show and tell, but still willing to play along. For now. "He made me train with them. It is easy to cut yourself if you aren't careful."

"What about this one?" I finger a crescent-shaped mark across his knuckles.

"Glass," he says without elaborating.

"And this one?" I turn to face him and place my hand over the center of his chest.

He sighs. "That one... Some of them I don't remember the cause of." His eyes darken, revealing his surprise at that fact. I wonder if he's ever stopped to tally up his marks before.

Or those inflicted *by* him.

Another question worms into my mind, and I don't bother swallowing it down. "How did Vadim get his scar?" I'm not brave enough to meet his gaze, but his fingers find my jaw and lift it anyway.

Anger isn't what colors his expression for once as far as that name is concerned. Just exhaustion. "Vadim?" The lines around his mouth strain, more pronounced than ever. He looks so worn. So tired. So alien from everything I know about the depth of human emotions and how normal people express them. He's more wolf than ever.

"Forget it," I croak. "You don't have to—"

"I tried to cut his throat." He lets me go and hones his gaze on the window.

"Why?" I whisper.

"We were children. I had a knife. I won't lie to you—" He snatches my hand, pressing it to the side of his face as if forcing me to feel the truth in every uttered word. "I wanted to kill him. It was only due to my inexperience that I didn't. Why? Because he stood in my way." His tone chills me to the core, despite the steam wafting from the water.

"He was an obstacle since birth. A potential replacement always compared to me. Always. By our father. By Anatoli. If I slacked for even a second, Vadim's name was on their lips. In some ways, they preferred him. He was smarter. More cunning. Charming in his own way. But when it came to a direct challenge, he always lacked the strength." He bares his teeth in a feral snarl, still trapped in that competitive cycle—even if it leaves him fighting against a memory. "Only one of us would be deemed worthy of carrying the Koslov name. I couldn't fail, not even for him. I refused to…"

He blinks as if forgetting where he is. Then his eyes fixate on me, and some of the tension constricting them eases.

"My entire life, I have fought for *this.*" He nods as if to indicate his entire being. His identity. "I've won—" He grips my chin in return, inspecting my expression. Whatever he finds, makes him recoil in disgust. "And yet, you are the only person in the world to ever look at me as you do. With *pity.*"

"It's not pity." I lunge for him before he can push me away. Trembling, my lips brush his chest, sensing the heart racing within. His taste is a world apart from melting ice cream. Dangerous. Enticing. Addicting. Alarming. And I lick my lips to savor every drop. "I do not pity you—"

"So what is it then?" he gruffly demands. "Disgust?"

"I… I feel for you," I find the space above his heart with my fingers—coincidentally where one of his worst scars is. He goes rigid every time I graze the ropey, uneven flesh.

Regardless, I can't stop touching him. "I know what it feels like…"

To fight.

To sacrifice.

To suppress.

"Oh?" He laughs. "You know what it's like to stab your own fucking 'sibling'? I respect your intent, Francesca—" His use of my name stings, anything but an endearment. "But, I strongly suggest you avoid comparing yourself to me in this instance."

"I know what it's like to lie to yourself," I insist, ignoring the warning in his tone. "To crave an escape. You wanted to destroy your brother. I… I wanted to destroy myself."

Suddenly, he captures my wrist and extends it for his inspection. Something, in particular, draws his interest, making him stiffen, a curse on his lips. It's a nasty scratch, stretching the width of my forearm, still weeping fresh beads of blood. "Do not tell me that what happened with Vadim caused this…"

I frown at the sudden seriousness of his tone. "No." But it's not like a fresh wound is an unusual occurrence between us. Then it hits me—he thinks I did it to myself.

"These have lessened," he points out as if reading my mind again. His thumb travels down my arm, grazing over countless healed scars and weeks-old scabs. "Since you've been with me. Did you think I didn't notice them?"

I wrack my brain, surprised that he might be right. Apart from a few nicks from my nails, I haven't hurt myself the way I used to. Not with a knife or razor. Not with my teeth.

"You enjoy pain," he says carefully. "But it wasn't until I noticed these—" he fingers another old injury of mine. "That I understood why. You crave the release of it."

"And what do you get out of it?" I counter, though I think I've finally deciphered the real answer on my own.

His mouth twitches, part grimace, part frown. "Pleasure."

A lie.

I can put the pieces together, even if the picture they make terrifies the shit out of me. One example comes to mind.

"You made me kneel for you." I brush my free hand along his forearm, sensing the power lurking beneath the healed, scarred flesh. "When you whipped me. You made me kneel. Like your grandfather made you—"

"Don't. *Please.*" He shakes his head, his teeth gritted. He's quiet for a moment. "I do not take for granted what you give to me. What no one else could, you do—" he returns his attention to the scratch. "But I don't want you seeking control out of fear."

"I didn't hurt myself," I admit. "Ainsley scratched me by accident. She's afraid."

"I know." He shifts, stiffening against me. "I will do everything in my power to prevent what happened from happening again."

"But you can't, can you?"

He doesn't respond.

"She's a little girl." My voice breaks. "She doesn't deserve to grow up afraid."

"I can make her happy," he counters. "Happier than today —all of them. I can keep you content. You can keep me sane."

"Is that what you really want?" It sounds like yet another way of phrasing the give and take of our entire relationship.

"I want understanding with you," he corrects. "No more mincing words. I want you on my side."

"As a partner?"

"Or a lover."

My cheeks burn at the raw heat in his tone. "You don't normally talk like this."

He returns his gaze to the view, eyeing it blankly, unimpressed. "You weren't listening before. Maybe this language will convince you?"

"So what are you suggesting?"

"At night, you give me what I need. And by day…" His eyes rove slowly to my face. "I give you what you want."

And what is that?

He doesn't say, but a few options come to mind. A Maxim who talks. An open Maxim. And unfiltered Maxim.

An unrestrained Maxim.

"What are you thinking?" His thumb slips beneath my chin, lifting it. So rich and deep, his eyes seem to stare right through me, impossible to escape.

"I'm wondering...how you'll indulge without traumatizing my family if we're all staying in the same house." Mikie's right. He's no idiot.

"Is that all?" Maxim's mouth quirks, and it's like the world fucking falters. "I have two methods in mind that should work in tandem."

Something warns me not to ask what they are. Not yet.

"But as for today?" He reaches out, grasping my hand. Raising it to his mouth, he brushes his lips along my knuckles, inhaling deeply all the while. "I will do nothing to alarm your family. You can trust me on that."

And I think I can.

At least for now.

CHAPTER TEN

The house itself turns out to be far more incredible than I initially realized. The open floor plan is centered around a breathtaking view of the square-shaped pool and the ocean beyond it. Wide, open windows allow in a sea-salt tinged breeze that displaces some of the heat, making the air feel more comfortable than the most intense air-conditioning.

There aren't many rooms in total either. The girls share a spacious suite in one wing while the boys share another. I'm struck by the careful planning of the layout as Maxim leads me on this impromptu tour, his hair still dripping wet. Our only detour is a trip to the closet of the master bedroom, where he changes into another linen shirt and plain slacks. There I discover an array of women's clothing hanging alongside his, conveniently coordinated to match. I slip into a loose-fitting white sundress and make a mental note to explore the rest of my wardrobe later.

"It's a fairly new acquisition," Maxim explains as we follow a wide hallway next, accented by windows that look out onto the terrace. From here, I can see the kids, clamoring to ride the carousel. "Even I have yet to explore it fully. Though there are a few...necessities that I insisted upon before closing."

Necessities? I decide to overlook voicing such a loaded question in favor of something far more harmless. "Where is my room?"

"Where? You've seen it." He gestures in the direction of his master suite. *Our* master suite, apparently.

"Oh. But when I was with Ainsley, you said..." A sudden realization chokes me off. He suggested I sleep with her in "my room"—which really meant he would forfeit his own bed entirely.

"Come." I look over to find him inclining his head. "There is one final feature I want to show you."

I follow him warily into the suite. This time, he approaches a door opposite the bathroom, near the bed. Another closet?

"Open it," Maxim says without explanation. "My one request before I would commit to buying the property..."

The grim commentary comes as I reach for the curved, metal handle. I tug, but rather than open automatically, I sense a slight give, and my ears pick up a mechanical sound before the door finally comes loose.

"It is now bio-metrically activated." I look over my shoulder to find Maxim advancing, his expression unreadable. "Only you or I can unlock it."

"Really?" I observe my fingers, too terrified to face what might be waiting beyond the door just yet.

"Come." As if aware of my hesitation, he takes my hand and steps around me, leading the way into the mysterious space. His bulk blocks my view initially. I can only make out a short hallway though the echoing sound of our footsteps alludes to a much larger area beyond it.

"It's still…rough," Maxim says as he maneuvers me to stand beside him. "I had the construction rushed to ensure it would be usable, but it will suffice. For now."

It being a near-identical replica of the "toy" room from his penthouse in the city—only white marble flooring makes the space seem even more isolated than the black. It's a stark canvas in a sense, incapable of hiding any stains; something I suspect he's planned on. A marble altar-shaped platform sports a thin, white pad for comfort, and a row of metal cabinets must contain whatever a man like him might need to indulge his inclinations toward sadism.

"Do you still agree to this?" His fingers slip beneath my chin, guiding me to face him directly.

Do I? Deep down, I sense that the answer is more important to him than the fact that we're standing in a sex room designed for pain and pleasure. He still wants my consent.

"The rules won't change," he adds. "If you want me to stop, you—"

"I know," I say.

"And?" His thumb traces the ball of my chin, making my breathing hitch with every traversed inch. "You aren't one for nuance, but I sense there is more you want to say."

And he's right. I suck in a breath and release it on a single question. "When we return to the city, will things go back to how they were before?"

Him dwelling primarily alone in his secluded penthouses while I live apart from my family.

He strokes my cheek. "Only if you want them to..."

WE RETURN DOWNSTAIRS, and Maxim leads me through an impressive kitchen with a view of the terrace. Without a word of explanation, he proceeds to stockpile several items from the fridge and a walk-in pantry into his arms. Meat. Veggies. Bread. I watch him in silence, intrigued by the potential uses for the ingredients. Fodder for the kids to throw at the shooting game, maybe?

Once on the terrace, he approaches a metal grill and confidently rolls up his sleeves. As he fires up the range, his true intent becomes crystal clear, and I suck in a startled breath.

He plans to cook dinner. For *us*.

As impossible as it seems in theory, the scent of grilled meat wafts across the lawn within minutes—a far cry from the polished, cold dinners I've come to associate him with.

The backdrop of the ocean breeze and the distant murmur of crashing waves create a cozy, casual aura. Even the kids are enticed enough to trudge in from the dispersing carnival, exhausted and dripping with sweat.

"I thought we might try something different tonight," Maxim says while dropping cooked hot dogs onto a plate. "Something…informal." His gaze cuts in my direction, and I squirm. Again, it's as though he's reading my mind.

Or even more unsettling—he's starting to know me too damn well.

"I want that big one!" Ainsley demands, appearing beside him, her eyes fixated on the food. "Or maybe that one. Or that one…"

The rest of us scatter onto nearby lounge chairs. Ironically, it's no different from how we used to eat, but with actual silverware and a mansion backdrop rather than a filthy living room.

And a newcomer whose presence is impossible to ignore.

As if sensing all eyes on him, Maxim tosses a fresh wave of food onto the grill. "Did you enjoy the attractions?" he wonders as the meat sizzles—his attempt at small talk, I realize. It doesn't come naturally to him, at least not in this context. But as stiff as his voice sounds forming the words, they land innocently enough.

"Yes!" Ainsley beams, practically bouncing on her toes. "I had so much fun, though I rode the spinny ride too many times and threw up on Mikie's—"

"No reminders, please," Mikie pipes up from his position near the pool. He cradles his head in his hands, and I notice a damp splotch on his shirt. "It took two bottles of water to get it out."

"Don't be such a baby," Ainsley snipes. Then she turns to Maxim and points to the spatula. "Can I help? Please?"

"Well…" His movements slow as he processes the request. "If your sister doesn't mind, then I suppose so—"

"Ainsley," Daisy says from a nearby chaise, "leave him alone. You're bothering him."

"No, I'm not!" Jutting her chin into the air, Ainsley tugs on Maxim's pant leg. "Right?"

"Right." No match for her, he surrenders the spatula and stoops to help her tend to the sizzling food. Under his guidance, she flips a hot dog by herself and howls in triumph.

"See?" Her impish grin could easily be classified as smug. "He *wants* me to help."

"You don't have to be a little brat about it," Daisy bites back. "But all you're doing is getting in the way."

"Hey!" I stick out my hand, inserting myself as the referee. "I think it's okay as long as she is careful—"

"You would say that, wouldn't you?" Scoffing, Daisy crosses her arms. "Like you give a damn about her safety."

"Daisy…" I resist the urge to groan out loud. "Do we have to do this now?"

"Do what? Lie? Eat dinner like a good little family?" She rolls her eyes at the plate of food balanced on the end of the grill. "Are we really pretending like everything's okay? Like we weren't shot at the other day? Like we aren't missing school? Like this is *normal*? Oh, I'm sorry. I guess we're just going to keep acting like what happened at the other house really was a gas leak—"

"Daisy." I stand and start toward her, fighting to keep my voice level. "We can talk about this in private—"

"Private? Like you give a damn about *privacy*! We don't even know who he is!" She points at Maxim and jabs the same finger at me. "Or who you are to him. Are you dating him? Screwing him? Are you some kind of high-class hooker? His mistress? What the hell is it? Or—" She hisses, her eyes narrowing. "Are you going to act like Mama and want us to call him 'Daddy?'"

"Knock it off!" Mikie snaps, appearing at my side. "Stop being a bitch."

"Don't be so stupid!" Daisy laughs at him, her voice high-pitched.

Whatever triggered this, it isn't about fucking hot dogs.

"She hasn't denied it," she points out, propping her hands on her hips. "And don't pretend like you don't know how she got her money before, Mikie. The slutty dresses? The late nights? Do I have to spell it out? She was a fucking prostitute. And this? It's just a fucking buy-off—"

"I care about your sister," Maxim interjects from his position near the grill. Silence falls instantly. It's as if the entire world stops, heeding the authority he exudes in every word.

Daisy grits her teeth, ruthlessly defiant. "I'm sorry, but what is that supposed to mean to me? Because all it's meant so far is bouncing around from place to place with no fucking clue as to what's going on." Her voice breaks. Tears spill down her cheeks, and it's painfully clear what today, despite all of Maxim's effort, truly was at the end of it all. A Band-Aid. "I'm not the only one who thinks it's fucking weird," she adds. "I'm just the only one brave enough to say it. I've already been through four stepdads, and I'm sorry, but I don't want another one. And it's not good for Ainsley, or Eric, or any of us to have strange men bounce in and out of our lives because they pay the bills for a few months."

"True," Maxim concedes, still tending the grill. "Stability is important, and words are meaningless. Which is why…I've asked your sister to marry me."

His statement is met with more silence. Unbearable, overwhelming fucking silence. I can't even look at Daisy, or the others for that matter. I stare at the sky instead. A swath of orange paints the horizon like fire, burning up the peace of the day, and leaving darkness behind.

"Um…okay." Mikie clears his throat, ever the peacemaker. "Is that true, Frankie?" I force myself to face him, prepared for the worst. But his expression doesn't convey anger or shock. Just confusion.

"Of course not," Daisy snarls, her cheeks red, eyes blazing. "Because you wouldn't do that, would you, Frankie? You wouldn't be dating someone without telling us. Your *family*—"

"Of course, she wouldn't. Which is why she rightly refused my offer," Maxim explains while flipping over a cooked burger. His shoulders are hunched, his posture rigid, and yet his voice doesn't hold a trace of annoyance. The relentless calm neutralizes even Daisy's hostility. Slowly, she sits back down.

"You mean more to her than anything I could offer," he continues. "More to her than any promise of money, or luxury. In fact, she threatened to leave me if I ever questioned that devotion again, and as you can see, there is no ring on her finger. Consider this vacation as my way of apologizing for insulting her. Nothing more. I can only hope that she will reconsider."

He finally looks in my direction, but I turn away and hunt for the first distraction I can find. "I…I'm going to take care of these dirty dishes."

I snatch up the nearest empty plates and cut across the terrace before anyone can recover enough to stop me. My hands shake so badly it takes me three tries before I can pry open the door to the kitchen. *Fuck!* I trip over the threshold in my rush, and the plates fall from my hands, smashing apart at my feet.

I can't even muster the sense of mind to clean the mess. Instead, I approach the sink, panting to control my breathing. Running the water as hot as it can go and shoving my hand beneath it is the only way to regain some semblance of clarity.

So much for our day of normalcy.

I close my eyes, mulling over the potential ways I can fix this mess. Apologize? Slap Daisy a second time? Run?

It's too late. My neck prickles with the awareness of someone behind me, betrayed by heavy footsteps.

"I know that is not how you wanted to tell them," Maxim admits. Before he can come closer, I turn off the water and tuck my stinging hand to my chest. "I apologize—"

"For what?" I force out a broken laugh. I don't know what's more disorienting, this entire conversation? Or the rare hint of regret from him? "You covered for my ass when you didn't have to. Thank you. But…"

"But?" he prompts.

"You wanted me to take your name, but what about them? Daisy's right, we've had our fair share of winners come through. And…have you thought about what kind of relationship you're comfortable with allowing?"

Melanie had her suckers throw around the word "Daddy" like it meant something. I could never do the same to the kids. Even with a description as harmless as *"Maxim, the brother-in-law for protection only."*

He doesn't say anything—but again, it's as though he's reading my mind, waiting for the real concerns to come spilling out.

"And what if…I don't want it? Your name. Even if your grandfather removes the bounty. And not because of you," I add in a rush. "But…he *abused* you—"

"Don't." He grits his teeth and glances at the doorway. Thankfully none of the kids have followed us inside. Yet. Returning his attention to me, Maxim's tone deepens in warning, "He has nothing to do with it."

"Doesn't he?" I rake my gaze over him, sensing the scars lurking beneath the polished exterior. "Your uncle was a pedophile," I add softly. "Only God knows about the rest of your family. You care about the Koslov name, but do you really want Ainsley to share the name of people like that? As you can tell, we aren't exactly the most perfect family to start with."

"You're upset," Maxim concedes. He crouches and grabs the broken plates with his bare hands. After tossing them into a garbage can, he heads for the door. "Come and eat." For whatever reason, his voice still holds that persistent calm. His posture, however, stiffens, his jaw tightening. "Give me this night to prove that I meant what I promised you, and the rest…" He blinks, suppressing whatever emotion might threaten his composure. "We can discuss later."

"That's it?" I wave halfheartedly in the kid's direction. "We just spring a bomb like that on them and then pretend it never happened?"

"You wanted normalcy," he says. "I may not be an expert, but I believe this might be part of it. Honesty. Or have you changed your mind?"

He waits near the doorway of the terrace until I finally leave the sink and follow. Outside, all six kids remain seated, but none of them seem willing to make eye contact. We merely coexist in awkward silence until Maxim reclaims his spot before the grill.

"Who wants another hot dog?" he asks, breaking the quiet.

Easily distracted, Ainsley perks up and raises her hand. "Me!"

"Me too," pitches in Mikie.

Then Ray, Ollie, and Eric all voice their assent.

Finally, Daisy sighs, lifting her hand. "I'll take one, too."

"Alright, then." Maxim continues to cook, and I force myself to reclaim a lounger, watching him. Them. It's a slow, clumsy return to our previous rhythm, and it doesn't come easily by any stretch of the imagination.

But it happens.

Eventually, it happens.

CHAPTER ELEVEN

As night falls, the kids stagger off to bed, exhausted. I tuck in Ainsley and press a kiss to her cheek while Daisy ignores me from the other end of the room. I let her sulk, preferring a tense truce over starting another war.

After checking on the boys, I finally steel myself to approach the master suite.

The sheer distance between it and the other rooms becomes apparent as it takes me a full minute to traverse it. The spaces are close enough that I would hear any bloodcurdling screams emanating from the kid's rooms—but little else. And they, theoretically, wouldn't hear anything in return. Like a cracking whip or a hiss of pain.

Or, more reassuringly, any brutal sex.

Inside the master bedroom, Maxim stands with his back to me and sheds his shirt, tossing it aside. "If you've changed your mind," he begins in a hollow tone, "if you want to stay with your sister—"

"I'm okay," I whisper.

Who cares if it's a lie? We had a deal. But the weight of our trade-off truly sinks in the longer I watch him. He's lost within his head again. Radiating tension, his muscles ripple and coil beneath his skin, threatening to rip from it.

Lucius' wolf analogy returns to mind. A beast can only remain caged for so long—and that's the word to describe how he looks now. Caged.

And I'm the bitch who twisted the key.

"I'm sorry," I croak, advancing a cautious step. "I had no right to mention your past like that—"

"You are ready?" With those three words, he cuts me off, and his façade of control splinters. He gave me what I wanted—peace. And now I have to return the favor.

"I'm ready..."

"Come." He crosses the room and opens the door. My breaths quicken as I approach him, my palms slick with sweat.

He looks so on edge. So fucking haunted.

As I near the threshold, I can't resist touching his forearm. "What's wrong—"

"No!" He wrenches beyond my reach and storms into the room. Deep down, I know the answer anyway. I brought up his past, ripping open old wounds he'll never acknowledge out loud. "No talking. Not now. I just... I need—" He moves to one of the cabinets on the other end of the room and tugs open a drawer. From it, he withdraws a single, coiled strip of leather. My heart lurches as he unfurls it with a graceful flick of his wrist and then turns to face me. "Kneel." When I don't move, he exhales, practically swaying on his feet. Corded muscle flexes in his throat as he rasps a second time, "*Kneel.*"

It's not fear that has me frozen. It's shock. This is the closest I've ever seen him come to...begging. And I never want to see it again.

Relief escapes him in a harsh sigh as I sink to the floor, my head lowered in obedience.

His steps resonate like thunder as he approaches me, and here, in this new arena, the rules of the game change once again...

Entirely at his discretion.

A GROAN RIPS from my lips as my eyelids part to a stream of blinding sunlight. It's morning, but I doubt I've slept a full hour. Minutes, maybe?

Or seconds.

Revenge might be too petty a concept to apply to someone like Maxim. Perhaps retribution instead? Whether to exact payment for yesterday's events, or out of anger for what I said, he kept me in the room until every inch of me throbbed in punishment...

I only remember snippets. *The whip. His commands—kneel, kneel, kneel.* I huddle beneath the sheets as one image remains in my skull no matter how hard I try to block it out —his face the few times he allowed me to glimpse it. I'll never forget that expression. Cold. Icy. Detached. The only comparison that might come close to it is the day he took me into that dank room already lined with a tarp.

And yet...

I can't escape the feeling that, this time, he held back. That's the most alarming part of it all. Neither assault broke the skin. He didn't fuck me either. Locked within himself, he merely raged, fighting against phantoms I couldn't see.

And by the end, I realized...he was never angry with me.

Afterward, I vaguely remember him carrying me to the bed. However, his steps then retreated, alluding to a night spent wandering throughout the house. Even now, he's not in the room.

And I don't know whether to sigh in relief or despair. The true cost of our bargain hadn't been put into explicit terms until now. His silence, for my comfort.

Closing my eyes, I contemplate sleeping again, but a scent tickles my nose, and confusion draws me upright. Food? Either Maxim hired another private chef, or Daisy—the only kid brave enough to tackle the stove—is trying to cook again. Though fuck, burning this fancy house down could be her latest act of rebellion.

Morbid curiosity outweighs my exhaustion, and I take a quick shower before throwing on a light linen dress. Then I head downstairs only to find everyone in the kitchen, camped out around a center island.

Everyone.

Maxim stands at the heart of the commotion, as stern as a drill sergeant—though one wearing gray slacks in lieu of a uniform. Armed with a pair of tongs, he dishes out various portions of pancakes and scrambled eggs to the eager troops jockeying for position around him. When his eyes find mine, there is no hint of the coldness from last night. He merely nods in acknowledgment while balancing a platter of food on his opposite hand. "You're awake."

"Frankie!" Ainsley rushes to me and throws her arms around my waist. "He made pancakes! And they were good and not burned like Daisy's—"

"Shut up," Daisy snaps, but she eyes me sheepishly. "Morning, Frankie."

I blink. The lack of a scoff directed my way might even be her attempt at an apology. Is this a hallucination? I resist the urge to pinch myself.

"Have a seat." Maxim pulls out the stool beside him and ladles food onto a plate for me. If I were sleeping, I figure the shock of this moment might snap me awake. He actually made pancakes, not steak, or some variation of bleeding meat. "Eat."

My gaze darts around the room as I chew mechanically, uneasy for reasons I can't name. Maybe the feeling has something to do with the mischievous way Ainsley keeps eyeing Maxim from over my shoulder?

It's fucking weird. Normal even?

Once I've cleared my plate, Ainsley nearly bounces off her seat, and the jig is apparently up.

"So can we ask her now?" she pleads, batting her eyelashes. "Please?"

Maxim eyes her and sighs. "Your siblings were wondering if you would consent to a day at the beach," he says.

And that simple phrase triggers all six kids to start speaking at once.

"Please?" Ainsley whines.

"He said he has a boat," Mikie pitches in. "And a jet ski—"

"And there's a cabana," Daisy adds hesitantly. "I could tan, and—"

"Okay." I hold up my hands in surrender. "Okay."

"Yes!" They race off, clamoring for the stairs while I try to process the concept with more scrutiny. A day at the beach, like a real fucking family. Have we ever had one of those?

It doesn't take long to settle on an answer. *No.*

"Lucius is a trained swimmer, as is Tomas," Maxim explains while piling dishes into the sink. "Both will accompany them for now."

I frown at the phrasing. "We won't?"

"No." It takes me a second to classify his expression. *Wary?* After rinsing the last of the dirty plates, he dries his hands and then heads for the stairs. My only clue as to his intent comes in the form of a single phrase uttered from over his shoulder. "We need to talk."

Left with no choice, I mount the stairs in his wake and trail him down the hall. As we enter the bedroom, I can't suppress a shudder. My eyes find the door to the "other" room. Will he insist on a round two, even in broad daylight?

Rather than head for that door in the corner, however, he steps onto the balcony. It's hot as hell out, and the sun beats down ruthlessly, illuminating everything in view for miles— from the terrace, to the beach, to a good portion of the open ocean.

"We will be able to see them from here," Maxim explains. As if on cue, a stream of tiny figures darts from the house to the beach, led by a taller person with a body shape suspiciously like Lucius'. "We can hear them as well…" His breath scorches the nape of my neck as he leans in closer to add, "But they cannot see us."

I've barely processed what that fact could implicate when his fingers find my shoulders and dig into the sore, tense muscle. Groaning, I relent to the pressure. He's damn good with his hands, kneading stiff flesh the same way he works his stone carvings. Before I know it, we're seated on the wide lounger, and he's massaging me in full.

Despite slipping his hands beneath the neckline of my dress, he keeps the contact purely clinical, focusing his attention where I ache the most.

"You're tight here." A rare hint of emotion colors his tone, leaving me reeling. Sympathy? Or maybe resignation at his handiwork.

This definitely isn't the worst state I've been in after a night with him. As the seconds tick by, I'm faced with the possibility that his hesitation has nothing to do with my soreness at all. Finally, his fingers still.

"Last night may not have been ideal," he starts, "but if you are satisfied with this arrangement, we can continue in this way from now on."

Normalcy for the kids by day, kink for him at night.

I lift my head and scan the stretch of beach until I spot where the kids have made camp. They fan out, darting from the waves to the shore.

"It could work," I say cautiously. "As long as Ainsley doesn't wake up from a nightmare and barge into the bedroom."

What I intend as a joke seems to have the opposite effect.

"Good." He stands, his hands held awkwardly at his sides. "We should go join the others—"

"But can we discuss the rules at least? Boundaries?" I can't forget how he looked last night. Closed-off. Isolated. "If we are to do this. *Really* do this, then I need to know what we keep in the room and what stays out."

He tilts his head thoughtfully and sits back down. "Some things... My past—" His gaze clouds over, distant. "That stays in the room."

The things he can't talk about. Such as Anatoli's abuse or his way of coping with it.

For a second, I wonder if it's worth arguing over—demanding to know more. But then I look at him. He's stiff, glowering at the ocean as if seeing hell where most people would only see paradise. There's so much about him I don't know, but maybe it's not my place to force him to reveal what he's not ready to.

"What about sex?"

He frowns, and I have his attention again. His fingers cross the distance between us, stopping short of my hip. The simple act conveys the power harnessed by him always. "In the room, I will have control."

"And outside of it?"

"Outside..." As he mulls over the question, he sweeps his hand along my thigh. There's no possession in this action. Just touching. Feeling. "Does my kitten crave another taste of vanilla?"

I look away, my cheeks on fire. Do I? Sex with him is one thing when pain is involved—mind-blowing. But without, like what happened in the shed?

It's a different taste entirely. One I'm not sure I want to write off exploring.

"Hmph." Maxim hooks his finger beneath my chin, coaxing me to face him. "I will admit that I am not familiar with this. Being...*domestic*." His accent thickens as though it's a dirty word.

The sinful, unknown kind of dirty—the way someone might sound describing his peculiar tastes. Taboo.

"I suppose that outside of the room, you may decide..." He trails off, seemingly unable to finish the thought. Outside of the room, I could potentially have control.

Over him.

It sounds too fucking good to be true.

"Really?"

"If it is necessary to your normalcy," he counters.

"So, during the day, I can touch you when I want to?" I rise up onto my knees, shifting to face him.

Dare I say he looks...curious. My heart jumps, rebounding off my ribcage.

"Touch?" he questions softly.

"Like this…" My fingers shake as I unfurl them one by one. When I brace my hand over his chest, he doesn't flinch. Emboldened, I undo the buttons of his shirt, and he shrugs his shoulders to help me remove it. Observing him this way is an experience unlike any other. I take my time, determined to savor every second.

His scars look ten times more grotesque in broad daylight. Beautiful too. I finger one, aware of his gaze tracking my every movement. Leaning forward, I press my lips against the most abused piece of flesh.

A low rasp catches in his throat. "You want to touch me in this way?" He sounds so amused by the prospect. As though any warm-blooded woman wouldn't crave a chance to appreciate his body.

I murmur in agreement, too intent on my task to form a coherent reply. But the more of him I inspect, the more doubt starts to sneak in. Could someone like him enjoy sex without control?

Once my hand travels downward, I discover my answer— oh *yes*. Hard, straining muscle pulses beneath the fabric of his slacks, conveying anything but discomfort. My breaths quicken as I press another kiss to an old wound on his chest. Another. I feel as though I'm marking them mentally for more detailed exploration in the future.

I can learn their secrets later.

Learn more of him later.

Right now, he's presenting me with a rare gift I know better than to waste. Patience. Time. Control.

True to our agreement, he doesn't command where I can touch him or how. He merely leans back against the cushions, at my mercy for once.

And I never knew what it could fucking feel like. Having *this* kind of power over someone. Studying them like an open book—far different from being a receptacle for their cock. I can't stop touching him. Kissing various parts of him. Learning his taste. The touch he likes—not what he demands, but truly *likes*. He jumps when I feather kisses over his pecs. Growls when I slide my fingers over his nipples. Inhales, the lower I go.

Lower.

Lower...

A guttural hum revs in his throat when I open the fly of his slacks, finally freeing his cock. This close, I can sense the sheer force of will it takes for him to keep from grabbing me. Forcing me. Controlling the act.

Were this to go his way, I'd never be able to caress him with soft, featherlight strokes. I'd never test the limits of his body, bringing him to the edge. Heavy-lidded, his eyes find mine, conveying the words he isn't capable of uttering out loud. *Witch,* I imagine him hissing. *What are you doing to me?*

I'm savoring him in every conceivable way. Like his taste when mingled with the hint of sea salt and the unbearable heat. His size. How thick he can be when barely aroused—

and how intimidating he can become once engorged, his body throbbing for release.

A gasp rips from his throat when I finally part my lips and take him in. It's fucking music, so beautiful. Noise I never knew him capable of making. This new, restrained Maxim comes complete with his own soundtrack—fabric hisses as he fists his hands in the material beneath us, nearly ripping it.

My brain buzzes, drugged on the atmosphere of lust, and the heady flavor of him. What would seem debasing in any other context is indescribable now. I take him deep, moaning at his taste. His feel. Everything. I don't care if I'm forced onto my knees, my ass in the air, my hair fanning out around me like some whore. He doesn't demand a single fucking thing from me.

Not even when he's pulsing against my tongue, practically writhing beneath his skin. I look up, meeting his gaze. Sweat slicks his forehead, his eyes unfocused, his lips parted. God, he's unrivaled like this.

But even now, doubt still sneaks in.

"Is this okay?" I blurt in a clumsy rush.

"I…" His throat cords around a thickened swallow. "I need to be inside of you."

That's all it takes to melt my brain entirely. A simple plea.

And I nearly come before I can even lurch against his chest and part my legs. He groans once he's seated to the hilt, his eyes closing in relief, teeth clenched. His hands find my waist, but he doesn't set the pace. I'm left to ride him of my own volition with no outside influence.

Slowly.

Harder.

Distant laugher and the roar of the ocean create an odd, unsettling backdrop that feeds the pleasure thrumming beneath my skin. This is insane. Fucking him beneath the sun in broad daylight is insane. Kissing him in between every thrust is maddeningly *insane.*

My orgasm hits me before I even register the depth of pleasure. He follows me, hissing partly in satisfaction, partly in agony.

"Fuck!" His hair frames him like a halo as he falls back against the headboard of the lounger. Utterly spent, I land against him, and his hand finds my hip, delivering a reverent stroke. "I *definitely* think I may come to enjoy vanilla…"

CHAPTER TWELVE

We wash up, change, and join the kids on the beach before noon. The youngest four are making a sandcastle at the water's edge, while Daisy and Mikie share a jet ski under the watchful gaze of Lucius, who wears his customary suit despite the heat.

A row of cabanas is positioned with a view of the water, creating a cozy, homey space. Maxim leads me to one, and we share yet another bed-sized lounger—though this time with a safe distance between us.

It should be so boring in theory. Lazing in the shade, watching the kids frolic in the ocean without a care in the world. To some people, maybe it would be. To me, this strain of peace is a new drug.

And I'm hopelessly addicted already.

Just when I think our "normalcy" has reached its peak, we're accosted by a whining Ainsley who begs Maxim to take her into the water. Which he does, utilizing a gentleness I would have never suspected him capable of expressing. I think he's surprised by it as well. The tenderness in his voice as he shows her and a bashful Eric how to plant their feet to withstand the waves. The playfulness he exudes while chasing them in and out of the water to help ease their fear of it.

A part of me keeps whispering that it's all an act—the real man comes out at night in that dark room. But witnessing him like this easily overpowers the doubt.

And I realize in the pit of my stomach that nothing else could come close to *this*. Not the supposed benefits he promised being with him would bring. Not the money. Not the ring.

I'd trade everything for this.

This moment.

This contentment.

Him, seemingly at peace, even for a second.

THE SUN IS in the process of setting by the time we return to the house. Dinner consists of leftover hamburgers eaten on the terrace while dipping our toes into the pool—another variation of our previous family meals.

I sit on a lounger across from Maxim while the kids chatter about random topics.

"Mermaids don't exist, stupid," Eric snipes in response to Ainsley. "But sharks?" He holds his hands up to his mouth, baring the nails like makeshift jaws. "They do, and they love eating little dummies like you!"

"Knock it off," I scold, but my voice lacks the old authority it used to. It's as though the warmth, and the breeze, and the hum of the ocean rob the atmosphere of everything but peace. Lifting my head to shoot them both a stern, warning glance, is about all I can muster in terms of refereeing.

Luckily, they both retreat.

"Mr. Sir?" Ainsley climbs from her lounger and crosses to Maxim's. Before I can stop her, she's already managed to crawl onto his lap, heedless of the discomfort turning him to stone.

I scramble to my feet, reaching for her. "Ainsley—"

"It's okay." Maxim raises a hand to halt my approach. One of his arms moves to cradle Ainsley's waist, keeping her from falling. The stiffness doesn't leave him, but the way he tilts his head receptively conveys that he's tolerating the contact regardless.

Oblivious to us both, she keeps chattering. "If you did marry Frankie, and you have kids. Would they be our brothers and sisters, or—"

"Ainsley!" Daisy rolls her eyes, shaking her head. "God, you can be such a moron sometimes."

"Not uh!" Pouting, Ainsley tugs on Maxim's sleeve until she has his full attention. "It's a good question, right? Are you going to have kids?"

Mikie groans, burying his face in his hands while the twins suddenly seem very interested in their food. The only person seemingly unbothered by the question is Maxim.

"I… I don't know." His voice sounds neutral enough. None of the kids seem to sense the hesitation in it that I do. From this angle, I can't see his face, just the hard, pulsating line of his jaw. "I'm afraid I can't answer that question."

But I can. That answer is one of the few things he's provided willingly without needing to be prodded—*no*. During my first few days with him, he ensured as much by injecting me with birth control without even asking for my consent. *You will not get pregnant,* he said by way of explanation. *That is the one thing you never have to worry about me inflicting upon you.*

Back then, I'd been more than relieved by that reassurance. But now, with the prospect of marriage looming overhead?

I'm not even sure what I want. But with his past…who knows how much of that affects his viewpoint on the concept of children? Which brings up the very good question as to where my kids fall into the grand scheme that is Maxim Koslov's fucked-up world.

"Oh, well." Sighing, Ainsley scampers off of him and returns to her seat. "I always wanted a baby sister. I hate being the baby—"

"Shut up, *baby*!" Eric balls up his napkin and throws it at her. Squealing, she throws it back, and they dissolve into a silent war while Mikie takes the reins of the conversation, steering it back to less volatile topics.

"How much does a yacht cost?" he demands of Maxim, raising an eyebrow. "Hypothetically speaking, if your only income came from cutting grass in the summer, how many summers might it take to buy one?"

Once again, we somehow manage to pass the awkward huddle and return to a smooth, easy rhythm of conversation and silence.

But as the darkness gradually claims the landscape, I sense a palpable shift in the man beside me. His responses slow to silence. His gaze grows more distant, fixated beyond this moment. Eventually, he stands and enters the house with a polite, "Goodnight."

At the same time, Ainsley starts rubbing her eyes, and I take the sign as a cue. "Bedtime."

The others groan in unison, but I follow them upstairs, surprised by the feeling building in my stomach. It isn't until I tuck Ainsley in bed and plant a kiss on her cheek that I can name the sensation for what it is.

Dread.

That cold, dark room awaits. But it isn't fear that sends my heartbeat surging as I finally approach the master suite. Maybe it's a little grief? The open, relaxed Maxim from earlier is dead and gone.

The figure standing hunched over the foot of the bed is a different creature—the other half of the twisted coin that is this beautiful, broken man.

"It's dusk," he says in a rasping tone. His hand gestures curtly toward the window. Sure enough, the horizon is a bloody, brilliant scarlet mingled with shades of orange. The sun is making its last stand. Technically, it isn't nightfall just yet. "If before... You can ask me one thing. The question I know is burning on the tip of your tongue."

My heart skips. His offer isn't a thoughtful request or a meaningless gesture. It's an olive branch. Reassurance—this is a true give and take. No matter how much effort it requires on both our parts.

"Do you want children?" I blurt out. He's right. That one question has been hovering in my throat, and I didn't even fucking realize it until now.

He sighs, lowering his head. "Would you trust me as a father?"

I'm unprepared for the question—one so different from his usual defensive responses. I think of how he can be with Ainsley, Eric, and the others—so gentle. On the other hand, it seems to take effort on his part. So much damn effort that at night, he needs to lock himself in a room just to express the pent-up violence. And with me...

He's slipped before, going too far, almost beyond reach. Could someone as small as Ainsley or even smaller be able to stop him?

No, a part of me whispers in horror. *But you know that. You've known it all along…*

I shake my head, banishing the doubts. "I don't know."

"Oh?" He laughs in a way that raises goosebumps, cold and distant. "You *do* know."

"Should I?" I swallow hard, watching him. He must have opened a window. A breeze drifts in, disrupting the golden halo of hair brushing his shoulders. For the first time, I toy with dissecting the real reason he's kept me with him, apart from the kids, except during our strained hiatus. I'd always assumed he preferred to live alone, but what if there is more to it than that? "Are you okay with my kids being here now?"

He doesn't answer.

I blink more rapidly, my eyes burning, my throat tight. "If this is all too much…"

"It's not," he says, and it isn't until now that I realize just how much I needed to hear that. My knees buckle at the genuine honesty in his voice. "I don't mind them. I will never lose control around them, I promise you that."

But something is on his mind, gnawing away at his previous composure. Something he can't—or won't—explain, no matter how many seconds tick by.

"Does this help you?" I finally ask, avoiding the real secrets looming between us. "The room. Even if you don't talk about it? Does it help?"

He nods, and it's like I can track the instability building within him. His spine goes rigid, his hands clenching into fists, his body hunched and angular. "Yes," he confesses hoarsely. "I need this… I need this from *you*."

"Okay." I turn to that infamous door, this time freed from hesitation. When I grip the handle, a mechanical noise sounds before it opens. I've barely stepped over the threshold when I sense him on my heels, herding me inside.

"Kneel."

Choking down a hiss, I sink to the hard floor. Every ache from last night throbs, renewed beneath his gaze. With him, pain takes on a sick connotation, enhanced by his reaction to it.

He inhales as if feeding off every flinch and twitch of sore muscle. I track his steps to the opposite end of the room. That one drawer, I suspect.

Sure enough, as he returns to me, the telltale snap of leather cuts the silence. Instantly, a stinging pain bites at my hip—a warning.

"Get on your hands and knees."

I do, bracing my palms over the frigid floor. He must control the air-conditioning in this room apart from the rest of the house. It's colder in here. My teeth are chattering, and yet sweat drips down my spine at the same time, a twisted dichotomy.

In this realm, even logic ceases to matter.

Another blow lands across my lower back. Another strikes my hip. My thigh.

"Strip," he commands.

I do so without bothering to stand up, shimmying from my dress. His footsteps echo, resonating in my bones as he circles my position, eyeing his handiwork. None of the lashings broke the skin, but they came damn close. The one on my hip smarts like hell, and I grit my teeth against making a sound. Attuned to my body like any true predator, he nudges that wound with the whip as if aware of the amount of pain inflicted in each particular spot.

Without warning, the whip hisses through the air and lands in between my shoulder blades. It hurts. I can't smother a groan, even as my thoughts start to dissipate, drunk on the burning sting.

Merciless, he hits me again.

Again.

Eventually, he forsakes the whip entirely and captures a fistful of my hair, wrenching me to my feet. Without explanation, he guides me to the marble slab and shoves me across it. Shivers ripple down my spine as he slides his hand between my legs, hissing at what he finds.

"There are things I want to do to you that would terrify you," he admits, stroking his damp fingers up the curve of my back, leaving a trail of moisture in his wake. "Things you aren't ready for. I've been patient, but fuck… Can you trust your body to me, even now?"

A part of me realizes in horror just what he's doing —begging.

Do I trust him? With his voice thick with lust, his fingers trembling with malice, my body on fire from his lashing…

Slumped against the marble slab, all I can do is nod. The intensity with which I do so makes my mind reel and has him grunting in relief. What dark, twisted fantasies has he held back from enacting?

For whatever reason, I'll take them without asking. Without hesitating.

His fingers dance over the throbbing skin of my ass, lingering there on purpose to heighten my anticipation. I writhe, too on edge to remain submissive. The disobedience makes him hum, and I know he's savoring the thought of whatever punishment lies in store.

"No one's ever fucked you in this way," he suspects, inching lower down the curve of my hip, to the center of my back. Then lower…

Oh. I have a grim suspicion as to what he wants.

"I can tell," he adds accusingly. "You stiffen whenever I touch you here. Why?"

My cheeks catch fire at the intimacy of the question. Because no matter how broke or how desperate I've been, no one could ever make me relinquish that one, small bit of myself. No one. Anal sex was never on the menu to any John, no matter the price.

"Do you trust this to me?" Maxim wonders, invading my thoughts so easily that it's pointless to speak them out loud. He *knows*. More than I should be comfortable with allowing. More than any other man ever will. "I won't take it from you—" He slides his fingers dangerously close to the entrance no one has ever touched. Not even him.

I tremble, my chest heaving. I'd be lying if I claimed I wasn't afraid. What little I know of anal is that it hurts. Like hell. If done too violently, it can cause lasting damage. Unimaginable pain…

And yet, my hips buck—*toward* him, not away.

"You're so perfect for me," he grates against the groove of my neck. It's both a praise and a curse. Perfect for him. Squirming and willing, thwarting the perfectionist in him that craves control. I'm ruining his careful, precise vision of taking my last shred of virginity. I'm far too fucking eager. Voice breaking, he commands, "Tell me I can have you—"

"Yes." The words escape me before he's even finished speaking. "You…you can have me."

He whispers something too softly to make out. An apology? His thumb grazes my lips before I can question. He parts them with persistent pressure, finding my tongue. Slowly, he wets his fingers—but I don't understand why until he moves behind me, urging me to lie higher across the altar.

I nearly jump out of my skin as he guides his thumb between the crack of my ass, finding that elusive opening.

One of his hands captures mine, gripping tight as his other pins my hip to the marble.

I only have enough sense to suck in a breath of air before he slips his thumb inside…

Out.

In.

This taking is brutal. No planning. No preparation. Only after a few tests of his thumb does he rub the head of his cock against that untouched opening, hissing when I flinch.

"Say that you trust me," he demands, nipping my earlobe. "Say it."

My lips part, devoid of hesitation. "I trust you—"

"Then take me." He bucks his hips, and the sharp pinch of his invasion takes my breath away. *Fuck fuck fuck fuck!*

I choke on a cry as his length slams into me, crushing me between his bulk and the unyielding marble. My fingers claw uselessly at the surface, scrambling for purchase.

He goes deep. Too deep. So deep.

It should be impossible to find pleasure in this— suffocating, crushing, writhing agony. In some ways, maybe it is. The heat of his breath on my neck burns like fire. He grips my hips without care, driving his nails in, forcing me to take every thrust with no mercy.

I'm convulsing around him anyway.

It's a feeling I could never find in his arms, lounging beneath the sunlight. Something violent and raw and selfish that lingers in the knowledge that only I can give him this.

True submission.

Even if it hurts. Even if the aftermath leaves me trembling on my knees, too exhausted to stand on my own. Murmuring against my skin, he lifts me into his arms, carrying me from the room. Still on edge, I gasp as the atmosphere changes. Warmth displaces cold. The air thins. Moonlight replaces the harsh, fluorescent lighting.

We re-enter the real world like creatures from hell, and it's a slow, cruel readjustment to reality.

He drapes me over the edge of the bed and disappears for a moment only to return with a cloth clutched in his fist. He bathes me carefully, but his touch lingers afterward. It's like I can read his mind as he weighs the prospect of taking me back into that space. Feeding this addiction with another round.

I've already resigned myself to exactly that when a frantic knock on the door shatters everything.

"Frankie? Frankie?"

"Shit!" I only have enough energy to roll onto my side, facing the door, and pray that it doesn't open. "W-What is it?"

"Can I sleep with you?" Ainsley asks in between sniffling cries. "P-Please?"

Double shit.

"Uh…" I can't even look at Maxim. "Not tonight, baby. G-Give me a minute, and I'll come to tuck you in—"

"It's okay." Maxim enters the closet and tosses me a robe. "Let her in."

He's already pulling on a pair of gray sweats and a shirt. Before I can call Ainsley myself, he crosses over to the door and opens it.

Rubbing her eyes, Ainsley barges in, trailing a pink blanket behind her that I assume came from her bed. She climbs in beside me and burrows beneath the sheets. From the corner of my eye, I notice Maxim already entering the hall.

"I'll be on the couch," he says.

"No!" Ainsley sits up, her eyes wide. "You have to stay in case the bad man comes back. You have to!"

"Ainsley…" I run my fingers through her hair and try to coax her into lying down. "Baby, try to get some sleep—"

"It's alright." Maxim lingers near the threshold before he returns to the bed. I can't read his expression. He circles around to the opposite end from Ainsley and me and then sits on the floor with his back braced against the mattress. "Get some sleep," he grunts. "No one will hurt you."

A faint reply comes muffled from beneath the blankets. "Promise?"

He sighs again. "I… I promise."

Satisfied, Ainsley snuggles against me, and within minutes she's sleeping deeply.

But her protector doesn't budge from his post. Even though he has no real obligation to, he keeps his promise.

He stays.

CHAPTER THIRTEEN

I wake up content—a fact that makes my heart beat faster before my senses fully return. There's no foot in my side, no tiny fingers tangled in my hair. Confused, I feel out with my hand, alarmed to find empty space beside me. "Ainsley?"

"She's eating breakfast," someone calls before panic can set in, their voice raspy with sleep. I look over to find Maxim unmoved from his previous position on the floor, his back to me. A familiar heat stirs as my eyes skim over his muscle, defined in the daylight.

But once I reach his face, the fire dies down, replaced by cold, hard fear. From this angle, I can only make out the stern set to his jaw—he's still in that room, brooding internally. Over regrets? Normalcy by day and BDSM by night could be a game that even he isn't up to playing for very long.

"Maxim?" I tentatively call out, rolling toward him.

He doesn't answer. Then he groans, stretching his arms above his head, and the tension leaves his muscles. "I believe they're having omelets," he says from over his shoulder, his voice neutral. "Courtesy of Lucius."

Slowly, I relax back into the mattress. "Is there anything he can't do?" I wonder tiredly.

"If there is, he'll rectify it somehow," Maxim replies with audible respect. "The man is the best money can buy."

That and loyalty. There's no denying that, their professional relationship aside, Lucius cares for him.

"You should go eat," Maxim suggests, rising to his feet while I shift to keep him in view. "I will shower and…"

He meets my gaze, and whatever he finds makes him trail off. The distraction is mutual. One look from him sets me alight despite the exhaustion weighing me down. I flick my tongue along my lower lip as I follow the line of his gaze downward. *Oh.* My robe fell open when I moved, revealing my breasts. Absently, I start to adjust it, but he lunges, grabbing my wrist.

I'm in his arms before I know it. He takes me into the shower, and we bathe together, saying nothing—verbally anyway. The way he touches me conveys a million different things, soothing over every sting inflicted last night.

A tendril of lingering doubt creeps in, feeding off the memories of him in that room. The anger. The repressed emotions. Again I have to wonder if this little game of give and take is more than he can handle. Is normalcy beyond his limits?

His fingers sink into my hair, grazing my scalp as if to banish all other thoughts but this. His nearness. Our nakedness. Heat. Cautiously, our lips meet. Once. Twice.

"I am curious about something," Maxim confesses, drawing back. My lips burn, mourning the loss of his as he turns his attention to my throat. His teeth knead the flesh along my collar, sending heat churning through my belly with every nip.

Distracted by how his mouth increasingly travels south, I can barely form a coherent reply. "Oh?"

"You didn't argue," he points out before cupping my breast in his palm. With a sinful caress, he squeezes, making me lurch against him. "When I told your family you refused my proposal."

"What?" I stiffen, but his tongue laves over my nipple, and any logic dissipates. "I-I…"

"You didn't deny it either. That I had pursued you—or 'dating' as your sister put it." Rather than annoyed, he sounds oddly…smug at that fact. As though in not refusing him outright, I hadn't closed the door on an engagement entirely.

"I…"

He returns his mouth to mine, robbing me of the chance to argue. Within seconds, he's buried within me to the hilt, and I lose track of everything but the sensation building between us.

Slow, lazy, unhurried sex is another first.

Experienced with him, it feels like some novel, newly discovered concept that I pity every other woman for never getting to enjoy firsthand.

Afterward, we dress, and by the time we make it downstairs, breakfast is long gone, and Ainsley is musing about lunch.

That meal is eventually supplied by Maxim as well—more grilled meat and fresh fruit from the well-stocked fridge. This time, we pack up the food and eat on the beach, wiggling our toes in the sand. That hazy, dreamlike feeling returns and I'm stupid enough to wish this could last forever.

But when Lucius approaches, a cell phone glued to his ear, I know reality is about to descend. Rudely.

Apparently, Maxim assumes the same. He lunges to his feet and races to meet Lucius first. Whatever words they exchange leaves the younger man scowling, and when he returns, he shoves his hand into his pocket and withdraws a wallet. From it, he takes several crisp hundred-dollar bills.

"Who wants it?" he demands, brandishing the bills in his fist.

Predictably, all six kids shout in a deafening clamor.

His voice booming, Maxim easily overpowers them, "Alright. If all of you can make it to that end of the beach —" he points to a spot in the distance "—and back, you can divide it amongst each other. Go now."

Oblivious to anything but their challenge, they take off, jockeying for the lead.

The second they're out of earshot, Maxim grabs my wrist and pulls me to my feet.

"What's wrong?"

He doesn't answer in favor of leading me back to the house. As we enter the living room, I see the cause of the disturbance for myself.

Dressed in a tan suit with a crisp white shirt, a few buttons open at the neck, a tall man commands the massive space. He stands rigidly, casting a cynical glance at the bright, neutral décor. Once he spots Maxim, he inhales as if steeling himself for a battle. "I will explain—"

"Explain, Milton?" Maxim echoes in a dangerously soft tone. "You don't *ever* come to me unannounced. Which means, you've suddenly picked now, the first time in twenty years, to drop by for a surprise visit. Or…" His eyes narrow. "You've decided to spring something far more unforgivable on me. Which one is it?"

The other man inclines his head toward the foyer. "You can come in."

"Many apologies," a new figure simpers with mock contrition. Dima. But in comparison to Milton's polished appearance, I don't know whether to laugh or stare as he strolls into the room. In lieu of a suit or linen ensemble, he wears an array of mismatched clothing as if he picked them out last minute from the bargain bin at Goodwill. A large, oversized pink sweatshirt shrouds his lanky frame, sporting a yellow heart in the center. A gray knitted cap obscures most of his dark hair, and a ratty pair of jeans completes the overall look.

He could easily fit in with the entertainers Maxim hired for his makeshift carnival—except for his expression. It's calculating, matching his easy, cautious posture. He keeps his hands in his pockets and scans the interior of the house in a way that makes me suspect he's memorizing every single detail.

But overall, he looks more cold than comical. *Physically* cold, hunched beneath the sweatshirt as if freezing despite the heat.

"I apologize for my ensemble," he says with a contrite nod. "Oh, how I wish I had the foresight to pack my own priceless suit before dear Milton forced me onto his private plane. Luckily, his sweet flight attendant gave me the use of *her* clothing—"

"Get the fuck out! And you—" Eyes flashing, Maxim whirls on Milton, poised on the balls of his feet. "What the hell were you thinking, bringing him here? Have you lost your fucking mind—"

"My mind? No." Milton smooths his hands along the sleeves of his suit, inspecting the ebony cufflinks, securing each one. When he finally meets Maxim's gaze, there's no hint of fear in the dark irises of either man. They stare each other down coldly, two opponents equally matched. "My *patience*, on the other hand? I'm running out of it. You could have avoided this if you picked up my calls. I made myself fucking clear to Lucius."

"Clear?" Maxim exhales sharply, his body practically humming with anger. "Don't speak in fucking riddles," he commands. "You want to say something, then fucking say it. Start with why you would dare to bring him here. Around my—" He grits his teeth, his eyes narrowing to slits. "You bring him here, knowing the risk you just put me in. Why?"

"Dima won't hurt you," Milton says tiredly, as if bored by the mere thought of it. "No one else will learn of this location. Proven wrong—which I won't be—I will personally fix it." He turns his head in Dima's direction, the politest version of a lethal threat I've ever witnessed burning in his eyes. "You have my word. But you know who *does* intend to harm? Danil. The motherfucker landed in Fair Haven not too long ago. Rumor has it, he's planning an assault, with or without Anatoli's backing."

"All of this over fucking Danil?" Maxim turns on his heel, leaving me at the doorway, his hands in fists. Several thunderous steps carry him across the room, parallel to Milton's position—but no further. It's as if the man serves as an invisible wall, preventing him from reaching his actual target. So he paces. "That bastard can't button his own fucking fly without Anatoli's blessing. You think he threatens me?"

"Your cousin may be a fool," Milton concedes, "but others will follow. Dima is the least of your concerns."

"If you believe that, then you really have lost your fucking mind—"

"I lost my *fucking* mind a long time ago. As *you* did. As Dima did." Milton says through clenched teeth, the unspoken history between them rotting the air. "Do you honestly doubt me?" There's a few seconds' silence. "I thought not. Now, let's get this over with. Give Dima the girl. End this childish idiocy between the two of you. Accept his assistance, and *together*, we can take Anatoli down."

Maxim stops short. "Were you anyone else, Milton, I would kill you for what you've just said."

"But I'm not anyone else, am I?" A hint of irritation disrupts Milton's polished façade. He's just as angry as Maxim, but in a very different way. "These are the facts you need to face. Anatoli has gotten bold in your absence. He's planning to attack your suppliers directly—a full-on assault. And, I apologize, but I don't want an open war. Not now. Not while..." He cuts off, shaking his head. "He and those loyal to him need to be dealt with. I suggest you return to the city as soon as possible."

Maxim laughs. "Give him *your* woman then. What? You thought I didn't notice her? The blond you've kept so close to you? Give her to Vadim, if you are so eager for peace."

A shadow falls over Milton's face, and this room becomes the world's smallest cage despite its size. They're both wolves, snarling for dominance in the center of it, leaving little room for anyone else.

All I can do is pray that none of the kids wander into the house—but I seem to be the only spectator concerned. Meeting my gaze from across the room, Vadim playfully waggles his eyebrows. *"Brothers,"* he mouths with a smile.

I cringe away from him, returning my attention to Maxim. If I thought the hidden room upstairs brought out the worst in him, I was wrong.

"What is it, then?" he demands, cocking his head. "Your little whore is too good for precious Dima, but my woman isn't? In fact, shall we ask her?" He extends his hand toward me. "Francesca, are you my whore to be utilized as I see fit?"

All three men turn to me. Stunned, I clear my throat. "N-No."

"Good," Maxim hisses. "Then it's settled. Unless you want to force her, Milton? Perhaps you and Dima prefer to reenact the very bonds of slavery you escaped from?"

"I suggest you watch your words as well," Milton warns, advancing a single, dangerous step in Maxim's direction. "As for Dima, you know he won't hurt her—" He nods toward me. "You know he won't hurt *you* either. All he wants is to toy with you. Entertainment. And you're all but providing him the shit show he wants by resisting. I could easily convince him to relent, but I won't. Do you know why?" His eyes cloud over with an unreadable emotion. "You *owe* him. You owe him this one fucking request, no matter how childish and spiteful it might be. We both know why. What was it you called it? The bonds we all escaped from?"

"Is that so?" Maxim clenches his hands into fists, cracking the knuckles in the process.

"*Yes.*" Milton merely observes him, seemingly lacking the energy to match his vitriol. All he does is sigh. "I've humored this grudge of yours for over a decade, but I'm telling you now, I'm *tired.*" Another layer of his persona falls away, betraying his words to be the truth. Worn lines strain the flesh around his eyes, enhancing an expertly disguised exhaustion. Even Maxim's can't compare. "My little blond whore, as you call her? Is under *my* protection. And I won't stand aside and watch Anatoli turn his attention to *her* to get to you. I fucking won't, Maxim. End this fight with Dima—"

"Get out." Maxim storms past Milton, but rather than head for Dima, he comes for me. His hand cinches my wrist, yanking me to his side. "Both of you. *Now.* As for Anatoli, I will return to the city in the morning and handle this myself."

Milton sighs again, more heavily. "You and I both know that you can't."

"So, you've come to insult me as well as threaten me?" I've never heard Maxim's voice so guttural. "I suggest you leave. You want to turn on me? Fine. I don't need you, or your pet—"

"You do," Milton insists. "You need me just like when we were kids, and we had *no one* but each other. Or have you forgotten that, too? I do not doubt your strength or ability to defeat him on your own. You just never had the *will* to. Dima isn't the pet here. *You* are. You've always been that little boy pining under Anatoli's shoe, desperate for his attention. His acceptance. Even if it bloody kills you."

"Don't use your fucking degree on me," Maxim snarls, his lips curling from his teeth. "Go!"

"My degree?" Milton laughs, a disarmingly beautiful sound. With his head held high, he faces Maxim directly and moves to stand within his path. "One of many I got from an education that wasn't free. That I paid in blood for. You want me to use it? Fine. You never hated Dima, not truly. You just can't stand what he signifies. Freedom. Independence. Someone who can live outside the shadow of your grandfather unscathed by his poison. You've let jealousy consume you for over twenty years. Dima never wanted his name—and *that's* what bothers you. Anatoli bred you like an animal, and you don't know a life outside of that brutal, violent existence. Do you deny it?"

He waits, but Maxim says nothing.

"I thought so." Flicking his collar, he strolls for the front door, deliberately unhurried. "When you change your mind, contact me, and I'll make the arrangements." He stops and cocks his head before adding. "What happened today doesn't change anything between us. Not to me, anyway. You know I'll always stand by you—but I won't enable you. I *can't*."

"Well, this was lovely," a cheerier voice cuts in, a surreal contrast to the anger crackling in the air. "A wonderful reunion, much better than I could have ever hoped for—"

"Race ya!" The high pitched, childish shriek cuts through the tension like a knife. It takes my brain a second to identify it as not belonging to any one of the three men before me. Which can only mean…

"Fuck!" I race to the glass door leading to the terrace to find Ainsley skipping toward me, her hair streaming behind her. She waves, giggling even as I shake my head and fumble for the door.

"No! No, no, no…"

Suddenly, a deeper voice calls out, and Lucius appears in her wake, running to catch up.

Whatever he says makes Ainsley turn to him, and he manages to take her hand and lead her away. Relief rips through me, and I brace my palms against the glass just to stay standing.

"Thank God."

"A child? Hers?" The question comes from Dima, or so I assume, given the lightness of the baritone. But his voice sounds different, suddenly devoid of amusement. Surprise colors it instead. Alarm. "You brought a child here. With him?"

He isn't speaking to Maxim.

"No. No one could be that reckless…"

"Come, Dima," Milton snaps, sounding farther away. When I finally have the strength to look back, he's halfway across the entryway. "Now!"

But Vadim doesn't move. His dark eyes remain fixated on me, narrowed with disdain. "You trust him with your child? I'd assumed you were his victim, but perhaps I was wrong. No *real* mother would ever put her children in danger—"

"Maxim!" In a blur of motion, Milton reappears as if from thin air to physically shove the other man back.

"Get out!" Eyes like coal, Maxim pivots, nearly barreling past Milton, who has to grasp his shoulders just to keep him back.

"Go, Dima!" Milton snarls.

Vadim doesn't seem to even notice the commotion. Or care. An expression crosses his face almost too quickly to process. Only my time with Maxim gives me a faint hope at interpreting it—an icy veil of memory, trapping him in the past.

"Your little daughter? He'll carve her to pieces," he tells me softly, while brushing his hand along the scar on his throat. "But you know that, don't you? You *know* he'll see her beaten. Raped. He'll sell her to the highest bidder himself, if his true master tells him to. You know this to be true." He nods as if my expression alone gives him all of the confirmation he needs. "And yet you stay. How dare you put an innocent in harm's way?"

Pain lances through my chest. It feels as if he punched me though he never moves a single inch. My lungs throb regardless, and it's harder to breathe. Think.

Is that what I'm doing? *Selling...*

Maxim bellows something, followed by another frantic warning from Milton.

But all I hear is Dima's calm, relentless murmur, sneaking past the clamor to easily reach me. "If you keep your child around him, you're no better than he is. You condemn her, and any other children you may have. The Koslovs. That name is more than *just* a name," he insists. "It is a creed. A brutality. And you've already sold your daughter to them just by taking his ring—"

"Get... Out!" My chest heaves as I spit out the words one by one, surprised by their ferocity.

From the corner of my eye, I see Milton and Maxim pause, panting in their struggle.

"As you wish," Dima says with another gallant nod. He turns on his heel, strolling for the door. Once he's out of view, Milton follows, adjusting his mussed suit. Near the threshold, he pauses.

"I'm sorry. You may not think Danil as a threat, but you didn't ask why he—of all Anatoli's pawns—would be so desperate to attack you directly. But he wants the bounty, Maxim." He sets his gaze on me and then back to Maxim. "And if you want to protect yours, as I am mine, reconsider this place. If I found you, he will, fool or not."

Finally, he exits the house, and both men leave, taking all hope of normalcy with them.

CHAPTER FOURTEEN

M ilton's visit shatters what little semblance of peace we'd managed to cobble together—but the most alarming part in the aftermath is how everyone, from Maxim to Lucius, still manages to pretend like nothing is wrong. At least around the kids. It is "normalcy" pushed to its very fucking limits.

I should be grateful for that.

Maxim doesn't brood around them, becoming a vicious stranger in a heartbeat. He disappears instead, leaving me alone to keep up the façade.

But I'm a sleepwalker, trapped in the nightmare of Dima's insinuation. *How dare you put an innocent in harm's way?*

When the kids return from the beach, we eat pasta around the center island in the kitchen, courtesy of Lucius, who serves as head chef in Maxim's absence. They chatter on about jet skis and swimming, innocently oblivious to the looming danger. Danger, I put them in.

That guilt robs me of my appetite. All I can do is pick at my plate while my mind spins in turmoil. When the kids finally trickle off to bed, I'm on edge, and Maxim is nowhere to be found.

Unease creeps in as I start to search for him.

He isn't in the bedroom or the bathroom, or even the infamous "other room" when I gather the nerve to check. For all I know, he could be gone already, heading back to the city without so much as a goodbye.

Would that bother me? I'm surprised by the ache knotting in my chest at the possibility. *Yes.* It would.

It fucking would.

Even as the fear sets in, I can't ignore the intuitive sense that he's still here—as if there's a taste lingering in the air, unique only to his brand of rage. My nostrils flare as I try to pinpoint his exact location. In a way, doing so feels a bit like some creepy, childhood game. *Find the mafia boss in the haystack.* And yet…

There's a skill to it. Knowing where he'd go to rage in peace. Somewhere where he can presumably do the least amount of damage to avoid alarming the kids—if he truly does care about their comfort. Somewhere open and unconfined, too, like the wild expanse of lawn beyond the terrace…

I slip out through the kitchen doors and cut past the pool, guided by the last shreds of daylight. A blood-red sunset bathes everything in a fiery glow, enhancing every nuance of the landscape.

Namely the lone figure pacing on the very outskirts of the property, far beyond the view from the house.

The dusky glow ignites his golden hair, illuminating the panes of his face and enhancing the rage shaping them. When he spots me, his entire body goes rigid, a creature apart from the man I spent the last few days in paradise with.

Fear nearly paralyzes me. Only God knows what keeps me moving, tiptoeing through the grass on bare feet.

"I'm leaving in the morning," he declares when I approach him. I jump at his tone. His voice resonates as deeply as a roar of thunder, and I half expect lightning to strike. "You and your siblings will be moved to another location. I'll send for you when I'm ready."

My heart lurches. Another move. Another gameboard. Another stint as a pawn. "Please, just slow down," I say. "We should talk about this—"

"Talk?" He whips around so swiftly I stagger an instinctive step back. Alarm stimulates every nerve in my body, urging escape. *Run!* "Do you really think you can dictate to me?" he wonders, his teeth bared.

No, a part of me whimpers in defeat. I'm no match for him when he's like this. Some things can't change. You can't cage a wolf—eventually, it will go for your throat.

The only option is to give in. Surrender to the inevitable fact that we'll always be back at square one. He'll always be a stranger, lost to rage. To him, peace was never worth chasing.

And a future with him will never be normal.

"Go into the house," he growls, resigned to the same outcome. "Now—"

"Please…" I take a step toward him. Then another as he falls silent. Cracks disrupt my brave façade however—my fingers shake when I reach out, finding his chest…

And all of my fear vanishes, replaced by a throbbing, inescapable concern. His heart is hammering, his chest heaving with shallow breaths. Up this close, I can sense everything he uses the rage to mask. He's panicked. He's breaking. He's losing control.

"You believe him, don't you?" he surmises, his eyes narrowed. "That I will hurt you. Hurt your children. I saw your face. You believe *him*—"

"I don't know what to believe," I say, taking another step. "But I want to trust you."

"Go." He turns away, glaring into the distance. "I need to be alone."

"You need *me*," I whisper, surprised by how true that statement seems the more I touch him. I slide my hand up to his shoulder, tracking how he flinches in response. "Talk to me—"

"Go!" He shrugs me off so violently that throwing my arms out is the only way I can keep my balance. "Don't be a fucking fool, Francesca." He toys with the syllables in my name to inflict the harshest sting. "I need you in the sense that I require the use of your cunt at my discretion. Now go into the fucking house—"

"You need me now." This time I step into him, lacing my arms around his neck. Before he can react, I feel along his jaw. It's a reckless move—he could bite me; he looks so fucking unstable. Lost. But he doesn't, and the slightest contact is enough to keep me talking. "You need to talk to me. Tell me what's wrong."

His hands fall to his sides, but he's still staring into the distance, far beyond here.

So I stand on tiptoe, bringing my lips near his ear, so it's harder for him to ignore me. "If you need to leave, fine, but you owe me—us—the chance to hear why. Do I worry about the kids? Maybe. But they trust you. *Ainsley* trusts you…" Emotion thickens my throat. I swallow hard and choke out each confession one by one. "Don't you dare forsake that. *Ever*. We don't deserve to be tossed around like objects. I won't let you throw them away, either. I can't. So talk to me, if you want us to work. This is what real families do. Talk—"

"Family?" he echoes gruffly.

"Yes… That is what I need from you if you want me to stay. More than protection. I need stability. I need my *family*."

One word, and it's like a candle being blown out. The stiffness leaves him all at once, and he sways, nearly bringing me down with him. At the last second, his hands cinch my waist to the point of pain, but we remain standing. I endure the discomfort, smoothing my fingers over any part of him I can reach. He holds me so tightly I know I'll bruise in the aftermath. At the same time, I savor this pain more than any other agony he could ever inflict.

It's *him* inflicting it, not the monster living in his head.

Cautiously, his fingers creep into my hair, parting the strands as if memorizing every one, using me as an anchor to ground himself. His breathing eases first, and then his stability returns, and I can let myself relax into him fully without fear of falling.

"A family with you…" Soft, his lips nudge my throat, coaxing me to meet his gaze. He's here again, his expression hollowed, but here. His lips brush mine almost in apology before he devours them, demolishing my defenses with his tongue.

We kiss hungrily, heedless of the heat and the chirping insects around us. I don't resist as he shoves me down, pressing my body to the ground.

He slams into me from behind, his mouth at my throat, his thrusts frenzied. Desperate. I don't move when he finally collapses against me, breathless and dripping sweat.

His hands smooth the hair from my face, his lips feathering over my shoulder. "You will marry me," he murmurs, but he sounds crazed. Russian words mingle with more broken bits of English. I doubt he even knows what he's saying. "Marry me. You will. I need you to marry me…"

His hand captures mine, forcing our fingers together.

"I won't lose you," he grates in between pants. "I can't."

It's minutes before he's coherent again, nudging me to face him as darkness fully descends, drenching us in shadow. "We will leave tomorrow," he says. "Your siblings can stay here for a week, long enough to make arrangements for them. But then…" He fingers my chin, ensuring I can't turn away. Visible even in the faint moonlight, his eyes glow. "We stay together. You have your normalcy, but we stay. Like this…"

I nod, unsure if he can even see me or not. "We'll stay together."

CHAPTER FIFTEEN

Maxim leads me to the terrace but doesn't follow me inside. "Sleep," he says. "We'll leave first thing in the morning. I'll make the arrangements."

I don't bother to ask him what "arrangements" could be made alone, outside in the middle of the night. Despite our breakthrough, I know better than to push for more.

So I enter the master suite alone, though I don't sleep. Eventually, I wind up in the shower and linger there for hours until dawn finally paints the horizon.

When I creep downstairs to find two suitcases near the door, I *finally* risk hoping that last night wasn't a fluke. For once, we might have communicated beyond sex.

Unscathed by the recent chaos, the kids are already awake and out on the terrace, still wearing pajamas.

"Are we leaving already?" Ainsley whines the second I join them, fully dressed. "But we're having so much fun!"

"Your sister and I are leaving," Maxim says. I jump and turn to find him exiting the house behind me. His outfit alone signifies the end of his vacation. The customary suit has made a reappearance, a striking shade of ebony. "We all would be returning to the city today, but the gas leak damaged the other house. Do you trust your sister to find a better one?"

Mikie mockingly rolls his eyes. "I guess."

"You have one more week of paradise," Maxim adds. "Then I'm afraid it's back to reality."

He steps back a respectful distance so I can say goodbye to the kids one by one. When I reach Daisy, I wrap my arms around her, but say near her ear, "Whatever you might think of me. It doesn't matter. I still love you. But that also means I expect more from you. Watch out for Ainsley and make sure she cleans up properly. Got it?"

She nods.

"Sir," Lucius calls from the doorway. "The pilot is ready."

Maxim nods and places his hand on my lower back. "We're on our way."

Together we travel through the house and exit from the front door to find a black car already waiting out front. Maxim leads the way and ushers me inside before settling beside me. His hand finds mine, interlacing our fingers.

And with that, we return to the real world.

My second plane ride unfolds a bit more memorably than the first. Like everything in Maxim's world, his private jet is nothing short of impressive. Custom leather recliners are comfortably spaced around the climate-controlled cabin, conveying an aura primarily for business over pleasure. The overall color scheme isn't surprising given Maxim's tastes—black and gray with modern accents.

"We will need to move," he says. His voice conveys a sense of calm that contrasts sharply with his tense, stiff posture. Poised on the very edge of his seat, he keeps eyeing the silver watch on his wrist, his gaze turned inward. But for whatever reason, I recognize his attempts at conversation for what they are—a stab at maintaining our fragile sense of normalcy. "And quickly," he adds. "I'll leave the house hunting up to you, this time. You'll start tomorrow. I have a real estate agent I can connect you with. He works fast, and the cost is no option."

I raise an eyebrow. Compared to the danger looming overhead, house hunting sounds like a rather unusual priority. Not to mention the time frame. "Can you really buy a new house in a week?" I ask, the most innocent of questions to probe him with.

Something that could be a laugh trickles out of him, and he sits back. "*I* can buy a house in a week. But you will need to arrange the furniture as well. For everyone—" Sitting back, his hand falls over the end of my armrest, but he doesn't reach for one of mine. "I don't think I'll have the time to assist you…" He spares another glance at his watch. When he faces me again, his expression is strained, though he flashes a lethal grin as if to disguise the unease. "I have a list of non-negotiable items I require, however. I'll leave it up to you as to how to disguise them."

My head swims at the thought of it—for the first time, I'm the one responsible for the manic move and décor. As well as stocking our sex room, apparently.

The term *domestic* is turning out to have a surprising amount of new meanings when it comes to him.

"The kids will stay with us?" I ask next.

His slow nod is all the confirmation required.

Relieved, I sink back into the leather cushions of my recliner. His responses so far make me bold enough to risk letting a more direct question slip out. "What about your grandfather?"

He stiffens, and I nearly kick myself for bringing up that dilemma too soon.

"I will handle him," he snaps. "Parading you beneath his nose so soon would not be my preferred course of action… But he will not be so bold as to attack me out in the open. As for the others? I can handle them as well."

Such as the mysterious Danil, whom Milton mentioned.

"Why did you bring me, really?" I can't resist leaning toward him to brush my fingers along his forearm. He lets me trace a path from his shoulder all the way down to his wrist before he grabs my hand in return.

"Because of business," he says, his gaze thoughtful. "Apart from me, you are in no less danger. Perhaps more. Some would be emboldened to harm you in my absence."

"Oh." I lick my lips. Does the answer sting? Maybe, but I swallow hard to disguise it.

"And…" He tilts my fingers for his inspection and settles on the one coincidentally meant to bear a specific type of ring. "I could enjoy your presence," he adds tonelessly, as if remarking on the weather. "Your scent. Logistics aside, I could enjoy knowing that no other man could even look at you without my consent. Or that with one glance, one word, one touch, I could have you wet and ready for me."

He withdraws slowly, dragging his fingers along my flesh in retreat. Then he turns his attention to the window on his end and strokes the collar of his suit. "I will let you decide which answer to accept."

Minutes later, the plane descends, and Maxim recaptures my hand, smoothing his thumb along the back of it. "We're landing," he explains as the cabin shudders around us.

It's nightfall when we finally touch down outside of Fair Haven, and it's like waking up from a dream for a grim, colorless reality. The chill hits like a slap as we exit the plane for the night air. A black car waits nearby, helmed by an unfamiliar driver. Unsurprising, since Lucius stayed behind with the kids, ensuring their protection.

"Come." Maxim draws me to his side, and we begin our descent toward the tarmac.

"Good evening, sir," the driver greets as we approach. "The arrangements have been made for—"

"Fuck!" Maxim reacts first before I even process the events unfurling in front of me. The driver stopped talking, cut off mid-sentence. Why? I look at him, trying to discern a reason but nothing makes sense.

He's falling. Red liquid goes flying as his body slumps against the side of the car, but something is wrong with him. His head? It doesn't look right...

Because it's missing.

"Get down!" Maxim shoves me to the ground at the base of the stairs. His weight crushes me down, shielding me entirely.

But I can still hear. Footsteps. They approach in a barrage, betraying more than one person. Judging from the tension radiating through Maxim's body, they aren't friends of his.

"Not so fast, little Maxi," someone calls amid the echoing sounds. "I wouldn't be so hasty. Don't even think about reaching for your gun or calling for backup. Now stand, the both of you."

Maxim stiffens. Then all at once, the pressure pinning me down recedes, and he grabs my shoulder, urging me to my feet. I blink to adjust to the darkness. Only a few spotlights illuminate this section of the tarmac.

But we aren't alone.

At least ten men advance from the shadows to converge on our position. They're bulky, but even as panic sends my thoughts scattering, my time with Maxim made an impact. Several details stick out. For one, they don't move in crisp unison like Maxim's trained men do. They're disjointed. Sloppy. Some wear polished suits, but others—like the man who seems to be leading them all—wear a T-shirt, jeans, and a leather jacket. But all are armed, with weapons trained on us.

"Danil," Maxim says. "What a pity. I always thought you were the smartest of your inbred branch of the family tree, but I was wrong. Obviously, you have a death wish to approach me like this."

"A death wish?" A balding man, presumably Danil, wearing the leather jacket, chuckles, waving his gun casually through the air. His accent reminds me of Sevastyn's, cold and crisp like the hiss of a snake. "Maybe I am just not as mischievous as Anatoli? I don't like to make my prey sweat before I make my move. I prefer to simply—" He aims his weapon at the sky and fires. "Move."

Maxim's grip on me tightens, and he all but shoves me behind him. "What do you want?"

"Don't play dumb, boy," Danil warns with another hearty chuckle. "Anatoli requests your presence, but as for me… I'll take the girl."

"Take?" Maxim cocks his head as a low laugh resonates in his chest. "Is that so?"

"Usually, I wouldn't go after such petty bait," Danil adds with an apologetic sigh. "But, you see, Bruno here?" He reaches behind him and grabs the ear of a thinner, younger-looking man with long blond hair, dragging him to the front. "The fucker screwed up and got himself disowned. Botched robbery." He tugs on the man's ear, forcing him to kneel. "He has prostrated himself before Anatoli to no avail. Perhaps this little bounty will get him back into the fold? As a bonus, I'll let him play with the girl beforehand, so he can finally learn what it's like to fuck a woman outside of his little video games. Yes? *Wait*—" Suddenly, he aims his weapon over Maxim, his eyes narrowed. "Not so fast, Maxi. I've heard of your temper, but even you know when a man is outnumbered, yes?"

The men around him adjust their weapons as well, and Maxim's grip on my arm turns bruising.

"Now," Danil says, shrugging. "I suggest we do this the easy way. You will come with us for your spanking, Maxi." He nods toward an approaching black van. "And the girl will go with Bruno."

"Touch her, and you'll be dead before your withered cock can even enjoy the thrill," Maxim says.

Danil smiles. "If you wanted me dead, I would be dead, boy. But no hard feelings, eh? This is nothing more than the love of a father, helping to right his son's pathetic mistake. Though you wouldn't know anything about that, would you?" The corner of his mouth curls in disgust as his gaze rakes over Maxim, settling over his waist. "I've heard the old man likes to castrate little whelps like you. Render you sterile so that you can't spread your seed without his say-so—"

"I suggest you watch yourself, Danil." Maxim stands rigid, his fingers flexing at his side. "Between the two of us, only one may experience a castration firsthand."

"Hmph. I think you and I will catch up first before I tend to your little friend. *Then* I'll give you to the old man," Danil taunts, his eyes gleaming. He gestures to the men behind him with a wave. "Come on, boys! Let's go—"

"I'm afraid *not*." The door to the back seat of Maxim's car opens, and a lanky figure gracefully climbs out. Like a dancer, he unfurls his limbs, stretching them one by one as if oblivious to the violence surrounding him. An oversized black sweater adds artificial bulk to his slender frame, and his dark curls spill from a knitted hat lazily perched on his head.

Dima.

"What the hell?" Maxim's grip loosens over me for a second, revealing his shock. Dima looks back at him with a wink before he whirls on his heel to address the hoard of men behind him.

"So predictable, Danil," he says mournfully, eyeing the body of the driver nearby. "I mean, I told myself that even you wouldn't be so dreadfully sloppy. So unimaginative. Alas, I was wrong."

"Vadim?" Danil's mouth contorts into a scowl, but he lowers his gun a fraction of an inch. "Have the two mutts reunited? How sweet. The last I heard, you were still selling your ass for treats, *dog*."

"That is the nicest rumor I've heard floating around about me," Dima says, slapping a hand over his chest in gratitude. "Now, your plan sounds marvelous and all, but I'm afraid Maxim and I have a previous arrangement regarding the girl. *I've* claimed a moment with her first, you see. Your wayward son will have to find another way to crawl back into Anatoli's good graces. *Adieu*—"

"Oh?" Danil laughs. "And you'll just wave your pretty little hands and make us leave?" He glances at the men around him. "I've heard you were a crazy son of a bitch, but you can at least count?" He aims his weapon at Dima's head. "You were always a sniveling rat, but Maxi here? I've heard the stories. Any other day I wouldn't dare come to you without an army at my back. But the rumors were right. A woman has made you soft, and I can assure you that Bruno —as well as the rest of us—will surely enjoy fucking her. And then there's Anatoli… I'm sure he'll take what's left, eh boys?"

The men around him laugh, voicing suggestions that churn my stomach.

But the loudest laughter of them all spills out like music and comes from none other than Dima. "Come now, Danil," he says. "You may be the most useless of Anatoli's pawns, but even you must see it?" He gestures around us. "The girl is the only reason you are still standing where you are. Were Maxim any other man, I'd assume he wanted to spare her the trauma. As it stands, I think he's merely biding his time to inflict the most…impact." He brushes his fingers over his heart a second time, his head bowed. Then he raises his hand and cuts the air in a sharp motion. "I, however, have no such qualms."

Maxim grabs my chin, forcing my face against his chest. "Close your eyes," he growls.

It's too late.

Blood goes flying, and Danil falls over, his limbs splayed in unnatural directions. A heartbeat later, his son slumps over as well.

I breathe in, resisting the instinct flooding my veins. I don't scream. I don't go numb. I inhale the salt-tinged air, and when I pull away from Maxim, I don't cringe from the violence at my feet.

I take it all in. Every grisly, horrible fucking bit.

"You can go now," Dima says, dismissing the remaining men with a wave. They continue to raise their weapons, eyeing each other warily. "Quickly, before I change my mind and have my snipers take out the rest of you. And don't even consider firing a single bullet."

The men exchange another round of wary glances. Then, all at once, they turn and pile into the black van. Seconds later, it takes off, its wheels skidding in their haste.

As the vehicle lumbers out of view, Maxim advances a step toward Dima. "Give me one reason why I shouldn't kill you."

"This was fun," Dima exclaims, utterly unconcerned by the other man's nearness. "We should do this again. I mean, who knew sibling bonding could be such a rush—"

"How did you know?" Maxim demands, his throat cording. "I had ten fucking men on the perimeter. Danil and his shitheads had no hope of getting through."

"Yes," Dima concedes with a thoughtful nod. "That is, if Danil didn't happen to bribe the airport manager into calling in the Feds on suspicion that your plane might be smuggling drugs from a foreign country. A smart move. Too smart. I believe his son came up with it, given the plot of one of his rather amusing video games. Have no fear, I was able to defuse that nasty situation, though it allowed Danil enough time to sneak past your defenses—"

"So, you come to the rescue?" Maxim spits at his feet. "Bullshit. Why? And why not warn Jacob if you were so fucking smart?" He nods to the slain driver.

"Hmm..." Dima slips his hands into the pockets of his jeans and shrugs. The simple gesture makes him look even younger than he already appears. A boy in grown-up clothing—but his eyes portray anything but innocence. "I'm afraid that poor Jacob had to be sacrificed for the sake of research. Call it a hunch."

Maxim snatches my wrist and nearly drags me to the car he moves so quickly. "Talk in riddles if you fucking want to. You have five seconds to get out of my sight before I have you killed. Thank Milton for that shred of mercy—"

"You've killed in front of her before, haven't you?" Dima wonders as Maxim wrenches open the door to the back seat of the car. It's covered in blood, and he hisses, wiping his hand on his jacket. Then he slams the door shut and fumbles for the front passenger-side door.

"You were afraid to kill in front of her again. You hesitated, I saw it," Dima insists. "You had every chance to call your snipers to take out Danil, but you *hesitated*." Awe colors his voice as if that simple fact is the most fascinating discovery. "Were you going to wait until the bastard was right on you before you reacted? By then, she certainly would be scarred for life, considering his brains would be in her lap. And you trust him around your child?" His attention turns to me, his lips quirked in an amused grin. "There is so much we must discuss when we finally have our talk—"

"You will never even touch her," Maxim swears. "Now get the fuck out of my sight."

"Why do you even want to talk to me?" I'm surprised that the steady, level voice is mine.

"Why?" Dima raises an eyebrow as if perplexed by the question. "To learn you, of course. The woman who fucks a beast apparently in the hopes that he may one day become a house pet. You fascinate me more than the concept of

Maxim seeing a woman outside of the role of a warm, wet hole. Yes, we must discuss!"

He laughs as I turn away from him, my face on fire.

"Oh, yes. Though I have been waiting patiently, haven't I, little Maxi?"

Maxim says nothing. Finally, he gets the door to the car open and shoves me inside it. Then he storms to the other end and claims the driver's seat while I fumble for my seatbelt.

"Goodbye for now," Dima calls as Maxim slams the car door. Muffled, his voice still manages to seep inside. "I'll be waiting for your call. I am anticipating our meeting more than ever, Francesca—"

Maxim slams on the gas, sending the car lurching forward and leaving Dima behind. At the same time, he snatches a cell phone from his pocket. He must speak to more than one person, switching from English to bellowed words of Russian before he finally tosses the phone aside.

"Are you alright?" he asks me.

No. I think I'm dazed. In shock, maybe. My brain seems delayed, processing everything in comically innocent terms. Like how, as we approach the city limits, Maxim completes his transition from budding "domestic" into a calculating mafia boss. I observe him, noting the shift in his posture and the subtle tensing of his jaw. But before any real doubt can set in, he grabs my hand and places it on his lap.

"Talk to me."

I flinch, recognizing my own words mirrored back to me.

"I…" Tears spill from my eyes before I can hold them back —but I'm not afraid. I'm too tired for that. Too exhausted. All I can do is squeeze his fingers, conveying a million things I can't say out loud.

When the car finally skids to a stop, I'm surprised that we're at, of all places, the penthouse he'd brought me to before we left Fair Haven. In silence, he escorts me from the car and up to the suite. It looks exactly how we left it, but it's a stark contrast to the warm, open beach house and its brighter décor.

I miss it—more than I thought I would. More than the other houses and mansions we've left behind. I miss the man I discovered there, sampling ice cream beneath the hot sun.

I miss the begrudging smile of content he'd tried to suppress after relinquishing control on the balcony. And how he had comforted Daisy and went out of his way to provide the others with what they wanted. What they needed.

A part of me despairs at the memories—we might never get those moments back. That peace. That…normalcy.

A different man entirely, Maxim drags me into the bathroom of the master suite and strips me naked before shoving a washcloth into my hands. He leaves, and when minutes creep by without him returning, I manage to wash mechanically and dress in a thin nightgown and a robe.

The murmur of distant voices creeps into the silence, coming from the front of the suite. Still oddly numb, I wander into the main hall and follow it out to the foyer.

There, my dreamlike haze shatters. I'm in a nightmare now.

Two demons star in it, dominating opposite ends of the foyer like the living incarnations of light and shadow. A violent, gleaming gold, Maxim takes up one corner, while a glowering Milton claims another, clothed in black from head to toe.

"How many more times do I need to tell you to end this? Letting Danil off his leash was a direct message to you. You *know* that," he warns. "For fuck sake, end this. Before even Dima gets bored of this game and decides he'll have more fun watching your livelihood destroyed by Anatoli than trying to make amends with you—"

"Stop pretending like you give a damn about me, or my fucking 'livelihood,'" Maxim bellows, his chest heaving, his hands balled into fists. "Otherwise, you would be the one to grow bored with this game. Bored of humoring Dima. For years, I've let you play the role of the so-called peacemaker. But what fucking use are you now?" He looks around mockingly and scoffs. "You manage our investments, only to withhold them when it suits you just to placate your childhood pet. You put your women and your interests above mine. And now you pretend as though I'm the one abandoning you? Why don't we call in the other investor, then? If I need so many allies? The truth is, you were never *my* ally, were you?"

"You fucking *idiot*," Milton hisses, his upper lip curling in disgust. "Don't talk shit. You're so blinded by fear and hate that you can't hear how bloody ridiculous you sound. You know what…" Tearing his fingers through his dark hair, he lets out a deep breath. "Fine. I'm done. You want to pretend as if it's you against the world? Even after everything we've been through? After everything I've done for you. Be my fucking guest. You accuse me of putting my life above yours, even though I'm the one risking my life every day for *you*. Well, maybe it's about time I did, for once. Go for it, *Max*. Knock yourself out."

He turns and storms from the front door of the suite. He's still visible within the hall when Maxim calls after him. "Don't tell me you're leaving little Dima to my mercy, Milton?"

"Dima?" Milton cocks his head and laughs coldly, the sound more unsettling than any I've ever heard. "Dima can handle himself. It was never *him* I was protecting when it came to the two of you. You're just too damn stubborn to see that."

He presses forward, vanishing into the shadows.

Roaring, Maxim pivots and slams his fists into a nearby end table. It shatters in a violent display of glittering glass. He stands alone in the aftermath, surrounded by countless jagged shards. Blood drips down his left forearm, originating from a gash sliced into the flesh, but he doesn't even seem to notice.

"I'm sending you back," he declares, spotting me standing at the mouth of the hall. "I need to handle this without any fucking distractions. Fuck Milton. Dima can play his little games. I won't let him win. I won't let him get inside your fucking head—"

"Maxim, s-stop." I exhale the plea, but he breaks off, his throat cording. Swallowing hard, I weigh my next words. This is a true Russian Roulette. To pull the trigger, or run away? "I don't think you spook easily," I add, my voice rasping. "So, something had to happen to make you change your mind…"

He cocks his head, his eyes flashing. "I don't want to hurt you," he rasps, as if the words are being ripped from his throat. "I *don't*."

But he has. He's left marks on me that will never truly heal, and I don't think I'll ever fully be able to suppress the lingering fear from that. At the same time, he's done so much for me…

So much it's pushed him to the fucking breaking point.

"You won't hurt me." This time I think I actually believe it. Reaching for him, I take a hesitant step, and he nearly jumps out of his skin in his rush to maintain the distance between us. His blood paints the floor with every step, coloring the monochromatic world of his own making.

"Go," he snarls, and my body shivers in recognition of that deep, resonating tone. He's beyond even the past now. He's trapped within his fucking head, and only God knows what he's seeing.

"Talk to me," I plead, inching another step forward.

"Talk?" He scoffs. "I'll talk. I'll talk about the fact that Anatoli is toying with me. Attacking my business like one would spank a naughty child. The bastard thinks he can *summon* me—" He breaks off, and the tension coiled within his body reveals just how much that simple command is affecting him. "Like I'm still a boy beneath his boot. Should I talk about that? Or I can talk about the fact that Milton has turned his back on me. And I can talk about Vadim, always having the last fucking laugh—"

"Tell me about him." I take another step, narrowly avoiding a streak of blood. God, the wound looks even worse the closer I come. Carefully, I strip my robe and wad the fabric in my fist.

"Vadim?" He laughs again more darkly, his eyes still fixated on a world I can't see. "I was four, I believe, when we first met. My mother must have upset my father more than usual. That day he left and reappeared with another child. *His* child, nearly my age. 'You think that since you have my heir, you are untouchable?' he asked her. 'Well, I have plenty of spare bastards to take my pick from.' He kept Vadim around after that, parading him before us periodically just to prove his point."

"That's awful…" Horror constricts my throat as I finally come close enough to him to risk brushing my fingers along his injured arm. He stiffens, unmoving. Cautiously, I peel back the sleeve of his shirt and wrap my robe around the worst of the wound.

"He should have looked smug then, Dima," Maxim continues, oblivious to the pain. "He wore rags, dragged into a home worth more than his whore of a mother could ever make on her back. In that moment, he had a taste of the mantle of being the heir and what it meant. He should have fucking smirked..." He sways, and I brace my hand over his chest, but my strength is no match for his bulk.

"Come with me." I glance over my shoulder and spot a nearby chaise. Gingerly I lead him toward it, still coaxing him, "What happened next?"

"I killed our father," he croaks, but rather than sit, he goes rigid, scowling beyond this room. Beyond me. "His mother died of some disease. Together, we were sent to Anatoli."

Uttering that one name drains the humanity from him. A darkness falls over his expression, and a stranger appears in his place—someone so cold and emotionless he could be formed from stone.

"I knew what awaited us the second we entered those fucking walls. *Hell*—" He balls his hands into fists, and my heart skips. An instinctive need to back away takes hold, but the second I withdraw, he staggers away from me, still speaking. "I knew. Dima... He didn't. That first night, Anatoli broke my ribs in retaliation for what I did to his son —" He flattens his palm against his chest in remembrance of that pain. "I didn't cry. But Dima? The old man didn't lay a fucking finger on him, and he wailed anyway. He never had what it took—and I couldn't forgive him for that. For weakness…"

He takes another step, teetering dangerously to one side. It's as if he's drunk off the rage, blinded to his own senses.

Renewed concern for him outweighs any fear for myself. I approach him again, keeping my voice as soft as I can. "Maxim…"

He recoils, as if his first instinct is to resist my touch. A heartbeat later, his hand captures mine, pinning it to his chest. When I lead him toward the leather chaise, he collapses onto the edge of it. His arm is still bleeding, and I race to apply more pressure, all while still stroking him. Speaking to him.

Keeping him here.

"*He* was weak," he tells me. "I had Anatoli's favor. I was his preferred heir. Everyone knew it. But Dima… He called the old bastard evil to his face once, can you fucking believe it?"

He laughs, partly amused, partly incredulous.

"I don't know why they didn't kill him then and there. Perhaps it was more fun to toy with him. He sniveled when they beat him. Cried when they whipped him. Cut him. Starved him. Did worse. But he never fought for his place. Not really. And when he looked at me, it wasn't in fear. He knew what failure meant. And yet, Vadim? He always looked at me with…fucking *pity*." His body vibrates with disgust at that word, mirroring his anger whenever he seems to sense it in me. "Can you believe that? As though I was the weak one. When I survived. I won. I took what I was owed and never looked back. I need no one's pity."

"Tell me what happened after."

"Anatoli grew bored," he adds, deflating. "He declared that only one of us would become the true heir, if we were willing to fight for it. The loser would go to Sevastyn…" He inhales sharply, and I press my hand to his cheek before that unsettling shadow can consume him again. With gentle pressure, I make him look at me.

"I'm here," I whisper. "You're with me. You're not there." He blinks, his expression blank, but I maintain the contact anyway. "Talk to me."

"He should have won." His gaze refocuses, fixating on mine. Hints of him return, peeking from behind the dark irises. The more I stroke him, the more of him I see. A man so confused the frustration haunts him. Poisons him.

It's tormenting him.

"He should have." Voice rasping, he insists, "The bastard should have fucking won. He wasn't stronger, but he was faster. Smarter. He could handle a blade better than anyone. He should have won."

I don't say anything. I can't. All I can do is stroke his jaw and staunch the bleeding from his arm, utilizing patience I never knew I had.

Gradually, his nostrils flare, and his expression regains some semblance of definition.

"There it is," he accuses in a surprisingly hollow tone. "*Your* pity. Worse than his in so many ways…"

"No." I shake my head and lean forward, resting my forehead against his chest. "It's not pity. It's never pity. Never…"

He doesn't argue. He's not here fully yet, but his breathing eases, and when I attempt to stand, he tightens his grip as if to pull me back.

"You're covered in blood." I take his hand and tug him to his feet. "Come with me."

Despite everything, I'm shocked when he lets me take him into the bathroom. He sits in the tub, watching skeptically as I gather supplies. I strip him slowly and then wash him inch by inch. When I finally reach his head, he pulls me in, kissing me deeply. The rest of my clothing comes off easily beneath his touch, but he doesn't settle me over his cock.

His hands find my waist instead, his chest meeting mine. He sinks his fingers reverently into my hair while pressing his lips to my collar, right above my breast. "You… Life was never a mystery to me. I knew what I wanted. Money. Power. Control. I took all of it. But never could I imagine you… I won't lose you. But…"

A raw, pained expression contorts his features, triggering an instinctive alarm in the pit of my soul. I've never seen him like this. In agony, but the physical wound isn't the cause—and I don't think he'll ever truly heal from it.

"Dima was right," he croaks. "Can I give you what you need? I don't know. You are young. You will want children —do not deny it. You *will*. And... In my world, children are met with strictness. Violence. What happened to Vadim and me is typical—they are beaten into submission and traded like chattel. And you will not understand, but this did not bother me. It is all I know, and therefore I made a choice. No children of my own."

His voice is a monotone hum devoid of emotion. I don't even think he's talking to me anymore—not really. This is for him—a confession of the things he can't express, even in the dark room.

But he's not alone, forced to use whips and knives to express the pain he won't ever admit to out loud. Silently, I brace my hands over his chest, reinforcing my presence.

I'm here.

"I expected no different," he adds. "Even with your siblings. I knew I would have to restrain myself from beating them if I was to keep you near. I was prepared to. But..." He frowns, and the expression breaks my heart into a million fucking pieces. He looks more confused than ever. So lost—a boy trapped in his memories with no way out. "I didn't. I didn't want to harm them. Not once. I didn't want to beat them down for insolence. I felt no urge to hurt your sister when she defied you. Your brother does not deserve to be whipped for daring to question me. And the youngest..." His voice breaks, hollow and hoarse. "I couldn't imagine hurting her.

Selling her. If Dima threatened her that day, I would have killed him."

I believe it. He practically levitates with repressed emotion. Brushing my lips along his shoulder is the only way to ease the tension from him again.

"I've never considered being a father," he tells me. It is honesty delivered as efficiently as one of the blows from his whip. Devastating in its aim. "But now? You think I struggle with this life. I *let* you believe that—" He tiredly meets my gaze, and all I see reflected in his dark eyes is a man pushed to his breaking point, exhausted beyond belief. "The truth is that…I feel clearer, the more I'm with you. With them. At the same fucking time, I feel like I'm losing myself. The man I've been for so damn long." He eyes his hands warily and then lets them fall into the water. "If you leave…who will I be in the aftermath?"

"You," I whisper against his skin, curling myself against him. I take one of his hands and thread our fingers together. "This is *you*. You don't have to suppress your past with me."

"I don't?" He laughs, but the sound trickles from him as a sigh more than anything. I look up to find him observing our clasped hands. "Dima is a different breed of monster from me, but he is right. You will never be safe in my world. Trying to convince you otherwise was a lie—"

"I like your world," I interject, my voice small. "Not your grandfather's fucked-up empire, or the twisted games, or the lies. *Your* world. A beach house with rules we decided on. Lazy days and vanilla sex, with kink at night. That world."

His expression shifts, and I choke out a startled laugh. He looks comically skeptical, an eyebrow raised. "I will have to fight to give you that world."

"I know. Which is why you need to let me help you." I weigh the danger of pushing him too far. But hell, that's the only game to play with him. Reckless, Russian Roulette. "If it will make a difference like Milton said, then let me talk to Dima—"

He makes a low sound in his throat. "I will grant you anything... But I will pretend you didn't request *that*."

"You need his help," I say, parroting Milton's insistence. "I don't want to come between you and your friend. And..." A part of me shies from voicing more, but I don't have a choice. It's the truth. "If he hurts me, I know you'll kill him."

"And if he toys with your head?" he counters, tightening his grip on my hand. "Plants devious, vicious lies? He is a snake."

"That's why you need to trust me. Like I trust you."

Trust. The line of his mouth softens at the sound of that word, but in the same damn breath, his nostrils flare. "No—"

"Maybe I can help you find the truth?" I suggest, trying a different line of attack. "Learn what he really wants? It's been bothering you, don't tell me it hasn't."

"The *truth* is, he wants to destroy what I have. He couldn't take the Koslov name, so he'll take you from me."

"And I won't let him."

His brows furrow as if the idea of my free will never factored into his thinking.

"You gave me a choice before," I add, recalling how he questioned me in front of Milton and Dima. "Or was that for show?"

Sighing, he repositions me so that I straddle him. It's a devious ploy only a true game master would enact to regain control. His hands feel huge against my hips, cradling me with a gentleness he rarely utilizes. Our foreheads meet, and his teeth tease my lower lip, dissolving my will to argue with every sensual nip.

"I trust you," he confesses as my thoughts start to scatter. "My kitten who can be so affectionate when she chooses, sucking me off for all of the world to see. And ice cold the next, lashing out with her claws. But I will never trust Dima."

Thinking fast, I slip my tongue between his lips, stealing his taste. He groans in shock, his nails grazing my flesh. As the upper hand shifts in my favor, I'm bold enough to propose, "What if we trade?"

A frown tugs on his mouth—he's suspicious. "I am curious as to why you are so determined in this instance. Vadim seems to catch your interest more than marrying me."

"I want to help you," I confess, brushing off the uncharacteristic note in his voice. Jealousy? In silent reassurance, I press my lips against his skin over and over. With each affectionate kiss, his breathing quickens, and the balance of power teeters again in my direction. "I only want to help you."

Can he really not see the toll this is taking on him? Though hell, he doesn't even seem to feel the wound on his arm. I swipe my thumb near it in sympathy. A normal man would be rushing to the emergency room, demanding stitches.

"You think I need helping?" he wonders.

"Maybe we both do? I want a future with you." I sound so damn tired, and I am. This is my last-ditch ploy to win this round—and not for Dima's sake or anyone else's but my own. And his. For him, I have no shame in resorting to selfish begging. Maybe later, I'll let myself examine what that might mean.

"I do," I repeat against his collar bone, cutting my brain off to any thoughts but this. "I'm willing to fight you for it, and if I'm wrong. I'm wrong. We've been through worse. So what do you say? At least consider a trade?"

"I will think about this." His lips find mine before I can argue, silencing me with a kiss so deep my head reels when he pulls away. Robbing me of any chance to recover, he rocks beneath me, settling between my legs. Before I can even steel myself, he's thrusting in deep, groaning at the feel.

"In the meantime, we will trade in this way," he grates through gritted teeth.

A thrust for a thrust. Pleasure for pleasure. A kiss for a kiss. All of it is currency we're both squirreling away for leverage later.

So is the way of the game.

CHAPTER SIXTEEN

Hell doesn't contain an ounce of fire. It's just so fucking cold. Wet. There's red everywhere. Painting the walls, sloshing over the floor, flooding the air with the scent of salt.

It's blood.

Screaming, I try to swim as the level rises higher by the second—an ocean of violence, washing me away.

And I'm drowning in it...

"It's alright," a heavy voice drips into my ear, persistent over my cries. Patiently, the owner coaxes me back to a reality of silken sheets and a darkened room. "You're safe. Wake up. Look at me, Francesca."

For a twisted, painful few seconds, all I can do is struggle to breathe as I take stock of my limbs. I'm drenched—but the liquid isn't blood, just sweat. I'm not in hell either. A nearby window displays a view of Fair Haven bathed in darkness, illuminated with accents of neon.

"You were dreaming," Maxim murmurs, brushing his lips over my forehead with a rare gentleness. He's beside me, his heat like an anchor, giving me strength against the tidal wave of fear threatening to swamp my thoughts. All those memories…

It's getting harder to ignore them. Harder to keep them at bay.

I saw yet another man die in front of me. More than one.

Sooner or later, I'll have to face that fully. I can't hide from the horror forever.

"Sleep," Maxim insists as if reading my mind. He eases his fingers into my hair, parting the sweat-soaked strands. "What happened changes nothing. You'll meet with the realtor in the morning—"

"What if your family tries to attack you again?" I'm shaking at the thought of it, and more terrifying worries sneak into my brain. The constant danger. The crippling paranoia. It will always be like this with him. Always. "What if—"

"I will ensure you have a team of security on you at all times," he says, raising his voice to gently overpower mine. He sounds different, though I can't name how. *Exhausted?* As if what happened in the tub drained parts of him away. His cold baritone resonates warmer than usual as a result, and it sinks into my bones, easing my fear. "As you said, I do not spook easily," he adds. "So sleep. If you trust me as you claimed to, then trust me now. No one will ever harm you again." His eyes scan my face intently, hunting for any sign of doubt. When I finally start to drift off, he sighs, relieved. "I'm here…"

HE'S GONE before I wake up. The mass of sheets twisted around my body reveals that he didn't lay beside me for very long. Just enough to soothe me back to sleep before rising again. Then I suspect he paced until dawn before the windows, mulling over the prospect of his kingdom in peril.

A gray dawn bathes said kingdom, and the room itself, in a soft, neutral glow now. It's such a jarring contrast to the chaos of last night, but I know better than to enjoy it for very long. Instead, I rise from the bed and stretch to wake up my sore limbs. After grabbing a clean dress from the closet, I shower alone and leave the bedroom to find a plate of lukewarm food waiting for me on the dining room table, along with a note.

I will be gone until tonight. The realtor has a list of my preferences. I insist upon them all. — Maxim.

My lips twitch as I fold the note and set it aside. I don't know whether to laugh at the rare attempt at a joke on his part, or…

Shiver. I suspect his "preferences" go far beyond a request for a particular architecture style or double sinks. The more I stress over what he could want, the more I start to second guess going out alone at all.

But intuition warns against the panic. Trust goes both ways. If I want him to include me in his life, I can't attach myself to him forever. I can't always kneel in his shadow.

I need to make a place for myself and determine my own rules as to what I'll allow within it.

So I eat, and when the realtor comes, I'm ready. Hours later, we've explored every fucking mansion within a twenty-mile radius, and some of my previous confidence starts to wane.

Who knew that a "family home" was a foreign concept in this city? Sure, there are plenty of spacious mansions like the few Maxim's shoved my family into before. They look beautiful, with plenty of space and "curb appeal," according to the realtor.

But none of them seem…real. Stable. Like a *home*, not that I'm a fucking expert on those. Even with money being no obstacle, I can't bring myself to sign off on any of the sprawling, lifeless structures I tour with Jonathan, an Italian man who peppers nearly every sentence with architectural terms.

"As you can see, this atrium will provide your family maximum privacy while allowing in some sunlight and the allusion of the outdoors." He beams at the plastic-looking trees and flowers cramped within the narrow space in the center of the last home on the list.

Suffice to say, it's a no.

I'm exhausted when I finally return to the suite. I've spent my entire life in the slums, and yet a day touring fancy homes worth millions has somehow left me feeling filthier than I ever did in Horn Hill. Disgusted, I strip my clothing right at the door and head straight for the bathroom. When I finally emerge from the shower wearing a robe, I discover that someone is already in the bedroom, ripping a suit from his muscular limbs.

"You found nothing," he says without looking in my direction. Am I surprised that he's kept tabs on my progress?

Maybe not.

"No." I awkwardly fiddle with the strings of my robe as he continues to strip, tugging at his shirt next. "Nothing really stood out to me…"

"It's a house," he points out gruffly. "What needs to stand out?"

I bite my lower lip. He has a point. What does a house need?

"Safety?" I ask, thinking out loud. "Someplace that Ainsley can play in, and Daisy can sulk, and Mikie can have his own room for once. A home."

"Hmph." He pauses, his shirt still clenched in his fist as if the concept is as foreign to him as it is to me. Then he snatches a clean one from a hanger and wrenches it on over his head. "I've added more men to the team on you. Lucius is still with your siblings, but I will need time to ensure the security of the new home before they can return. As long as it's secure, I'm sure any place will suffice rather than have their return delayed."

Which makes his week deadline more pressing than ever.

"Are you leaving?" I wonder as he swiftly buttons his shirt and straightens the collar.

"Yes. I've been busy strengthening my security overall," he adds while stripping his pants in exchange for a fresh pair. "Restructuring my assets. Letting Danil confront me at all was a mistake on Anatoli's part." His grim expression reinforces the guttural edge to his voice. "A mistake he will not make again."

Once fully dressed, he marches to the doorway. Only then does he seem to remember my presence enough to add, "I won't be back tonight. Tomas can bring you dinner—"

"Wait." I reach out, brushing my hand over his shoulder. He falters, but doesn't fully stop, rocking back and forth on his heels with barely suppressed impatience. "Is something wrong?"

"No." Without warning, he captures my chin, kissing me hard with an intensity that leaves me clinging to him. Up this close, I can sense the unease bubbling beneath the surface of the stern façade he's crafted beneath the fresh suit and aloof gaze. His lips linger over mine until he finally pulls back.

"I've made up my mind," he says, his voice cold. Final. "I won't let you near Dima. There is nothing worth trading for that risk. Nothing."

I watch him go in a daze, too stunned to argue.

At least he was honest. The man can offer me the world, but there is nothing I possess he deems worth having. Nothing apart from complete possession.

Even the prospect of us living together doesn't seem to appeal to him beyond the surface practicality of it. What he said won't stop taunting me, echoing in my brain on repeat. *"What needs to stand out? It's a house."*

Maybe he's right.

Or maybe…he is capable of viewing it from just one angle. It's not the house itself that matters but what it symbolizes. This cold, isolated penthouse reflects the many aspects of him he's clung to. What's helped him survive in his world for so long. Few personal belongings. A bed he rarely sleeps in. Furniture picked solely for its functionality.

Lucius had a point, but I think I misinterpreted his original warning. You can free the wolf from its captivity, but if all it knows are iron bars, the forest doesn't seem like home anymore.

But no real family can survive within the confines of a cage.

The only way to bridge the gap is to find a compromise. Learn what bait might tempt a wolf…

Enough for him to forget he was ever a prisoner at all.

CHAPTER SEVENTEEN

The next morning, I wake up to the realtor, Jonathan, knocking on the door of the suite. When I open the door, hastily dressed, I find him flanked by two armed members of my expanded security detail. One is Tomas, who nods stiffly in greeting.

"Mr. Koslov strongly suggested we close on a property soon," Jonathan says while tugging nervously at his purple tie with one hand and juggling a briefcase in the other. Crossing to a—newly replaced—end table, he fishes a stack of documents from his bag and shuffles through them. "I believe you'll love a series of homes in the exclusive Knight Heights district—"

"I think I want to look at some places near the water," I suggest, cutting him off.

It's the one feature that separates Fair Haven from most other shitholes in the country—a bay on the outskirts, which serves as both a focal point for what little tourism there is, as well as the main reason why it's such a hotbed for crime in the first place.

We're open to the world in a way that leaves it ripe for the taking by men like Maxim.

Jonathan's brows furrow. "The bay? An interesting choice." His skeptical tone betrays his true thoughts on that front. "I will admit that location holds a more *rustic* charm. You won't come anywhere near to the elegance of say, this property here—" He gestures around us, referring to the penthouse. "Though, I suppose you could always renovate…"

On that optimistic note, we take a car staffed by one of Maxim's drivers. Within an hour, we're pulling up to the first property to fit my preferences. My initial impression is that Jonathan was right. These homes are nothing like the highly modern mansions we toured in and around the city. They look older, like something you'd see in one of those small-town dramas. Still huge and impressive, but in a less obvious way.

The place a mob boss might live, only when retired or under witness protection.

The one we approach now is sprawling, made of sturdy brown wood, and supported by stone accents. Positioned on a hill, it overlooks a quiet, semi-private section of the bay, complete with a rocky beach and a wooden dock.

Inside, the mixture of stone and wooden architecture continue, creating an open, simple layout centered around three large windows overlooking the water.

"There are ten bedrooms in total," Jonathan remarks. "Plenty of acreage if you're into outdoor activities, and there is a pool in addition to a private section of the waterfront. Basic amenities, but they possess a certain charm, I suppose."

I crane my neck back to take in the high, vaulted ceilings above a living room dominated by a stone fireplace. The beautiful, "rustic" design will amplify every single sound the kids make. When Ainsley and Eric fight, it will resonate with the intensity of an army skirmish. Daisy's whining will echo times a million during one of her rants.

And Maxim's voice alone will have no trouble filling the space, reaching every inch of it.

"Ms. Marconi?" Jonathan wonders, an eyebrow raised. "Are you ready to move on?"

"No." I sigh, turning my attention to the view of the water beyond the windows. It's no tropical paradise, that's for damn sure. Shitty Fair Haven can't compare to endless blue waters. But in some ways…

This is so much better.

Turning to Jonathan, I square my chin. "I'll take it."

MAXIM WASN'T LYING about his ability to purchase a home within days. All Jonathan seems to require from me is simple confirmation. Afterward, he devolves into a flurry of phone calls and shuffling paperwork. Before seeing me off, he presses a folder into my hands. "Oh, Mr. Koslov requested I give you this once you'd settled on a property. Tomorrow, I'll connect you with an interior designer to get the furnishing process underway."

My heart pounds ominously as I tuck the folder beneath my arm and enter a car driven by Tomas. It isn't until we're nearly in the city that I finally gather the nerve to open the folder and observe the documents within.

I scan the first line, expecting an explicit, detailed list of sex toys. Instead, I find a series of names with a sentence or two scribbled beside them, denoting that particular person's requests. All of it is written in Maxim's handwriting, with curt phrases implying that he personally interviewed every member listed.

Ainsley – Pink walls. A playroom. A pony. Please, a pony? I don't need a room, just that!

Daisy – My own space. Seriously. MINE. Please. Yellow. A deck to tan.

Mikie – Blue. An arcade. (he's rich enough, right?) A boat.

Ollie – Bunk bed. A pinball machine. A skateboard ramp.

Ray – A video game room. A bed shaped like a pirate ship.

Eric – A room made of LEGO.

Tears well within my eyes and spill out before I can blink them back. They distort the ink on the page, making the words blur and run together. At the very end of the list, its author made sure to denote—*I will attend to my own personal requirements in time.*

He could do this for me, while having the confidence to claim that nothing I could offer him would ever be enough to make him bend where it really matters. His psyche. His security. *His* peace.

That wall will always remain between us—literally. Only in some dark room, deep in the night, can he ever face the trauma shaping him. And he will always choose to face it alone.

"Are you alright, Miss?" Tomas wonders from the driver's seat. Alarm deepens his tone as he reaches for his pocket, presumably for a cell phone. "Did you change your mind about the house? If you are not satisfied, I'm sure Mr. Koslov will—"

"No," I croak, waving him off. "I'm fine. It's just…"

I look down, surprised to find my fingers interlaced, the nails digging in. I'd been pinching myself without realizing it. I've already broken the skin—a bead of blood bubbles from the tiny wound, and my eyes fixate on the color.

Red. That fucking hue dominates my life now, a reminder of the violence that comes with Maxim Koslov. The insanity. The death. The rage.

If I ever did marry him, there is no way in hell I could ever wear white. Just this goddamn color that's come to drench our lives.

Red.

"Ms. Marconi?" Tomas inquires, sounding more alarmed.

"I want you to take me somewhere," I say, wiping at my eyes with the sleeve of my coat. "I don't want you to ask for Maxim's permission either. I don't want him to know where I am. If you don't know the address, Lucius will—"

"Do you understand what you are asking?" Tomas wonders, his voice soft.

I'm asking for him to risk pissing off an employer who isn't like any other. But I'm learning that it takes more than desperation to win a game. It requires a reckless willingness to gamble.

Everything.

"Please," I insist. "I need to do this alone."

"Miss…" I can visibly see him wrestle with the dilemma of informing Maxim or deferring to me. The second directive, must outweigh the first. At least in this instance.

"As you wish," he concedes with a sigh. "Though if you are in any danger, I will be forced to inform Mr. Koslov immediately. And I will only be able to maintain silence for a few hours, at the most. You understand."

"I won't be in any danger," I admit. "Though I'm afraid that you'll probably be incredibly bored."

Not for the first time, I face my reflection and barely recognize the woman staring back. Yards of silken fabric spill from her slender body, conveying a cruel, twisted imitation of the perfect, beautiful creation most girls spend their entire lives envisioning.

In my case, the concept is more abstract than that of a beautiful gown fit for a princess, or a symbolic representation of what should be the best day of my life.

This dress is a promise, conveyed in glaring, contrasting shades of white and bloody red.

This is the life I'm willing to sign up for. The trade, I'm finally able to make—a harmony of violence and security. Death and life. Blood and the purity left behind once it's all washed away.

Looking at myself now, I realize that this is the only gown befitting of someone insane enough to marry Maxim Koslov.

"I must admit the overall effect is stunning," the designer exclaims as she races around me, pinning various pieces of fabric in place. "I do adore the original, more traditional concept. But traditions were made to be…adapted." She adjusts the scarlet bodice that hugs my torso before flaring out into a wide, billowing skirt. The base is every bit the beautiful dress Maxim first envisioned. But as the viewer's eye rises, swaths of scarlet intermingle with the ivory, consuming the gown entirely by the level of my chest.

I don't look wide-eyed and innocent in this design. I look like I'm bleeding from my heart, drenched in the color I've come to dread. In some ways, it's beautiful. In others, it's fucking terrifying.

But I'm tired of hiding from it.

"I can finish the alterations in a few days," the designer says while continuing to make more adjustments. "I think the color is lovely, but if you wanted to add a deeper red here —" She breaks off, gasping as a monstrous thud resonates from the entrance of the boutique—the door slamming hard enough to rattle the fragile glass.

His expression like thunder, the culprit storms in, his dark eyes flashing as they find me. "I've been looking everywhere for you," he growls, brandishing a clenched fist at Tomas, who stands alert beside a rack of clothing. "You order *my* men to hide you from me? I had to have fucking Lucius—" He breaks off as he finally takes in my appearance. "I…"

His mouth opens and closes wordlessly. Then he blinks and rakes a trembling hand through his hair. In the end, all he seems capable of doing is staring. His gaze traces the contours of my dress, tracking the blend of color and the bold shape. It's impossible to tell what he's thinking from here.

Rather than dwell on it, I face him with my head held high, my shoulders back. "How is this for a trade?"

He swallows hard, his throat rasping until he finally manages to spit out a handful of words. "I…I'll be in the car."

He turns and leaves the boutique, decidedly quieter than the way he entered.

It's nearly an hour before the seamstress manages to carefully dissect the gown, preserving the construction.

When I finally join Maxim out front, he's in the driver's seat and doesn't say a word as I claim the space beside him. He doesn't even look at me, turning his full attention to the road. Rather than the penthouse, I'm surprised when we arrive before Club XXX minutes later, just as night is beginning to fall.

Maxim climbs out and marches inside almost too quickly for me to keep up. Before I can fall behind, he grabs my wrist, dragging me down the hall to his secluded room in the back.

After stumbling over the threshold, he shoves me against the wall. The cold surface braces me as his bulk crushes me from the front.

"Fuck," he breathes, as his fingers bunch up my skirt and find the wetness already slicking my inner thighs underneath. He wastes no time, testing me with the width of his thumb.

When he flicks his wrist, nothing is preventing him from going deeper on the second explorative touch. Further than he meant to, judging from his raspy grunt. His free hand crawls up my spine, cinching my neck, forcing me to meet his gaze.

"Say it," he growls, grinding his pelvis against my hips. "You'll marry me?"

I suck in air through my teeth and release it in a single word. "Yes…"

"In that dress." He lowers his mouth to my throat, inhaling me. "You will wear my ring?"

My eyelids flutter at the intensity of his voice. "Y-Yes."

"And you'll take my name, even if it means nothing?"

"Yes."

He groans, cursing under his breath. "You truly were made for me." A crime in his book—and my punishment comes swiftly—his lips dominating mine, nipping teeth giving way for a tongue that batters me open and overtakes any resistance I may have felt. With the club full, someone might be able to hear us, even from here.

And when he finally wrenches up the skirt of my dress and plunges inside of me, anyone within a goddamn ten-mile radius probably hears me.

Hears him. His guttural roars echo every mewling cry to spill from my throat. Together, the sounds meld into a blistering crescendo—the only thing I can hear as my world comes apart.

I come clinging to him with all I have, my limbs shaking and ghosted with sweat. "Holy…fuck," I breath out against his skin.

"I'm going to fuck you in that dress," he swears as his hands cup my ass, lifting me into his arms. With staggering steps, he brings me to the bed and climbs onto the mattress, pinning me beneath him. "Mark you in it," he adds, describing more of his X-rated wedding day. "Take pieces of the silk. Make a whip. I'll use it on your pretty skin until all of you is painted red…" His voice shakes with need, and he hardens against my thigh, rousing an answering twitch in my belly. "And the ring," he adds, sliding his hand down my trembling stomach to the space between my legs. I'm forced to buck my hips into him further, relishing the sinful contact. "The things I will do to you with that ring." He swipes the pad of a finger over my entrance, swirling the moisture already there. "But that is nothing compared to your name." He chuckles deeply, and my breathing hitches at the foreboding sound. "I'll train your sweet ass to react to it," he tells me, nuzzling his open mouth against my shoulder. Without warning, he bites down. Once. Twice. I'm too tired to scream. I just moan, weakly clutching his arms. "I'll make you come every time I fucking say it. *Francesca*…"

He bites off the rest and groans again, sounding pained. Starving. Mad. "I will be the only man who can call you his." His hand sinks into my hair, and he uses a chunk of it as a leash to draw me into him, letting our mouths meet. He isn't content with claiming just my lips. His mouth travels across my jaw and finds my ear as he shifts his hips against mine, drawing his erection between my legs. "And how I will own you."

"Own?" I counter, finding my voice again. "I thought this was a trade?"

"Trade… Yes." He nuzzles my throat as if addicted to the taste of me. I doubt he's actually processed what I've said. He finds my nipple and captures it between his teeth through my dress, making my back arch off the mattress.

"A t-trade," I insist, sinking my fingers through his hair. I stroke through the damp strands until he finally faces me again. "Do you accept my terms?"

Rather than annoyed, his eyes glow, heavy-lidded with lust. A low hum revs in his throat, deepening the more I touch him. Could this be victory?

"My kitten," he grates, sounding pained. "She drives a hard bargain. Regardless, I accept the terms, but can you accept *mine*?"

He gives me a taste, entering me again. I'm sore and breathless from the first time—but my body gives me no say. It yields to him, dragging him deep. So deep that I forget what it feels like to ever go without him.

In the aftermath, he holds me tight, crushing my body to his chest. His hands stroke through my hair as if memorizing every strand.

"I want you in my dress," he admits. "My ring. You've made a tempting offer. So I'll take it. And in return…you get to play your dangerous little game."

"Dima?" I say, dread thickening my voice.

"Is that what you truly want?" His skeptical tone resonates cold in the wake of his lust—but his fingers absently stroke my hips, countering any real anger.

"I want to help you," I reply. "I wasn't lying when I asked you for a partnership." I press myself against him, sensing how his body relents to me as if in defiance of his stubborn frown. "I want your trust."

He grunts and parts his lips over my shoulder as if a mouthful of my flesh is the only thing worthy of silencing him. A jolt runs through me as he bites down, conveying his agreement.

He'll let me talk to Dima.

But as he rolls over and drags me to his side, I can't resist wondering who got the better bargain out of this trade.

CHAPTER EIGHTEEN

After we dress, Maxim makes a single phone call. To Milton, I presume. Their conversation passes quickly, surprisingly devoid of a shouted argument.

"It will happen here," Maxim announces once he hangs up. "Soon. Before I come to my senses and change my fucking mind. Come." He takes my hand, and we return to the main club, finding it empty.

In our absence, someone rearranged the furniture, leaving a single table in the center of the room, set with two chairs.

"He has an hour," Maxim warns as he leads me to one of the chairs and holds it out for me. "One fucking hour. He can't touch. And I have my men watching…" He hesitates, as if he wants to say more. Demand I reconsider, maybe? In the end, he retreats, presumably returning to his private room. "I won't be far," he calls back to me. "Him, I do not trust. But you? I trust that you can handle him. And

I trust that if you feel that you cannot, you will call for me…"

I shiver beneath the weight of his newfound confidence. Do I deserve it? I won't know for sure until the time comes when I'll have to pull the trigger in this ultimate game of roulette.

It isn't long before I sense the entire atmosphere in the building shift with the arrival of my opponent. Dima. For him to arrive so quickly…I can't escape the feeling that he knew well in advance this moment would come. Maybe not the exact time or day—but with enough certainty to stick around closely, awaiting Maxim's summons.

Oozing confidence, he strolls into the club dressed in a gray sweatshirt, with a red beanie crushing his curls to his skull. When he spots me, he flashes a grin, wiggling his fingers.

"I'm impressed," he exclaims, taking the chair across from me. "Very impressed. I'd assumed it would be at least a few months before Maxim would break down enough to humor my little request."

I fight to keep control of my expression. Do I smile and aim for politeness? Or do I copy Maxim's inherent hostility?

I mull over both options only to settle on neither. Something warns me Dima would see through the act either way.

So all I do is ask, "You were willing to wait that long just to talk to me?"

He smiles. "Oh, no. By then, Anatoli would have already beaten his favorite boy back into submission. I would be speaking to you through the iron bars of your cage after the old man tired of you and Maxim had already moved on to another pretty fool."

A shiver runs through me, constricting my throat. So much for uncertainty as to how to treat him—I'm starting to agree with Maxim. This is pointless, humoring a psychopath whose main goal only seems to be sowing chaos.

But I'm the idiot who decided to play the game. All I can do is see this round through to the end.

"So, what do you want?" I ask, making my tone as neutral as I can.

"Let's not waste time discussing such boring matters!" He snaps his fingers, beckoning a waitress who appears from nowhere with a bottle of wine. Her hand shakes as she sets two glasses onto the table and fills them to the brim. I try to meet her gaze, but she avoids me and scurries back down the hall the second Dima dismisses her. I watch her go—she isn't heading toward where I assume the kitchen to be.

Will she report to Maxim that I'm unscathed so far?

"Ah, dear Maxim has supplied us with the absolute best," Dima exclaims, drawing my attention back to him. He lifts a glass and hands it to me.

"Thank you," I say while setting it aside without taking a sip. "So why did you want to talk to me?"

"This is a marvelous establishment," Dima admits, eyeing our surroundings with an approving nod. "Such a unique atmosphere."

One he obviously doesn't feel comfortable within. It's warm enough inside that I feel fine, even in my short-sleeved dress. He, on the other hand, seems to sink into his sweatshirt, and a slight tremor in his jaw draws my notice. He's shivering.

"Are you okay?"

"I'm fine. Just cold," he says offhandedly. "Nothing abnormal. I am always cold. My therapist tells me that it's partly psychosomatic. All in my head," he explains, tapping his skull with his finger. "Mostly, it is due to medical reasons. Alas, you could stick me in the middle of a raging inferno, and it would never be warm enough. Anyway, as for why I am here?" He shrugs and shifts to face me directly. "I must admit you fascinate me."

"Why?" I counter, unnerved by the way his eyes flicker across my face as if missing nothing. Not my unease. Not a single fucking pimple.

He chuckles, eyeing his own glass. "You think you're special to him, don't you? You think you're the only woman to tempt him. The only woman to soften him. The only one..." He lifts his gaze to mine. "And you would be right. He's been through women the way most men change out socks. Rarely the same one twice. None of them have lived with him. None of them have desired to. But have you stopped to ask yourself why?"

"No," I lie. "But why does it matter to you?"

"Why?" His eyes widen in disbelief. "Maybe it's because Maxim doesn't love. He's incapable of it, as am I. We are similar in this, you see—and I came to that realization years ago. Living within that family has damaged us both. Even Milton, to an extent. While *they* may have forgotten that, alas, it can't be helped." He shakes his head, sending his curls bouncing beneath the rim of his beanie. His smile doesn't disguise the glimmer of darkness lurking beneath the cheerful expression. He's angry. *They have forgotten…*

"Perhaps I seek to warn you?" he adds.

I hate how confident he sounds. Smug. As if I'm an idiot he's decided to take pity on and inform that the sky is indeed *blue.*

"Warn me?" I say, forcing myself to stay focused. "About what?"

"Or maybe I seek to test him?" His lip quirks, transforming his expression from concerned to playful. He peeks toward the hall, where Maxim presumably is, and lets loose a wistful sigh. "He's stewing now, you do realize? Wondering what lies I'm telling you. What secrets I'll let slip about him. He's always been a jealous boy, too possessive for his own good. That is why he could never father children, you see. He would only ever see them as competition—"

"Just get to the point," I snap, losing my neutral tone.

His words sneak into my brain long after he's gone silent, sowing seeds of doubt that blossom into full-on panic.

Could there come a day when I'll have to choose between my family and Maxim...

No. I shake my head, picturing the way he acted at the beach house. He's already proven the steps he'll go to in order to avoid that very situation—I can't deny that the effort pushed him to the breaking point.

"The point?" Dima sits back and sips from his wine glass. "Maybe Maxim and his love life are the least of my concern? My motives may be more selfish in nature."

"You just want to taunt him, then?" I deduce, pushing back from the table. Irritation prickles my skin. I'm such a fucking idiot, falling for his trap. "You just want to play with him for entertainment like Milton said."

"Yes." He nods thoughtfully. "Or closure. According to my therapist, I will never be truly happy unless I close old doors, so to speak. He's a bit of an old fuddy, duddy. He claims that I must discover what's been bothering poor Dima since he was a wee, little lad and finally slay that monster."

I stiffen in horror, still perched on the edge of my seat. "You want to kill him?"

"Maxim?" He frowns. "No. Where would the fun in that be? I *want* something from him, though. I want... acknowledgment. I want him to admit that he is as weak and as human as the rest of us. That he is a violent, broken, damaged fool, as am I. To pretend otherwise is simply unproductive. Having him say as much might do wonders for my psyche. His too."

"By toying with him?" I croak. Dima is still smiling, but the vitriol in his words stings deeper than it should. Perhaps because Maxim all but confessed the same thing? "Why do you feel like he can't change?"

"Because I cannot," he says simply. "I've tried. It's no fun. No family for poor Dima. No woman to ply with some ring. I've chosen against pretending it's even a possibility."

His lips part in a beautiful, chilling smile. "Therefore, I've decided my dear brother should realize the same before he hurts you in more ways than by using a whip."

I cringe, but he beams in triumph. "It isn't my place to kink shame," he adds. "Maxim's been known to dabble in masochism for a long while. Though who am I to judge? I have my own…quirks."

He waits as if daring me to ask him more. When I don't, his smile widens, baring all of his white, perfectly straight teeth.

"I don't prefer to tie up my women, but I do enjoy the odd mind game or two. Convincing some poor, desperate bachelorette that I may be the answer to her financial dreams—only to watch her run in disgust the more I put her desperation to the test. Love is relative, you see. A little humiliation here. Some deception there. You find out quickly what price some might put on their so-called happy ending."

I can't disguise my disgust this time. "That sounds insane—"

"Insane, yes." He forms a steeple with his fingers and perches his chin on top of it. "Because I am. *Clinically,* though I assume you were being a tad dramatic in your assumption. The old man had us both rigorously tested, you see. And I was tested yet again when I was separated from my brother and sold to...let's call it a 'boarding school.'"

I nearly choke. Maxim put it a different way. *The loser would go to Sevastyn,* he said. *Sevastyn,* the pedophile who gained influence through corruption. The same man Milton despised for equally murky reasons.

"So he *has* told you something," Dima suspects with a knowing grin. "Maxim is a very smart man. In fact, he possesses above-average intelligence, though he goes out of his way to disguise the full extent. Milton, now he is just a tad smarter. But me?" He waggles his eyebrows. "My intelligence was deemed immeasurable *twice.* My sanity, equally confounding. Depending on who you ask, I am afflicted by a long list of ailments and disorders. Asperger's. Dissociative identity disorder. Antisocial personality disorder. Generalized anxiety. Paranoia. Post-traumatic stress. Attachment disorder. It goes on and on..."

He gestures with a bored flick of his wrist, and I nearly contemplate surrender. My fingers grip the sides of my chair, rooting me in place. Fear of Maxim's potential reaction is the only reason why I don't lurch to my feet and head straight down the hall.

Yet.

"So yes, I am insane," Dima continues, oblivious to my discomfort. "Though I wouldn't take it as an insult. In fact, I'm grateful for my many quirks. They've kept me humble, you see. In touch with my feelings." He extends his slender arms and hugs himself. "But as I work through my many… hang-ups, I was forced to confront the reality that there are some things in my past I must address. Even if the other parties involved may not be inclined to revisit such memories. I need to bury them once and for all."

The violent phrasing draws my interest enough for me to question, "Like?"

"*Like,* did Maxim tell you about the day he tried to kill me?" He tugs at the collar of his sweatshirt, revealing his scar. For the shock value of it, I realize. He wants me to jump in disgust at the raised, ropey strip of flesh.

But I don't.

"Yes." Does that surprise him? I can't tell. His amused grin doesn't reveal an answer either way.

"Let me guess. He told you some sob story about how I ruined his perfect, innocent childhood via our father's ruthless need to assert his authority? He told you that I was a weak, worthless rodent always scurrying underfoot? And I'm sure he boasted about taking a knife to my throat as well. So typical."

I school my expression to match his—hopefully unreadable.

"He did." Unconvinced, Dima leans forward, his eyes sparkling. "Do you want to hear the truth? The *truth* is that, one day, a stranger barged into the bordello where my mother worked and lived—she was a prostitute, you see—and he dragged me out by my hair. I'd never seen him before in my life, mind you. Still, he took me to a strange house, full of strangers who looked at me like I was nothing. Then he said I was his son." He wiggles his fingers, his eyes comically wide. "Quite the surprise, you see. But my newfound brother, didn't take the news too well. Not long after our meeting, he attacked me. Punched me in front of our father, who egged him on in approval. Always the showoff, he made a spectacle of it, dear Maxim. He knocked me down. Fractured my cheek—" he points to his left eye. "He spit on me. Told me I was a rat, unworthy of living. *Blah, blah, blah.* Given my previous life circumstances, those words were nothing new to me. But..."

He frowns, eyeing his hands, and a rare real emotion slips through his façade. Confusion. His slim fingers grasp at the air as if trying to capture the memory and dissect it properly.

"You know what was new? Later that night, I realized that he had slipped something into my pockets without me realizing it. Do you want to know what I found? It was the oddest, strangest thing..."

My brain shies from the dare. What kind of object could make him look so conflicted? Nothing good, and I'm not afraid to admit it. "No—"

"Socks," he says simply before I can fully voice a refusal. "A single, scarlet pair. Hand-knitted by his mother, I suspect—she was the crafty sort. They were worn enough that I knew they had to be his. Possibly his favorites. He'd noticed that I had none of my own, you see—" He points to his ankles. "There was also a piece of candy hidden inside one—extravagant chocolate he must have stolen from our father's private collection. The bastard was quite the glutton..." He chuckles only to trail off, his lips pursed. "But do you want to know a secret? That was the first time anyone had ever given me anything. I couldn't wrap my mind around the concept. A present? Such a mythical thing! When I saw him again, Maxim, I looked for any hint of that kindness, but alas, I found nothing. He continued to beat me. Berate me. I thought, perhaps I'd imagined it? But no." He frowns more deeply, stroking his chin. "I continued to find small, tiny things shoved into my clothing. Combs. Toys. Food..."

His gaze turns distant, and for the first time, I see a hint of similarity between the two brothers. They both express confusion in the same terrifying way. Via anger at whatever dared challenge their understanding.

"It went on until we both were sent directly to Anatoli. I won't get into the details of that time." He waves a hand as if dismissing the horror away. "Eventually the day came when the old man demanded we fight to the death with the gusto of some ancient Roman emperor. Maxim agreed with no hesitation, of course. No fear. But I was bored of that life." He shrugs. "I was tired. I didn't care. That time was so...unstimulating. I was ready to die. I made it so easy for him—and death, you see, is one aspect of life the Koslovs fear more than anything. It's for the animals, in their view. Animals are slaughtered, not men. How to kill is one of the first things you learn in that fucking family. Maxim had already done it before, of course. It should have been nothing. But…" He frowns and picks up the bottle of wine. "More? Oh, you've not taken a sip." Laughing, he takes my glass in addition to his and alternates sipping from both. "Where was I? Oh yes. Killing me should have been nothing. If anything, it would have been too easy. Anatoli demanded it, and the first, most important rule of being a Koslov, is to never disobey. And Maxim, like a good boy, dug his knife into my throat. But…he failed to do it."

Failed. That's not the word I would use to describe the scar snaking down the column of his neck. "He still hurt you," I point out hoarsely.

Dima laughs. "Hurt me? Even a child knows which direction you cut a throat in." He drags his fingers across his own, perpendicular to his scar. "Maxim didn't spare my life by some fluke or pathetic mistake. He went *out of his way* to. I just want to know why. Is that so wrong?" With mock sadness, he bows his head and sighs. "I want to know why my brother spared me, and yet shuns me. Why he despises me enough to ignore my very existence for twenty years, and at the same time, never once, *ever*, attacks me directly. Even when I get bored enough to play with his little toys or disrupt his supply lines. He can use Milton as an excuse all he wants, but the man isn't stupid —" He extends his hand to me as if demanding the answer. "I want to know why he's decided to challenge his nature, especially now. Perhaps the first thing isn't all a mystery, though? To acknowledge me is to acknowledge that he was never really a Koslov. He failed the first test, after all. But I admit that lately, my curiosity has been piqued—because although he refuses to acknowledge any hint of kindness extended toward me, he seems more than eager to claim some young, average prostitute as his wife. No offense."

I stiffen. Am I even insulted? I don't know.

Laughing, Dima continues, "And I know one must be patient when it comes to these things. Milton—I mean, my therapist—" He winks. "He claims that '*you cannot rush him, Dima. He is not like you. You push him too far and… poof!*" He mimes his head exploding with wiggling fingers. "'*Be patient. One day he will reach out to you. Give it time, time, time!*" He rolls his eyes while mimicking Milton's accent. "The man babies him to an extent. Though I suppose it can't be helped. He's kept the promise he made to me, at least. For twenty years, he's kept that promise…"

Rather than ask what he means, I take my time putting the pieces of his verbal puzzle together. Then, it comes to me. "You asked him to be Maxim's friend?"

It sounds so strange when said out loud. Grown men with a twisted web intertwining them, all of it cemented in friendship.

"Maxim is a delicate soul, pretty girl," Dima says with a tired sigh. "He would have been eaten alive without Milton's…let's call it independence. I had hoped the man would convince him to finally break from Anatoli. But it seems that nothing can cut that bond. Even you." He flicks his gaze in my direction just in time to catch my reaction.

Rather than take the bait, I sigh. "That doesn't hurt me."

"Perhaps. But that's why you're here, isn't it? You want me to help Maxi defeat the big bad wolf once and for all."

Is that why I'm here? My motives feel less relevant the longer this twisted conversation goes on. Despite all this time, I still don't know what *he* wants.

"How do I know you can even help him?"

"How?" Dima cackles, sloshing wine from his glass. He swipes at the drops with the sleeve of his sweatshirt, clearing them away. "You are very amusing! I'm beginning to see the appeal. Pretty girl, Anatoli will do anything to get his precious Maxi under his thumb once more. Why? He is his legacy. His good, loyal boy. Without Maxim, he has nothing but a loosely connected family tree of sycophants and grifters. Maxim is his crown. And the crown belongs to the king—no one else."

"But you can defeat him?"

He laughs again as if knowing some wonderful joke that I'll never even learn the punchline to. "Do you want to know the secret? Come close. Closer…" He beckons me with a wave of his hand. He waits until I finally sit forward before saying, "The only way for Maxim to ever defeat Anatoli is… to break the throne. Give up the name. Walk away. Anatoli will never touch him directly. In some ways, Maxim knows this. The old man certainly does."

"What do you mean?"

"Milton is a powerful man, pretty girl." He raises an eyebrow. "But the third member of his so-called club has even more influence. He is a *very* powerful, very rich man. The bastard has a lot of stock in pharmaceuticals, you see. He controls more money, property, and people than Anatoli can even dream of amassing. Maxim is his only firewall against total insignificance—and he needs his golden boy now more than ever. Even a Koslov can't live forever."

"How do you even know who the third member is if Maxim doesn't?"

He winks. "Let's say, I know a little about him. He's incredibly handsome. Highly intelligent. Very charming, though some might say…unassuming. And of the three, he has the most impeccable fashion sense—"

"You?" I blurt out.

"Little me?" Dima blinks innocently and places his hand over his heart. "As a child, I learned my place in this violent, dangerous game of money, and men. It's better not to play at all. That's the only way to win."

I exhale in frustration. Keeping up with him is damn near impossible, and I know now that it's futile to even try. "So all you want is Maxim to what? Accept you?"

"I *did*," he admits, his eyes downcast. "I wanted my tortured brother to take my hand and boldly step out into the light of freedom. Call it childish if you want. I call it progress—but I've changed my mind."

He props his hand beneath his chin and observes me more intently than ever. "I *like* you, Francesca. So now I want to help you. I want to help you learn the answer to the question you're too terrified to ask."

Alarm prickles through my nerves, warning me to back away. But I can't without conceding defeat—and his fucking grin proves that he knows it.

"And what is that?" I ask tiredly.

"Does he truly love you, Maxim? You love him, or will you deny it?" He smirks as if he'd like nothing more than for me to challenge him.

So I don't.

And the man practically bounces in his seat. "It's a good question, you agree? Not only that, but you want to know if he is even capable of love. If the day will ever come when he loses control again. When he kills you finally, or takes a knife to little Ainsley and hacks her to pieces on a sheet of plastic tarp—"

"S-Stop!" I brace my hands on the table, and it takes everything I have not to lurch to my feet. The memories of that night still haunt me, threatening to descend. Gritting my teeth and closing my eyes is the only way to keep them at bay. "How did you—"

"Milton doesn't spill Maxi's little secrets," Dima says. "But I have ways of learning what he knows. The messes he helps his friend clean up. The women he examines for him. The blood he has to wipe off his hands when Maxim makes yet another mistake…"

When I open my eyes again, he isn't smiling. "How can you even help me prove that?"

"Oh, I can. And I always pay my debts, pretty girl. But in this case, I will want something from you in exchange for such a favor."

"I don't want anything from you—"

"But you do," he insists. "You truly do. I know my brother far better than you. I have years of research to draw from, and I will tell you now that he is stubbornly resistant to change. Some might say incapable of it."

"Research," I echo, picking up on that particular word. "Like you were *researching* when you let Maxim's driver be killed in front of me?"

"Oh, Jacob?" He raises an eyebrow as if he'd completely forgotten about the incident already. "Jacob Marsten had a wife named Ilia, and a daughter named Mariah. And he had spent the better part of ten years, terrorizing the hell out of them. It was fun to him, you see. And with his skill set, he was incredibly good at finding their new home or apartment, no matter where they went. He liked to send Ilia love notes, detailing the many ways he would eventually reunite with her. Chilling stuff." He makes a show of shuddering. "So pardon me if I don't shed too many tears for the man."

I watch him warily. Is he telling the truth? I can't tell.

"Maxim didn't know any of this, of course," he adds, before the suspicion could even sneak into my thoughts. "He is very thorough in his hiring process, but my methods are a tad more unorthodox. So believe me when I say that I can get you the answer you want—and relatively soon. But as in Jacob's case, it may not lead to a pretty ending. Nonetheless, I will still insist upon my favor by the end, no matter the outcome."

"What favor?"

He stands abruptly and bows at his waist. "This was a marvelous, *marvelous* conversation. Better than I could have ever hoped. So much, so much better!" He claps gleefully. "But I must bid you *adieu*. Oh, and before I go, remember! You cannot repeat a word of what we discussed to dear Maxim, remember? That's the rule."

He scampers away, passing Tomas and another guard on his way out.

"Goodbye, Francesca!" he calls back from the end of the hall. "For now…"

CHAPTER NINETEEN

The second Dima leaves, Maxim appears by my side. "Come," he demands from behind me. By the time I stand and face his direction, he's already lumbering toward his private room, his steps slow and deliberate. As I cross the threshold in his wake, he keeps going until he's forced to brace his hands against the far wall, his back still to me.

"I know he told you lies," he hisses before I can say anything. "I know he fed you twisted ideas. But if I let his claims go unchallenged, I only have myself to blame. So here—" He points to the bed. On it is a silver folder, and the sight of it unnerves me almost as much as his rasping tone does. "Open it."

I approach the bed cautiously and stoop for the file. It's surprisingly heavy, and my heart skips as I peruse the documents within. I have no fucking clue what it might contain. Another contract? The deed to the house? Or something far more puzzling…

A frown tugs on my mouth as I scan the printed documents. They're phrased in legal terms, and considering I have yet to finish one semester of college, I can barely make sense of them. Some kind of declaration? It isn't until I read the last few lines that I finally register one crucial detail that makes my knees buckle in alarm.

His name.

It's printed wrong. A single X denotes his last name on every single page instead of Koslov, and I rub at my eyes, refusing to believe it.

Maxim X.

"I don't understand," I start to say. But then it clicks, and a wave of shock knocks me off balance. I sway, grasping at the mattress, my throat unbearably tight. My head swivels toward him so quickly my neck throbs in response. "You... You changed your name."

I struggle to say it. Given his feelings on being a Koslov, I can't believe it, either. Not until I see him. Still hunched against the wall, he stands with his spine bowed, exposed to any reaction I might have.

"You gave up your name for me?" I whisper.

"You were right." His accent sounds so heavy, as if each word is being ripped from the pit of his chest. "That name isn't fitting for a family. Admittedly, this one is just temporary. But I am willing to take on any one you want to claim what I am owed."

Me.

"W-Why?" I ask hoarsely. "I thought—"

"Do you refuse it?"

"No!" I lurch to my feet and stagger toward him. My fingers claw at his forearm until he pivots. Our eyes meet, and the emotion in his takes my breath away. They're wide, so dark they're fucking fathomless. I greedily hunt down whatever emotions they might reveal, but he turns away, averting his gaze.

"Don't…" I'm begging. I'm too desperate to care. "Look at me. Please."

Sighing, he stiffens, and I take his jaw between my fingers, making him face me.

"Dima said the name Koslov was a creed," he admits, fisting his fingers through my hair, holding me captive in return. "And he was right. If I gave you that name, you would never be safe—and not from Anatoli or his fucking bastard pawns. But from me. You would never be safe from *me*. If I lost control, I could always blame it on that fucking creed. I have already, haven't I?"

He stares down at his hands in remembrance of the damage they can inflict on a whim.

"By hiding behind that name, I could lie to you and claim that it was all I knew." The line of his jaw tightens as he captures my waist, dragging me against him. Near my ear, he confesses, "Even before I saw you in that dress… I knew what needed to be done. What I needed to sacrifice to keep you. I've done it."

"But what about your grandfather?" I ask as my brain restarts, running through every potential danger his name change might enhance. *Anatoli. Dima. The future.* There are so fucking many. "What about—"

"I can't think about him." He grips my chin, guiding me to look up at him. Dark and hollow, his eyes bore into mine, going deeper than ever before. In some ways, it feels like he's ripping me open more intimately than he could with a whip or during sex.

"And I don't need Dima to come to my rescue either," he snaps. "Whatever happens, I will face it... But I will need you to do one last thing for me."

"Anything." My brain is still struggling to process the gravity of what he's done. I'm numb with shock, barely aware of what I'm saying. "I'll do anything."

His nostrils flare at the intensity of the promise. I've never seen him so fucking charged. Raw power emanates from him, putting any previous authority he commanded to shame.

"Anything?" I tremble in anticipation at the hunger thickening his tone. He'll put that word to the test later, I'm sure. But now? He smooths his fingers along my jaw, tracing every divot and curve in my skin. "I need you to play in one last game for me."

"What?"

"I want you to pick another dress." He runs his fingers along my spine, and cups my lower back, snatching me to his chest. I grasp his shoulders, forced to stand on tiptoe. The added height brings my forehead near his mouth, and his lips find my temple. "Not as yourself, or even for me— but as the kitten who dug her claws into me. Wearing it, I want you to stand by my side, no matter the outcome. Can you do that?"

I don't have to ask him for clarification this time. An ominous thrill shoots through my entire body as I grip him tighter in agreement.

We both know the final round that awaits at the end of this game.

The one in which he'll finally declare checkmate.

Or submit to utter defeat.

WE SPEND the night in the club, sharing the bed that feels more broken-in than those in any of his other dwellings. In some moments, a sliver of space separates us. Other times, I regain consciousness in his arms, cocooned by his scent. By the time morning comes, I stir to find Maxim already dressed, pacing at the foot of the bed, a cell phone held to his ear.

"I'm ready," he murmurs into the receiver. "With or without him… Only way. Be ready when I call."

He hangs up and spots me from over his shoulder, his expression obscured by shadow. "Tomas will take you to the suite," he tells me. "I'll meet you there. There is one thing I have to do first."

He doesn't say what. In silence, he picks up my discarded dress instead and helps me into it. When he leads me through the club, it's empty, bathed in darkness. Tomas is already waiting at the entrance, a car parked in the driveway behind him.

Before I leave, Maxim takes my hand, drawing me close. His lips find my temple, lingering for a second before he pulls away.

I watch him reenter the club alone, curious as to what task might be on his mind now.

A part of me warns that I'll soon find out.

For better or for worse.

CHAPTER TWENTY

The first time I came to this place in Maxim's shadow, I wore the clothing of a doll—the twin to the black velvet ensemble he originally intended for me to wear to this meeting. The simple dress had obscured my shape, its primary purpose being to convey the ownership of the man beside me.

Nothing less, nothing more.

Now, a swath of red silk boldly displays the shape of my body while leaving little to the imagination. Cut dangerously short, it's something the old Francesca might have pined over from the window of a boutique she could only dream of shopping in. The kind of outfit I would have assumed was far too good for me back then. Too classy. Too bold.

Maxim wanted me to choose a dress fit for his kitten. For whatever reason, *this* ensemble fits that bill.

In approval, Maxim's fingers trace my lower back, exploring

every contour exposed by the tight fabric. Even he looks different as we exit the car, flanked by his security. Instead of a suit, he wears a loose-fitting white shirt and black slacks that enhance his bulk more than a jacket and tie ever could. It's a stark contrast to the professional attire of his guards as they draw up behind him.

To my surprise, he waves them off. "Stay here."

Tomas and his partner share a questioning look but remain near the car rather than follow. "As you wish, sir. His guards weren't expecting us," Tomas adds, glancing at a security booth guarding the entrance to the property. "If you wanted to come unannounced, I would assume you have a minute or two before they alert him. They knew better than to deny you entrance outright, at least."

"Be ready," Maxim warns as he cranes his neck, observing our destination. Before us looms a sprawling mansion in Black Briar Hills—a part of the city reserved for politicians, or those with enough money to buy them. It towers above, casting a shadow that diminishes even the sun fighting through a layer of morning cloud cover.

And I can't lie and pretend that I'm not fucking trembling inside, fighting back the memories of my first visit. This is the place where I experienced the cruelty of Maxim's family firsthand—and my first introduction to his uncle Sevastyn.

"Are *you* ready?" Maxim wonders as if reading my mind. He captures my hand, lacing our fingers together.

Am I? Something won't let me answer. Instead, I feed off the strength in his touch and shift my focus to him. The more I take in the rigid set of his jaw, the more I suspect the question wasn't directed at me. Is *he* ready?

The determined tilt of his head gives me a clue. So does the cold, hard intensity of his gaze. Gone is that unnerving distance.

He's more than ready.

"Come." He pulls me forward, and this time, we don't wait for a timid maid to open the door. He barges inside and heads to the heart of the house, every step bold and assured. It's as dark within as I remember, adorned with a chilling décor devoid of any warmth.

But Anatoli isn't in his study today.

Instead—as if smelling him out like a predator—Maxim drags me past that room and into another, wider space. A long dining table dominates the center of it. At its head sits an older man with white-blond hair. In one hand, he brandishes a knife while a maid sets a plate of steaming food before him.

Spotting Maxim, the woman jumps spilling food onto the table's polished surface. "M-Mr. Koslov—"

"Leave," Maxim tells her as he advances. To his grandfather, he inclines his head. "You've summoned me, so here I am."

"Maximov?" Red spots appear over Anatoli's cheeks as he snaps his fingers. At the silent command, his maid struggles to scrape up the fallen bits of egg and bacon with her bare hands. She fails, and after another pointed look from Maxim, she scurries from the room, leaving the mess behind.

Anatoli scowls, barely noticing her absence. "You dare come here unannounced—"

"I'm not here on your behalf," Maxim says over him. To my shock, he bows his head in reverence, and the air sticks in my lungs. I back up instinctively, ripping my hand from his. *It was a trap all along,* Dima's disembodied voice taunts me. *Did you really believe he would choose you?*

But as Maxim draws himself back to his full height, his gaze is honed, radiating the intensity of a creature who is anything but a pawn. Snippets of his past still strangle his expression like shackles, but I can sense the effort it takes for him to resist their pull.

And he does.

"I am here for your blessing," he says. "As well as to offer my condolences on the loss of Sevastyn."

"Loss?" His grandfather echoes, his black eyes emotionless. Watching him, I realize that he has no clue as to the fate of his son. "Explain."

"I apologize for not making myself clearer to you before," Maxim adds. "But now, there can be no mistake..." He reaches into his pocket and tosses a small, metal object onto the table. It bounces over the polished wood, nearly landing onto Anatoli's plate.

Frowning, the older man snatches it in his fist, holding it to the light. Slowly, recognition dawns over his features, and shock rapidly displaces the disgust.

"It is Sevastyn's, yes," Maxim confirms, and I finally recognize the object for what it is. A ring. Silver and ornate, he must have taken it from his uncle's body. If I squint, I swear I can see remnants of scarlet dried over the gleaming surface. "I return it to you, along with a warning. I am no longer yours to command."

"And if I don't grant you such a foolish request?" Anatoli counters.

Something cold and cruel slips into Maxim's gaze. My breathing stalls. Thoughts sputter into incoherence. There is nothing more beautiful than anger on him. And nothing more fucking terrifying.

"I do not think you want a war, Grandfather," he warns.

"War?" Anatoli scoffs and leans back into his chair. "You sound like *him*. The failed mutt. Is he the one who put this idea in your head?" He bares his teeth, but a muscle in his jaw trembles. He sputters, and a series of heaving coughs render him gasping, gripping the arms of his seat for balance. "Did you come to mock me too?" he wonders breathlessly. "I'm sure he's told you already. I don't know how the little bastard learned of it—" Another cough rips from his chest that he struggles to smother into the sleeve of his tailored jacket. "He made sure to send his condolences. But Maximov, I never took you as one to gloat."

Eyes narrowed, Maxim examines his grandfather, from the worn lines around his mouth, to his pale, papery skin, and the ragged sound of his breathing, audible from here. His upper lip quirks the more he assesses the man who tormented him for years, now barely able to sit upright unassisted.

"You're dying," he says finally. Awe colors his tone, mingled with disbelief. "Is that why you've been so desperate to bring me to heel? You truly have no one else—"

"And you would walk away?" Anatoli spits back. "No. I know you, *boy*. I saw it from the first fucking day you came to me, sniveling and weak. You crave the safety of power. You were always desperate for it. That is what set you apart from the rotten chaff. Am I to believe you'll just walk away?" He chuckles, eyeing Maxim from head to toe with raw, open malice. "No. You were never that foolish. And if you did forsake your name, it would never be for the sake of some whore. The fact that you brought her proves my point." He scoffs and waves his hand dismissively. "Leave. When I send for you, you come. Alone—"

"Did you not hear me?" Maxim interjects, but his tone is softer. Something in his expression changes the longer he eyes the man across from him. The anger fades, and resignation sets in, hardening the set of his jaw. "I'm no longer yours to command. Keep your bounty if you want. None of your pawns have been able to claim it anyway—"

"And yet you bring her here," Anatoli points out, his grin smug, his accent thick. "Why else if not to prove where your real loyalties lie? I could always call in another one of my men to deal with her, as Sevastyn did—"

"Why is she here?" Maxim echoes. He extends his hand toward me. I don't hesitate to take it, moving to stand by his side. "Because I don't fear you. Dima was right. You've lost your power. You're merely afraid of losing more. The Koslov name was only ever a leash to you—and you no longer have a grip on it."

His words eerily echo what Dima let slip during our supposedly private conversation. Had Maxim been listening in? Standing here now, I have no trouble deciding on an answer. Of course, he did—though I doubt he heard everything, or he'd be raising hell about Dima's revelation as the third X. No, like a true predator, he'd eavesdropped only long enough to glean what he felt like he needed to win.

Leverage.

"Is it money you want?" Anatoli chuckles. "You want to broaden your holdings? Fine. End this game, and you can have it."

"No." Maxim turns for the door, pulling me with him. "Send your peons after me again, and Dima's little games will be nothing in comparison to the hell I will bring down on you. Oh, and I'll ensure you receive your invitation to my wedding."

He barrels into the hall, tightening his grip on me. As I cross the threshold, I look back to find Anatoli still watching him, his expression unreadable.

"You will come back," he says. "A dog like you can't survive off of his leash for very long…"

Maxim stiffens, his steps faltering. His fingers clamp down over mine, nearly crushing them. Right as the pain builds, he relaxes his grip. More than that—it's like something drains from him all at once. Something dark and twisted that festered within him for so long. He sways, registering the loss of it, only to right his balance within the space of a heartbeat.

Slowly, his chin juts into the air as his posture straightens, stronger than ever. "Goodbye, Anatoli." He strolls down the hall without looking back.

"You'll come back," Anatoli insists. "You will…"

As we exit the house, his laughter chases us, interspersed with hacking coughs.

I watch Maxim as he hustles me into the car, scanning his features for any reaction. Surprisingly he looks…calm. Too calm.

"Is it done?" he asks Tomas, closing the door behind us.

The other man nods. "Mr. Hood is already on the line. He's managed to track down Danil's associates, as well as the bank containing Anatoli's American assets. All that's left is for you to say the word."

Maxim's lip quirks in a lethal smile. "Do it."

The car takes off down the driveway as Tomas speaks into the receiver of a cell phone withdrawn from his pocket.

"What's going on?" I ask, glancing between the two men. "What are you doing?"

"I'm breaking Anatoli's leash for good." Maxim takes my hand, tightening his grip so that I couldn't pull away even if I wanted to. "This visit was merely a formality," he explains, bringing my knuckles to his mouth. He swipes his lips reverently across them, raising goosebumps over the flesh. "I could declare open war, but with this method, I can diminish his influence with little bloodshed. He won't have the strength to attack me directly. Not now."

"How?" I ask.

"As we speak, Anatoli's remaining pawns are being dealt with, piece by piece. He'll have no choice but to leave the States. And in the process, he'll be leaving the city to *me*."

"It's done, sir," Tomas pitches in from the front seat. "Mr. Hood claims that everything is in place. It's only a matter of time."

"Good," Maxim says, inclining his head. "Now, we wait."

But it's not that simple. After being around him for this long, I'm able to suspect the truth in what he doesn't say. He may succeed in driving his grandfather from the country now, but in the process, he completely forsakes any ties to his family.

Does he regret that?

No, his expression warns. Not one fucking bit.

CHAPTER TWENTY-ONE

"They're on their way," Maxim murmurs against my forehead. Sunshine spills in through the wide bay windows beside us, enhancing every nuance of his face. Two days after his meeting with his grandfather, and I can't tell if he's bothered by what happened. Or if he's finally at peace with the possibility that Anatoli might be gone from his empire—for now. I want to assume it's the latter. The gleam lurking in his gaze reinforces that hope, anyway.

"Lucius called and estimated they'll arrive within ten minutes," he adds. "Though, I believe everything is already sufficient."

I frown, skeptical of that. Within a little under a week, I've realized the power that money can buy. In some ways, it's like magic. Back in my old house, buying something like a new couch or mattress was an ordeal that required scouring the stores for a cheap deal, finding nothing, and eventually having to fish out whatever we needed from the dump.

In Maxim's world, a house can be fully furnished in a matter of hours, complete with a fresh coat of paint. Jonathan's recommended designer certainly knew her shit. A few minor touches and modest furniture work to transform the "rustic" waterfront home into a world befitting the aloof style of Maxim—combined with enough nuances to make six kids feel comfortable dwelling in the same space.

Muted, soft grays and pops of navy create a cozy interior. The kids' rooms each contain their various preferences—though Ainsley's pony will have to wait, according to Maxim. A stable was one thing that he couldn't guarantee within a week.

I hadn't had the sense of mind to decide if he was serious or not. Getting every detail perfected consumed my focus. Why?

I have no fucking clue. Nothing in our old house inspired the same obsessive need in me before. I never went from room to room, hunting for a single piece of dust that might be out of place.

I never felt invested.

"They will love it," Maxim insists for the umpteenth time. His hands snake around my waist, drawing me against him. "I will still maintain a property in the city for business reasons, but this…" He exhales raggedly, and I think I sense a hint of something that could be…contentment? "I am impressed with this."

My heart swells up as I scan our surroundings, attempting to see whatever he is. A house untainted by blood or death. A view of the water with the city in the distance. A home, untouched by the Koslov name.

"Thank you," I whisper, finding his hands with my own. "Thank you—"

"You thank me for a house?" he wonders incredulously. "I will thank *you* for this."

He tugs aside the collar of his shirt, revealing his chest. It takes me a second to understand what he wants me to see— but when I do, I gasp. There, scrawled amid the scarred flesh is a series of inked lines spelling out a single name —*kotyonok*. Inflamed skin around the edges of the tattoo betray just how fresh it is. A day? Hours?

As I gape, he takes my hand and slips something cool and round onto my finger. I look down, unsurprised by the sight of his ring.

His lips brush my shoulder, imparting more than words could ever say. Slowly, his fingers creep along my collar, slipping beneath the thin fabric of my dress.

"Sir?"

We break apart and turn to find Tomas in the doorway. "They are arriving now, sir."

Nerves flutter to life in my stomach as I follow Maxim to the front door. Two black cars advance toward us slowly, and the second they come to a stop, the kids stream out, craning their necks to take in the house.

"Holy shit," Mikie exclaims, using his hand as a visor. "We could actually have a fucking boat!"

"Watch your mouth," I scold, though my voice must lack the authority it used to.

"Holy shit!" The twins share manic grins and then take off, tearing into the house.

"Wait for me!" Eric calls, racing to keep up.

A hand tugs on my skirt, and I look down to find Ainsley staring up at me, wide-eyed.

"There is no pony," Maxim says coldly.

She blinks in shock, her bottom lip trembling. Before a single tear can fall, he extends his hand.

"But would you like to see where he will live when it's completed? Come with me."

"Really?" She practically squeals as he leads her on a path across the expansive acreage surrounding the house itself. There, near the back with a view of the water, a team of builders have already erected the base of a stable and cordoned off the footprint with caution tape.

Ainsley peers over every inch with Maxim in tow, her eyes bug-wide. "Is my pony really going to live here?" she asks him repeatedly.

"Yes. One pony, or two. Perhaps more…" He meets my gaze from across the structure. "Whatever your sister allows, of course. Do you want to see where you'll be able to ride him?" He points to a section of land a few yards away.

"Okay!" Ainsley merrily skips off while Maxim returns to my side.

"This is one small feature I attended to," he says while tucking a loose curl behind my ear, "I hope you aren't too offended."

Am I? I can't tell. The sun is shining, painting the property in shades of emerald with a pop of silvery blue marked by the water. It truly is a beautiful place. A private stable may not have been in my original list of requirements, but I can't muster the energy to truly care.

"She doesn't even know how to ride, though," I admit. "She just wants a pony because every girl her age is genetically programmed to want one."

"Even you?" he wonders, his voice uncharacteristically soft. When I nod, a rare smile creeps into the corner of his mouth. "Then I will have to ensure the stable is big enough for more than one pony. As for the riding, I can teach her. I would like to teach her." He frowns as if that simple phrasing surprises him—namely the intensity with which he says it. The man with a tortured past, forced to ignore his humanity, wants to teach a little girl how to ride a horse. He wants to live in a house overlooking the water. More importantly, he wants to shed his name and finally become someone different.

Himself.

"It's getting late," Maxim murmurs. As he speaks, he entwines our fingers. "I'm eager to see what surprises *my* room might contain."

I shiver at the innuendo. It's the one room in the entire house that we've yet to tour. My cheeks burn as I look back at the field. "Ainsley?"

"She probably already ran to tell the others news of her impending pony," Maxim says. "You go. I'll look around just in case she went further up the path."

When I reenter the house, I find the others on the deck in the back, observing the view of the water.

"This place is perfect," Daisy murmurs as I draw up beside her. "As perfect as you can get outside of a private island, but…perfect."

"You always gotta quantify shit," Mikie taunts. "It's amazing, Frankie."

"Yeah, amazing," the twins chirp in unison before scurrying off.

I can't ignore my smile anymore. It strains the corners of my mouth, making them ache. I'm not used to the expression —painful happiness.

"Maybe this Maxim guy isn't all that bad," Mikie adds. "Eh, Daisy?"

She stiffens, her eyes darting to me and away again. "Yeah," she says softly. "Maybe. Frankie…" She faces me, her eyes downcast, her bottom lip skewered between her teeth. "I'm sorry for what I said. I didn't mean—"

"It's okay." In some ways, can I even blame her for being suspicious? After everything we've been through, I can't.

She smiles, her posture relaxing. It's only when I register the lack of a distinctive, girlish bit of laughter that I remember my task. "Where's Ainsley?"

Daisy frowns. "I don't know. Last I saw her, she was with you."

"She's probably upstairs screaming inside her new room," Mikie suggests.

But when I enter the house, I don't find her in any room. Not near the waterfront either. Or outside. When I head back out by the stable, Maxim is walking to meet me, but Ainsley isn't with him either. Something in my expression makes him stop short.

"She wasn't at the house?"

"No!" My throat thickens as I race past him. "Ainsley? Ainsley?"

"I'm sure she hasn't gotten far," Maxim insists. "She's probably just playing—" He breaks off, frowning. His hand dips into his pocket, withdrawing his cell phone. Whatever number he finds on the screen makes his eyes narrow.

"I'm going to look for her near the shore," I say, starting for the dock. "God, I just hope she didn't go near the—"

"Francesca..."

I look back to find Maxim watching me with the cell phone pressed against his ear. Slowly, he offers it to me, his expression stone.

"What's wrong? Is it Lucius?" I take the phone warily. "Does he know where—"

"Did you give her the phone?" a man wonders, his accent distinct. "Ah, you did! I can tell from her breathing. Hello, Francesca!"

"D-Dima?"

"Yes, yes!" He chuckles playfully. "I'm afraid little Ainsley won't be coming home anytime soon. Though do not fear, Maxim alone knows what must be done to ensure her return—if he cares to, that is. In the meantime...I will show her every courtesy my brother ever showed me. Every last one. And just to give you a taste—" He breaks off just as a loud, high-pitched scream resonates through the receiver. "*Adieu!*"

I don't even know what I do next. What I say. My only coherent recollection is just...screaming. And someone holding me so tightly it hurts, his voice a persistent, echoing bellow.

"We'll find her."

CHAPTER TWENTY-TWO

Somehow Maxim gets me inside without the other kids noticing me. I'm vaguely aware of Lucius ushering them to another part of the house as Maxim calls in his guards, questioning them one by one.

Though he shouts, his voice eventually fades to an unintelligible murmur that serves as background noise to my own panicked psyche.

How could I be so stupid, stupid, stupid?

So reckless?

Of all the coherent thoughts to cross my mind again, the first is that I was right—this house was designed to amplify Maxim's voice until the rafters shake with it.

"How the hell did he get past the security?" he bellows at Lucius. He stands in the center of the living room now, bathed in the glow of a hanging lamp. It's already dark out, revealing the passage of hours. Hours while Ainsley suffers God only knows what…

"How?" Maxim snarls. "I demand answers—"

"As do I, sir," Lucius insists. "Heads will roll, I can assure you. As for his current location, we are tracking a vehicle most likely to be—"

"What if he hurts her?" I barely recognize the sound of my own voice. I can't stop rocking back and forth as a million twisted images run through my brain, each new one more horrible than the last.

I will show her every courtesy my brother ever showed me.

I should be out there, hunting for her. Kicking down whatever door I can to find her. But the fact that Maxim *isn't* betrays a truth even he has enough tact not to say out loud—*we would never find her.*

"God, what if he hurts her?"

"I've never known Dima to act this way," someone says from the back of the room. I look up, finding Milton standing apart from the other two. I didn't even notice him come in. He isn't wearing a suit, but a black shirt and a pair of slacks, his gaze distant. He stands near the window overlooking the bay, blending into the darkness of the sky behind him. "But I do know he would *never* be capable of harming a child."

"Then you don't know him as well as you thought," Maxim growls. He crosses to me, brushing my cheek with the flat of his palm. I'm too numb to react to the touch. I can barely look at him at all. "Leave. I should have never asked you to come—"

"Possibly," Milton says, fingering his collar. For the first time, doubt clouds his features. Then they harden with resolve. "I'm here. Whatever you need, I'll get it done."

"Start with where he might be," Maxim demands. "You know his haunts. His hiding places."

"I have my men on it already," Milton admits. "But Dima isn't stupid. He knows that you'd come to me, and he knows where I'd look for him."

"So your insight is worthless, then," Maxim snaps, starting to pace. "You can't think of *anything*—"

"It's my fault," I croak. "I talked to him. I fell into his trap."

And he was right. I put an innocent girl in danger. For what?

A sick game, a part of me wails. *One you knew you could never win.*

"Enough," Maxim commands, cutting through the hopeless thoughts. "You pitied him, but that does not make you weak. Whatever he's done…we can face it. Don't give him what he wants by doubting yourself now."

"He's been…different, lately," Milton admits, frowning. "You don't speak to him regularly, Maxim, so you wouldn't have noticed, but he's been gone for a while. Over a year, I believe. It's not unusual for him to go off on his own for long periods, as I do, but…" His brows furrow. "It isn't like him to stay away that long. He kept his usual accounts though, always supplying regular contributions to the club. He only resurfaced in person a month ago, but we haven't discussed where he was."

"Contributions?" Maxim inquires. His eyes widen and narrow in quick succession as if a sudden realization came to him. "No. You don't mean—"

"That's something we can discuss another time," Milton says gently. Dima's secret as the third member of their partnership is apparently out in the open now. "When he returned, he seemed more interested than usual in your relationships. Mainly with Francesca."

Even in my daze, I marvel at the fact that he says my name for the first time. Not *woman*. Or *her*.

"And my relationship with Heidi—" the name of the "blond woman," Maxim mentioned, I assume. "Although my personal life has no relevance to this situation, Dima seemed more disturbed than I'm used to. He's not erratic. But, whatever is behind this, I suspect it's to prove an elaborate point."

"So, you still defend him?" Maxim demands. "Even now?"

"Defend him?" Milton says softly. "I *know* him. Just as I know you, and who did I come to first when I learned of this? I'm not in my office waiting for a call from Dima, I can tell you that."

"You're right." Something dampens Maxim's expression, and he sighs, raking his fingers through his hair. "We won't find him," he confesses, even as Lucius continues to make phone calls rapidly in the corner.

"You are sure that he gave no clue as to his motives?" Milton wonders. "None at all?"

"He said Maxim would know what to do," I whisper. I still hear him taunting me. I still hear Ainsley screaming…

"Is that true?" Milton turns to Maxim, an eyebrow raised. "Do you know what he could want?"

"No!" Maxim curls his hands into fists, and his gaze is so hopeless, that I know he's not lying. "I don't know what he could fucking want. I would give it to him if—" Suddenly he breaks off and sways. "That son of a bitch…"

I scan his face, desperate to follow his train of thought. Our gazes meet, and something in the set of his jaw has me lurching to my feet. He meets me halfway, clasping my wrist, dragging me against him.

My throat aches as I rush to speak, "He wants you to—"

"I know." He nods, his eyes glinting with fury. "Lucius!"

"Yes, sir?" Lucius appears by his side in an instant.

Still holding my gaze, Maxim says, "Empty all of my accounts into the club accounts. All of them. Every last one. I don't care what favors you have to call in. Get it done now."

"Right away, sir." Lucius races off while Milton advances from his corner, an eyebrow raised.

"You think that is what he wants?"

"What else?" Maxim snarls. "He wants everything I have. But as for the money..." He flicks his gaze to mine, his voice resonating with authority. "He can fucking take it."

It's past midnight when Tomas enters the room, his expression tense. With an apologetic nod in my direction, he crosses to Maxim and murmurs something near his ear.

Suddenly, Maxim lurches to his feet and races for the front door. I catch up to him, just in time to witness a ruby red car appearing in the driveway. Flashy and bold, it's something Maxim or his men wouldn't usually drive.

Frowning, I place my hand on his shoulder, straining my eyes to see through the tinted windshield. "Who..."

I barely finish forming the thought before the driver's side door opens, and a lanky figure climbs out, his hands raised.

"I wouldn't do anything rash," he warns with a smile as Maxim tenses, poised to lunge for him. "I may not be armed, but I am not alone—"

"Where's Ainsley?" I croak. "Where is she?"

"Ah, yes…" Dima flicks his gaze toward Maxim again, lingering over his face. "That would depend on a few small variables…"

"What?" Maxim demands. "Just name your fucking price."

"Fine." Dima sighs and inspects his spindly fingers. He almost looks bored, irritated to have his fun cut short. "I want you to beg. On your knees, of course. Beg for this child's life. Though, I will warn you that what has already been done to her has alas…already been done."

My heart sinks. Tears sting at my eyes, but I blink them back, swallowing down any cries. A resolve unlike anything I've ever felt strengthens my limbs, keeping me standing. No matter what happens, I refuse to give him the satisfaction of watching me suffer.

"Dima," Milton says, appearing at Maxim's shoulder. "What the hell are you doing—"

"Enough." Maxim lurches forward, his fists clenched. Then he sinks down to his knees, his hands at his sides, his body rippling with tension. "Is this what you want?" he demands. "Well, you have it. Give her back."

"Hmm." Dima frowns, and for the first time, a hint of alarm crosses his smug expression. Confusion. He eyes Maxim in utter silence, tapping his chin with the tip of his finger. Then he reaches into the pocket of his black sweatshirt and withdraws a knife.

A gasp rips from me as I step forward, but Maxim raises his hand, still crouched. "Don't."

Dima intently eyes the edge of his blade. He takes his time, inspecting every inch of its gleaming surface. "I said beg," he remarks coldly. "Not pretend as though you're ordering dinner. *Beg* for her life—"

"I'm begging." Maxim's voice resonates like thunder, guttural, and deep. "Give her back."

"Are you *really*, though?" Dima throws his knife into the air and catches it deftly by the handle. "I don't know if I believe you—"

"You want to kill me, is that it?" Maxim demands with a harsh, callous laugh. "Do it. If tormenting a child is how you bring me to my knees. So be it. But don't beat around the fucking bush. Do it!"

"Fine." Dima shifts in a graceful movement of muscle and slashes at Maxim's throat with the tip of his blade.

"No!" I tear down the path, uncaring. All I see is Maxim, his body still upright. It isn't until I'm nearly even with him that I realize the amount of blood trickling down his collar doesn't match what would stream from a lethal wound. My eyes trace the base of his throat, noting only a small, delicate scratch.

Dima eyes the streak of scarlet painting his blade. Then he sighs and pivots on his heel to open the back door of the car.

A small figure bounds out, her light hair flying out behind her. "Frankie!"

The sight of her distracts me even from Maxim's injury. "Ainsley!"

I run forward and grab her mid-step, wrenching her into my arms. I bury my face into her hair, holding her so tight she squirms in discomfort.

"What's wrong? Why are you crying? I had so much fun!" she exclaims, her voice high-pitched with excitement. "I love Uncle Dima! We saw real ponies, and then we ate candy, and we played screaming games, and—"

"Hush, baby." I tug at her arms, scanning her tiny limbs for any injuries. Any hint of blood. Her clothes are intact, devoid of so much as a fucking stain. The only change I notice makes me grit my teeth—her usual pink socks have been replaced by a scarlet, woolen pair.

Apart from them, I can't escape one glaring fact.

"You didn't hurt her." Confusion thickens my voice as I meet Dima's gaze.

"Her teeth, perhaps," he admits, with a wink. "I did not regulate her sugar intake—"

"You son of a bitch." Maxim is still laughing, his head turned skyward. A smile shapes his mouth, but there's nothing joyful about it. "You son of a fucking bitch..."

"Hurt me?" Ainsley questions, frowning. "I want to hang out with him again! Can I? Next time, can Eric come so we can—"

"Get her inside," Maxim warns, rising to his feet, his fingers balling into fists.

"Come with me, Ms. Ainsley." Lucius steps forward to ease her from my arms. "I believe it's time for bed."

"Ah," she whines, her voice fading as Lucius carries her inside. "I wanted to say goodbye to Uncle Dima—"

The moment she's gone, Maxim barrels down the front path, and there's no stopping him. He's toe to toe with Dima within a heartbeat. His fist slams into the other man's cheek, sending him sprawling against the hood of the car.

"Enough," Milton warns, stepping forward. "You've made your point. *Both* of you."

Laughing, Dima cradles his jaw and staggers to find his balance. Blood adds a ghoulish flourish to his haggard appearance. In tiny rivulets, it dribbles down his chin unchecked. "You can have your money back, little Maxi. Every dime. All of it, I promise…"

"Why?" I demand. "Why did you do this?"

He frowns. "Perhaps old Dima grew bored of waiting for Maxi to be receptive? If I wanted answers from him, I would have to take them. And I did." He meets my gaze, and whether intentionally or not, he doesn't try to disguise the raw confusion contrasting with his gleeful mask. Beneath the façade, turmoil rages underneath, making me recoil. Maxim has his demons, but nothing like this…

"If he and Milton can form their little families and play their little games… If they believe they can change, then why can't I? Perhaps it's time I take my own family. Play my own game?" He eyes his trembling fingers and forms a fist as if capturing something within it. "I believe it is what I am owed… And in all honesty, if Maxim can attract a woman and children to him, any man can."

"That's it?"

"Francesca!" Maxim's hand swipes at my shoulder, but even he can't stop me from pushing past him, approaching Dima head-on.

Towering over me, the man meets my gaze, unfazed—even when I raise my arm. I lash out, tracking the amusement flickering through his dark eyes as my palm lands across his cheek.

"I deserved that, I suppose," he murmurs, brushing his fingers along his reddening flesh—but his smile is too feral to be contrite. I doubt he even feels the pain at all. *You got what you wanted, didn't you?* His smug grin tells me. *You got your answer.*

And I got mine.

"Anyway, this was fun! I agree with dear Ainsley, we must do this again." Beaming, he turns on his heel and enters his car. As Maxim glowers, he issues a lazy wave and kisses the tips of his fingers.

"*Adieu!* And no hard feelings, Maxi? I hear from a little birdie that you've sent Anatoli running back to Russia—"

He laughs, the sound booming. "He won't stay there for long… But for now, all is well, yes? You and Milton are the best of friends again, and poor Dima will take his leave. Though…" He chuckles before closing the door after him. As the window lowers, he adds. "I will be expecting my invitation to the weddings."

He drives off as Maxim glowers, his body rigid. A ferocity radiates from him like fire—fiercer than any rage I've ever sensed in him before. But I've come to know him enough to suspect that it doesn't stem from hurt pride or shame. No, this fury extends deeper than that. Into his core.

And it's expressed solely in the way he reaches back for me, yanking me against him. His touch conveys possession as he finds my hip, cupping it with his palm. Whatever he did just now—his capitulation to Vadim—was worth more than a thousand rings.

More than if he had slayed a million Anatolis.

More than any promise he could ever make through words alone.

CHAPTER TWENTY-THREE

T he bedroom is the one space in the house that didn't get as much attention as the rest. Maybe because I subconsciously knew that he deserved to have say in it. That he would insist upon it.

Dark and unreadable, his eyes take in the plain white walls and modest furniture mainly consisting of the massive, wooden-framed bed we're seated on now. He's perched on the mattress' edge while I'm on my knees behind him, dabbing at the blood still flowing from his neck.

A wave of emotion constricts my throat, preventing me from speaking—in fact I don't think I've said a word since Dima and Milton left. All I can do is clean him off, conveying in gentle caresses with my cloth just how much I appreciate what he did.

Defended his family.

With the worst of the bleeding finally staunched, I set the cloth aside and use my opposite hand to trace a path down his arm, seeking out his white-knuckled fingers. He's furious. I suspect the irritating pain is what keeps him from hunting down Dima—that and an emotion that swelters between us the longer my touch lingers over him.

Overwhelmed, I sink against his massive frame, pressing my lips to the crook of his shoulder. He stiffens, then gradually relaxes. This kind of intimacy is new for us both, as foreign as vanilla ice cream was to him just a few days ago.

As the seconds pass, my throat loosens, enough for me to croak out a single, tired question. "When do you want the wedding to be?"

He lifts his hand, bringing mine with it, displaying the ring on my finger. His free hand comes to trace the delicate circlet of marble, lingering over his name.

"When you are ready," he says, and that statement carries with it so many connotations. My thoughts swim at the prospect of deciphering them all. But, as always, he can never leave me with a solid choice—it always comes in the form of a game. The premise of this one, he proposes as a dare. "After we make this room suit us both."

Club XXX continues in Vadim: Control. Continue on for a preview!

When delving into the world of sexual promiscuity, it's totally okay to have *one* glass of wine beforehand, just to calm your nerves. Two is fine too. Okay, three—but there's a benefit to every sip of alcohol far beyond the use as a mental crutch.

Or so I tell myself.

For one, I'll be nice and loose for whatever millionaire I manage to snag on my first night on the prowl. Depending on how well it goes, I'll be closer to scratching the big-ticket item off my bucket list—joining a secretive, exclusive sex club. Through that act alone, I'll be giving my ex-husband the ultimate kiss-off, while indulging in years of repressed sexuality to boot.

Win, win.

Telling myself that makes it easier to down my fourth glass as I scan the offerings milling about the exclusive "Gray Bar" of Hotel Six—the most exclusive venue within ten miles of the area's major airport. It's a forty-floor haven for millionaire businessmen with too much money to spend and not enough time to look for a relationship lasting beyond a few hours. In theory, it should be a sexual revolution Mecca.

In reality, it's slim pickings tonight, go figure. The one night of the week I finally managed to gather up the nerve to assemble an outfit that—in the right lighting—makes me look like I almost belong here. Enough that I was able to slip past the stern-faced bouncer before he could do a double take.

Though, maybe I should have tried my skills on him first? The old guy could have been a nice warm-up for my rather lacking talent of seduction. Frowning, I do the math on my fingers. Six months since my divorce from Jim was final. Three years since we last had sex. Minus the odd dildo every now and again, I haven't been laid in…

Too damn long. Sighing, I let my fingers fall to the table before me and tap the polished wood with my hot pink nails. A normal person would try online dating, or maybe troll the grocery store for some horny single dad with a fetish for one-night stands to ease her way back into the dating pool. A normal person.

I, however, decided to skip the queue and jump into the big, wide world with a bang. Literally. Why feign interest in a long-term relationship or play the roulette game with STDs when you can aim right for the jackpot—exclusive millionaire sex clubs like the kind my uncle Conroy used to gossip about after one too many brandies.

The millionaire part is beside the point. Three big ones, actually—safety—both physically and health-wise—privacy and most importantly…kink. Weird, crazy kink. Enough to drown out say, seven or so years of a lifeless marriage and boring, missionary sex so lame that a nun wouldn't consider participating as breaking her vows.

Yes, Tiffy, I tell myself. *You're on a roll. A horrible, fruitless roll.*

An hour in, and I have yet to be approached by one of the three men occupying the lounge in addition to me. It must be the slow hour for rich bachelors.

One potential prospect sits at the bar, his back to me. A curtain of dark hair obscures most of his face, but he's scrawny. Too scrawny. *Next.*

Sighing, I shift my attention to another potential victim. Aged approximately seventy years, with a beautiful head of balding gray hair, he's only a moderately more appealing candidate. I bet rich old men have plenty of experience to draw from, though. Viagra can be a heck of a drug—and hell, to make their trysts last, those over sixty probably extend the foreplay too.

Bonus points.

Not that I would know how to recognize extended foreplay if it slapped me in the face. Jim thought oral sex was sinful —unless on the rare occasion he had two beers, it wasn't Sunday, and I was the one willing to open my mouth.

Stop it. I shake my head to clear away the negative thoughts —no more dwelling on the past. I'm the new and improved Tiffany Connors. No longer bitter about years of youth wasted. No longer hating on my prudish ex-husband. No longer sexually repressed.

So very sexually repressed.

I crane my neck to the corner of the room where the third and last potential victim sits thrumming through a magazine. The fact that it's Vogue, paired with his impeccably tailored suit, sends my gaydar pinging hard. *Strike three.*

After yet another sip of wine for courage, I cycle back to bachelor number one, the guy at the bar. He's not my type, but what's the harm in trying? Glass in hand, I leave my booth and approach him, praying to God I don't trip in these heels. It's the first time I've worn anything but neat, respectable flats in nearly a decade—yet another example of jumping headfirst into my new carefree life.

Forcing my lips into a friendly grin, I sidle up to my target. "Hello," I purr huskily—or at least I try to. "I'm Tiff."

He inclines his head toward me, and my eyelids flutter in shock. I'm so caught off guard; I nearly let my sexy rouse slip in favor of gaping at him.

He's pretty. Freakishly so. An angelic nose anchors his delicately crafted features—like a masculine but beautiful doll. Pale skin conforms to his high cheekbones and strong jaw. Jesus almighty, I've never seen a sexier jaw. Eyes so dark, I feel the need to strike a match take me in with little reaction, and my brain runs wild trying to decipher them. Is he bored? Surprised that I've approached him?

A half-empty glass of whiskey sits in front of him and nothing else—a testament to the brooding businessman stereotype.

Score.

"Gorgoshev," he says in a voice so rich my tongue dampens, my throat contracting. He has an accent I can't place. Russian, given the name? No. Something more musical.

French? I'm too distracted to put much effort into narrowing it down as he extends his hand toward me.

And it's as beautiful and slim as the rest of him. My nails look garish against his porcelain skin, and I'm ten times more self-conscious. Way to make a first impression. If he already doesn't think I'm a dumb bimbo, I'm halfway there.

"Do…do you come here often?" I ask, flicking my hair over my shoulder. I must flick too hard because one of my hoop earrings smacks off my chin, and I nearly slip from my stool.

A cool hand catches my wrist before I can lose my balance completely, anchoring me in place.

"T-Thank you," I stammer, smoothing my fingers over my skirt. He moved so fast. Already he's back to nursing his whiskey as if he never budged at all. "I've probably had way too much wine."

I groan internally. The fact that I acknowledge drinking at all is a sign I've definitely had too much wine. Surprisingly, Mr. Pretty doesn't seem to mind my sloppiness.

My heart races the more I watch him, and I dare to hope this could be working. He's handsome enough, and yes, he may be freakishly thin, but I can work with it. Jim— no, not thinking about him. *My ex,* has the body of a college linebacker five years beyond his prime, so I'm not picky.

Smiling wider, I try to engage the non-cheating, non-asshole person before me in conversation. *Say something smart, Tiff.* "Is Gorgoshev your first or last name?" I wonder.

Kill me.

"Last," he says, either oblivious to the stupidity of the question or he must get it a lot. "I'm not inclined to give out my first name to strangers." A playful smirk shapes his mouth, softening the rejection hidden within his words. *Touché.*

"I'm Tiffany Connors," I blurt. It could be the wine talking, but something about him makes me curious enough to extend the conversation, all embarrassment aside. "Age twenty-eight. I like long walks on the beach. I can assure you that I'm not a serial killer—"

"And I'm sure you carry quite the reputation in finance to commandeer a private booth in such an establishment," he says over me.

I clam up as my cheeks catch fire. Smart man—*too* smart, it seems. "I...I..."

"Relax." He cocks his head back and takes a small sip from his drink. "You're the first woman under fifty to come in here alone—" He meets my gaze directly, and my heart lurches. "Pardon me for being curious."

"Oh, yeah..." I flick my tongue along my lower lip, weighing the benefits of further engagement. He seems nice, but his lack of ogling my tits or trying to feel me up leaves me puzzled. Navigating the dating world beyond high school is a brand-new experience for me. Are we in good territory? Bad? Should I cut my losses and move on to an easier mark like the bald guy across the room?

Decisions. Decisions.

Jutting my chin, I decide on the spot to cut the bullshit and go for the balls. "Maybe I'm not a financier," I confess, eyeing him through my lashes. "Maybe I'm interested in something a lot more fun than comparing business ventures. What do you say? I'll show you mine if you show me yours."

A part of me cringes inside—the good, God-fearing part of me that wishes I was wearing a nice sweater instead of a dress that exploits my cleavage to hell and back. After two years, it's still hard to shake the old girl.

But as Mr. Gorgoshev's eyes flicker from my face down to my collar, I suddenly can't hear anything but the hard swallow contorting my throat. Good girl Tiffy can put a sock in it.

"Vadim," he says. "First name."

"Vadim," I parrot, playing with the syllables. I probably sound more tipsy than sexy, but a thrill runs through me anyway. I swear his eyes narrow slightly. So I say it again.

"Are you alright?" he wonders, a black eyebrow raised.

"Huh?"

"Your voice. It sounds strange." Frowning, he takes another sip of his whiskey while I pray I might sink through the floor and die. Just when the mortification becomes unbearable, he flashes one of those disarming grins. "If I didn't know better... I'd think you were coming on to me, Ms. Connors."

A teensy bit of my panic gives way to an excited flutter in my belly. "And if I am?"

He seems to mull it over, his dark eyes gleaming. "Then I would have to say..." With undeniable interest, his gaze flits over me a second time, and my heart lurches. "How much?"

Vadim's story continues in Control! Read now!

A WORD FROM THE AUTHOR

Hey there!

Thank you so much for reading! If you enjoyed the story, please leave a review and recommend the book to any friend you think would love this twisted world. You'd have my eternal gratitude. Even a short sentence goes a long way!

Then, come join the rest of us dark romance lovers in my Facebook Group where you can get snippets, sneak peeks of upcoming books and even help vote on aspects of future novels.

Come to the dark side:

https://www.facebook.com/groups/lanasbeautifulmonsters/

WANT MORE STUFF TO READ?

Join my newsletter and get a **free book**! Plus, you get to stay updated with any new releases, random giveaways and exclusive sneak peeks!

https://www.lanaskybooks.com/newsletter

Other Novels: https://lanaskybooks.com/

FREE BOOK - JOIN MY NEWSLETTER

Dark, Twisted Romance

Join my newsletter and get a **free book**! Plus, you get to stay updated with any new releases, random giveaways and exclusive sneak peeks!

https://www.lanaskybooks.com/newsletter

ABOUT THE AUTHOR

Lana Sky is a reclusive writer in the United States who spends most of her time daydreaming about complex male characters and parenting her Cockapoo Joey. She writes dark, twisted romance across several genres. Her titles include everything from mafia romance to vampires.

facebook.com/AuthorLanaSky

twitter.com/lanasky101

amazon.com/author/lanasky

pinterest.com/lanasky101

goodreads.com/lanasky

instagram.com/lanasky101

bookbub.com/authors/lana-sky

For more titles by Lana Sky, please visit:

https://www.lanaskybooks.com

www.ingramcontent.com/pod-product-compliance
Lightning Source LLC
Chambersburg PA
CBHW070743190726
48292CB00002B/388